SPOOK Squad

Allan Evans

IMMORTAL WORKS
SALT LAKE CITY

Immortal Works LLC
1505 Glenrose Drive
Salt Lake City, Utah 84104
Tel: (385) 202-0116

© 2024 Allan Evans
evanswriter.com

Cover Art by Ashley Literski
strangedevotion.wixsite.com/strangedesigns

This book is a work of fiction. Names, characters, businesses, organizations, places, events and incidents either are the product of the author's imagination or are used fictitiously. Any resemblance to actual persons, living or dead, events, or locales is entirely coincidental.

ISBN 978-1-953491-87-9 (Paperback)
ASIN B0DBZRDNJR (Kindle Edition)

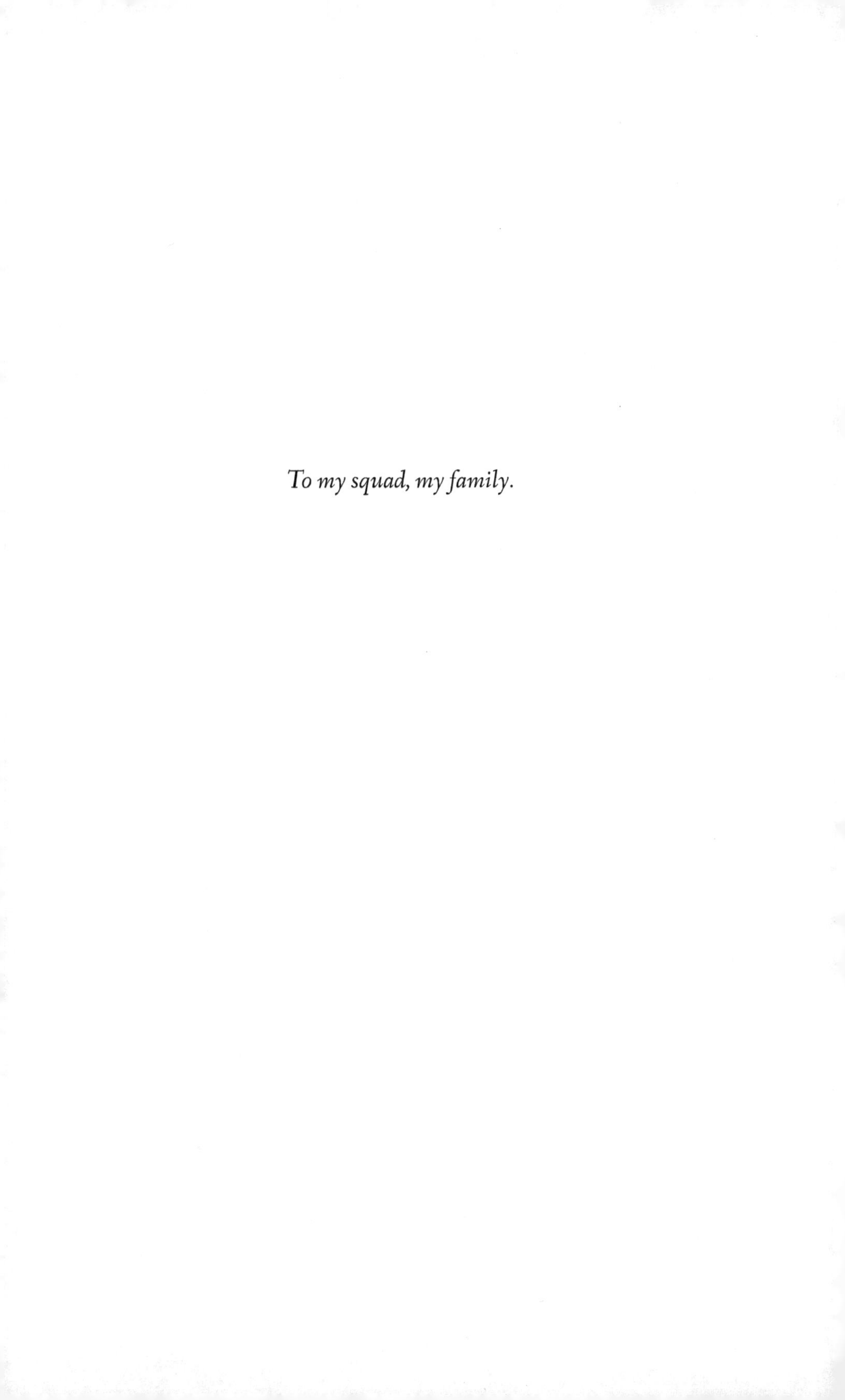

To my squad, my family.

A CALL FOR HELP

"Abbey." The voice was barely above a whisper, but two things were immediately apparent: I knew this voice, and she was terrified. Absolutely terrified.

"Are you there?" Stacia's voice had a pleading quality, but I couldn't reply. I'd answered the call without thinking when my phone vibrated in my back pocket. Using your phone in class is strongly discouraged at Pine Ridge High School. By discouraged, I mean the teacher collects the offender's phone and turns it over to the principal's office. It's not a place I want to visit again. Turning in my seat to hide the phone at my ear, I heard my name again.

"Abbey?"

Fear does something to a person's voice, constricting it, raising the pitch, and causing it to tremble. Stacia was frightened beyond anything I'd ever heard from her. And given our history, that said a lot.

"Stacia," I whispered. "I'm in class. What's wrong?" Bending down, I pretended to dig in my backpack to hide my rule-breaking phone usage. Our teacher, Ms. Sparrow, stood at the front of the class at the smartboard, lecturing about our country's entry into the

Vietnam War. However, most of the class watched me, wondering why I was doing something so stupid. Half of them had endured the confiscation routine.

Stacia calling during the first hour of the school day meant she should have been in class, too. She's at the high school in Stillwater, a much larger school in the next town.

Her words tumbled out faster than her usual lazy cadence. "Something is here with me."

Something, not someone.

"What's going on?" I asked as a feeling of dread washed over me.

"Here I Go Again," the eighties hit from Whitesnake flashed through my head. Thanks to my mother's influence, I am an eighties girl through and through. For good or bad, it's the soundtrack of my life.

"I'm trapped in the bathroom at school. The lights are flickering like crazy, and purple slime is running down the walls." The tremble in her voice had increased. "There's something outside the stall door. It's just waiting."

Now I know why Stacia called *me*.

Ever since I was a little girl, I could see things others couldn't: spirits, ghosts, and dead people. Call them what you will, but for some reason, I'm sort of a spook magnet. Ghosts have always been attracted to me. But it's not always as glamorous as it sounds. The dead can be annoyingly persistent. My friends know about my abilities, and when weird things happen, there's no question who they're going to call.

They're calling me.

"Abbey, you have to help me. Please." Her voice cracked with emotion, and my heart broke. There was no way I wouldn't help her, which meant I had to get out of class. Right now.

I stood, grabbed my backpack, and walked up to Ms. Sparrow as she wrote *Containment* on the board. "Now, class, preventing the spread of Communism—" She noticed me and stopped. "What is it, dear?"

"Umm," I leaned in and whispered, "I'm having issues."

Ms. Sparrow looked at me briefly and blinked, but she got it. "Oh, right, it's shark week. Go ahead. You're excused. Hurry now," she said as she ushered me toward the door. Thank God I have a woman teacher, I thought as I sped down the hall.

Right around the corner, I texted "911" to Lexi and Kelly. And since I don't drive yet, I added, "Need a ride, performing arts exit."

I got back on the call and walked as fast as possible. "Stacia, I'm coming. But where are you? Which bathroom?" With a school as big as Stillwater, she would have to narrow down the geography.

"In the bathroom behind the gym."

"Alright, just hang tight. Be there as soon as I can. Call you when I get there." I ended the call and picked up my pace, speed-walking to our school's performing arts wing. Lexi and Kelly replied to my 911 text with, "On the way" and "One minute."

I love these girls. Without question or concern for consequences, they're willing to skip out of school to help. I'd be lost without my friends. But for much of my life, I hadn't really had any. The ones I had disappeared quicker than a Twinkie at a weight watcher's meeting when they discovered what I could do. Losing friends over my so-called gift has hurt a lot over the years. But I get that it can be more than a little creepy to know your friend sees dead people.

When I rounded the corner, there they were. "What's up?" Kelly asked, her concern front and center.

"Stacia is in trouble at Stillwater." Glancing at them both, there was no hesitation, just determination. I've told them about my summer at camp with Stacia. They know about the near-death experience we shared.

"I'm guessing it's a spooky girl kind of trouble, then," Lexi said, not really asking a question.

I nodded.

"Okay then, I'm driving," she said as we rushed to the cold parking lot. The wind swirled the Minnesota snow, and the chill got underneath my jacket before we could get to Lexi's Ford Escape. The weather had recently turned cold, but Stacia's problem outweighed the weather.

Lexi threw the car into gear and headed straight for the exit. Not bothering to delay for the stop sign, she accelerated onto County 12. The Escape fishtailed as she fought to gain control, turning into the skid. It worked, and we were soon flying down the road at 70 miles per hour. Let the fun begin.

In the ten minutes it took Lexi to get us there, I filled them in on the few details I knew.

"What if the trouble isn't supernatural?" Kelly asked as we raced into the Stillwater parking lot. "Shouldn't we call the police just in case?"

We were out of the car the second Lexi slammed it into park. Sirens were in the air. A lot of them. "Sounds like someone's already called them."

Kelly grabbed my arm and pulled me toward the school. "Run," she shouted. "The school will be going into lockdown. We've got to get inside while we still can."

Fueled by adrenaline, we sprinted towards the entrance to the gym wing. The sirens came from all directions. Multiple squad cars screamed into the lot as students rushed out of the school. We grabbed a door before it latched shut, and once inside, I called Stacia to let her know we'd arrived.

"I hear sirens," she said in lieu of a greeting.

"Yeah, squad cars are coming into the school parking lot."

"Really? How many?"

Looking back, a lot of police cars were headed in our direction. "I think it's all of them."

"The more, the better," she said, her voice trembling.

"We're coming. Going to hang up. See you soon." I said, tucking away my phone as I needed my hands. Not sure what that meant, but the situation was not even remotely normal.

We raced down the hallway and took the corner. Partway down

the hall, a dense, swirling mist hung in the air—most unusual for a higher education establishment.

"That's different," Lexi said, summing up my thoughts.

"Sure is," Kelly agreed. They shared a quick look before gesturing for me to take the lead. "After you."

Someone once said bravery can only take you so far, and then determination leads the way. I might have been scared, but I knew my determination to save Stacia would lead me where I needed to go. I counted on it.

Moving cautiously, we entered the mist part-way down the hallway. It felt like we'd been transported to a jungle. A strong, musty odor motivated me to breathe through my mouth. Our feet sloshed on the wet floors.

"Hey," came a muffled shout from behind us. A quartet of firefighters caught up to us. "You guys shouldn't be here."

I spoke for our group. "Our friend is trapped in the bathroom, and we've come to get her."

The firefighter shook his head like he'd heard it before. "No, we've got this. It's not safe for you to be here," he said. "Leave it to the professionals." And just to make his point, he gestured for us to go back. They pushed past us, not waiting for a response.

"Where are you going?" Kelly asked when I started to follow. "You heard the man. We're not equipped for this. They're the professionals."

I shook my head. "There's no way the firefighters are equipped for what's in the bathroom with Stacia. We need to keep moving."

My friends shrugged, and we continued our journey as we moved deeper into the mist. It had become densely thick and seemed alive in the way it swirled and danced.

Strange things for a Tuesday morning.

We were about to turn the corner, and the firefighters were there, sprinting in our direction this time. They moved so fast, one slid into the far wall with a loud grunt as he rounded the corner. Another lost his footing on the wet floor and completely wiped out. None of the firefighters slowed down, let alone glanced back at their fallen comrade.

As the last firefighter got up and raced past us, I glanced at Kelly. "There go your professionals."

"They looked terrified," Lexi said.

I rested a hand on each of my friends. "It's up to us now."

"I forgot to feed my fish." Lexi said this matter-of-factly with an unreadable expression.

I was confused. "Lexi?"

"I forgot to feed my fish. And they like to eat."

Holding her gaze, I nodded. "We all do, sweetie."

"But I'm the only one who feeds them."

I nodded again.

"So, make sure we get out of here so they get fed." Her seriousness was adorable.

"I promise. You'll make it out of here safely."

Lexi nodded. "Okay, then let's go save Stacia."

The men's and women's bathrooms were in front of us, a smelly swamp outside their entrances. The women's had dark purple slime running down the length of the door. It leaked out of a crack above the door.

"This can't be good," I said as I opened the door. The smell hit without warning. Seriously, the rank odor was worse than a garbage truck stewing in 100-degree heat.

Stepping carefully into the bathroom, I avoided a glob of slime as it ever-so-slowly elongated down from the ceiling. Clearly, this bathroom was skipped on the custodian's morning rounds.

The lights flickered, winking on and off with a buzzing sound as we peered around the corner. A dark figure swayed in front of the closed stall door. It looked vaguely human, but with everything going on around it, I'd venture that it wasn't currently human. Maybe at one time, but not anymore.

Moving away from the protection of the wall, I stepped out into the bathroom. "Stacia, we're here."

Her response was instantaneous. "Oh, my goodness. Thank you." She hesitated briefly and then asked, "It's still out there, isn't it?"

"Yes, it's here," I told her as I moved past the thing, careful not to get too close. You never know what you'll get when the spirit world tangles with ours. "Stay put until I tell you to move."

"Okay," Stacia said. Her voice had a *wtf* tone to it. "But what's out there?"

I wasn't sure what to call it. Once a man, the thing's face was now a lurid shade of green that looked like it had been melted off in a vat of toxic chemicals. "I don't know what it is, but he's an ugly cuss." Its one intact eye fixed on me as it leaned closer and opened its mouth. What came out was a bellowing roar. The sound was near deafening, but I held my ground.

"Leave us alone. You're not wanted here," I said as forcefully as possible. But it wasn't especially moved by my show of toughness. Clearly, I wasn't going to push it away with my words. This encounter needed to move into the physical realm to get Stacia out. In the past, I've made contact by focusing my mental energy on my hand. But the thought of touching the slimy thing had me disgusted. Help arrived in the form of Kelly and the custodian's mop.

Tossing me the mop, she shouted, "Go get it."

With a firm grip, I swung the mop for the cheap seats. The handle connected with the gruesome spirit, and it took a faltering step backward. Wanting to push my advantage, I stuck the business end of the mop into the thing's midsection and shoved with everything I had. It was enough that it moved the thing away from Stacia's stall.

"Now, Stacia," I commanded.

She didn't hesitate and flew out of the stall as Lexi and Kelly grabbed her. All three hit the door and were out of the bathroom in a flash.

I gave it another shove with the mop, but it decided to fight back and grabbed onto the handle. But it didn't matter. I was done with the mop and let go. What I hadn't expected was what happened next.

Dropping the mop, the thing lunged for me. It locked onto my wrist with a bone-chilling grip. My wrist tingled where it gripped me. There was no way I would break free from the vise-like hold unless it willingly let go.

As I struggled to break free, it pulled me closer and closer. We locked eyes, and I saw what had to be a glimmer of humanness buried deeply within its green eyes.

"Let me go," I said. "And I can help you move to somewhere better."

It didn't respond, so I took that as my opening to continue.

"When I was a child, I was afraid of the dark. But as I've gotten older, I've seen people who are afraid of the light, which is far worse. The light is healing, purpose, and freedom. And it can mean that you're finally home. Death feels like a dark tunnel with no light at the end, but there's always a light."

The thing stared into me. My arm ached as the cold spread from where it gripped me.

"The light is there if you look for it," I said. "Look for it now."

The spirit's eyes lost their focus. "Do you see it?"

It felt like I was finally getting through to the thing as the grip ever-so-slightly loosened.

"Go to the light. You can pass Go and collect your $200, but you need to go."

The grip released as the green man in front of me faded. The last thing I saw was something I hadn't expected. A smile.

Lexi, Kelly, and Stacia waited around the corner. Wrapping me up immediately, Stacia's frame may be small, but her grip was immense. After all, she graduated from the same boot camp as me. Given the camp's intense physical training, we toughened up and found new strength. And it gave me the confidence to persevere through any obstacle I encounter.

"I knew you'd come for me," she said.

I pushed her hair away from her eyes. "That's what friends do. We help each other."

"Let's get out of here," Kelly said. "Maybe that thing has friends, too."

"Good point," I said in agreement.

One of the few positives of a paranormal encounter is the effects often don't linger. The mist was already dissipating, and the floors were no longer wet. We hurried back down the empty halls and stepped back out into the fresh, wintery weather. However, it was anything but calm outside.

Dozens of Washington County Sheriff squads and an equal amount of Stillwater black and white police cars had arrived. And several dozen guns were pointed in our direction.

"Whoa." I was never too eloquent when guns were pointed at me —I don't like guns. But we did what you're supposed to do when the police aimed their weapons at you: we raised our hands. "Hey, don't shoot. We're the good guys," I called out.

Out of nowhere, officers rushed in, grabbed onto us, and rushed us away from the building. We were swept into the mass of emergency vehicles and ended up in the back of a paramedic truck. Medical personnel surrounded us.

"Hold on," I said, holding up my hands. "We're fine."

I noticed it at the same time the others did. And judging by their reaction as they backed away, the medical staff didn't know what to make of me—the girl with the glowing hand.

2

NAUGHTY BEHAVIOR

A purple luminescence radiated from my hand where the ghostly thing had grabbed me.

My mind raced to come up with something I could tell the medical staff that didn't shout paranormal. I didn't need the world to discover the truth about me—that I'm the spooky girl.

"Purple Rain" from Prince came to mind as I examined my hand. My mom introduced me to eighties music, and I've shared her passion for it ever since. She said the music has stood the test of time because of its complexity and because everyone brought something new and exciting. The eighties were home to artists with rich voices and innovative visions. Though I doubt even Prince could have foreseen a girl with a glowing purple hand.

The female paramedic was the only one who didn't look like she wanted to run away or call an exorcist. She pulled on a pair of latex gloves and stepped forward. "Can you tell me what happened in there?" Her voice was calm and measured. "If I know what you've encountered, I can treat you. From what I understand, there is a very real possibility of a toxic chemical spill."

There. She'd given me my way out. "There was liquid on the

floors and purplish slime running down the walls. I guess I must have touched the slime. Accidentally," I added.

She simply nodded.

I made a fist with my glowing hand. "It doesn't hurt, though."

"The color goes with your eyes," Lexi blurted out. I glanced at her, and she gave me a very Lexi smile that I can only describe as the perfect mix of sweet, cute, and ridiculous. She can be such a goof, but I love her.

The woman ran a black device that emitted a series of clicks over my hand. The clicks remained constant, and I guessed I'd passed the Geiger counter radioactivity test.

"We need to get her flushed right away," the male paramedic said, gesturing for me to move. "The hazmat vehicle has flushing stations to decontaminate you."

As I slid off the bench, the woman paramedic now held a silver device with LED lights. The lights went from green to red when she moved it toward my hand. I had no idea what kind of medical device that was, but I was shepherded out the door by the other paramedic before I could ask.

"What about the rest of you? Anyone else touch the slime?" the male paramedic asked. Receiving negative responses, he returned to me and asked that I remove my coat. With quick cuts, my shirt sleeves were also removed.

"Hey, that was my favorite shirt," I complained.

A man in a full protective suit sprayed me with a yellow hose. "I need you to keep rotating your hand," the hazmat technician told me. "We have to ensure we get all of it." The spray was barely warmer than the chilly air, and it wasn't long before I shivered and shook from the cold. Hypothermia, here I come.

"You're going to need this," said the hazmat technician, holding up a blanket. My savior wrapped the blanket around my shivering shoulders.

"Thanks," I managed to get out between shakes.

The paramedic leaned in and held a stethoscope against my

chest. He listened for a moment. "Breath sounds normal," he said to a different female paramedic. Glancing around, I didn't see the first one.

"What was that silver device the other paramedic used on me?"

The paramedic with the stethoscope shrugged. "I don't know. I've never seen her before." He looked around and shrugged again. "She's gone now, though."

The flushing continued as the snow drifted down around us. After an eternity, the tech cut off the flow and wrapped my arm in a towel. When he pulled it off, my supernatural glow was gone.

"You'll need to follow up with your doctor. Make sure you're okay. Don't want your hand falling off."

"Not like that last guy," the paramedic chimed in. He must have seen my panic-stricken face because he quickly added, "We're just teasing."

"I knew that," I said, but still shivered at the thought.

He patted me on the shoulder. "We're through here, but I'm guessing they want a few minutes of your time," he said, gesturing to the four waiting officers.

The police asked for our names and contact information and took our statements. I gave them a mostly true narrative of the phone call from Stacia, who was trapped in a bathroom stall. I left out any mention of the ghostly figure.

They asked why Stacia would have called me. I told them how we had been trapped together in a burning building over the summer and how bonds forged in adversity tend to remain strong. And that's why I was the first to be called when she was in danger again.

Happily, our story was accepted, and we were given the okay to leave.

"Anyone up for lunch?" I asked. "Going back to school doesn't feel right." I got a unanimous nodding of heads.

"I know just the place," Stacia said. "After all, this is my turf."

Piling into Lexi's Escape, our boisterous atmosphere carried us into downtown Stillwater. Outwitting death and living to talk about it can do that. We loudly sang along with the radio as "Everyone Have Fun Tonight" by Wang Chung played. After that, we laughed and enjoyed ourselves for the rest of the ride. It felt like we could take on the world.

Which might be why Stacia had suggested our destination in the first place.

"The Water Street Inn," Stacia announced as we pulled alongside an ancient brick structure. The three-story building was a stone's throw from the St. Croix River and took up an entire city block. Wrought iron fire escapes and balconies clung to the structure.

"The food is terrific, as is the atmosphere," she said, gesturing for us to enter. The plaque by the entrance reads, "Est. 1890."

When my hand touched the door handle, I felt a weird vibration. It was enough to make me go, "Hmmm."

Suspecting something, I glanced at Stacia, but she simply gestured for me to continue. Something about how she held the other two girls back led me to believe there might be more to our visit than just lunch.

We were seated at a table with a view of the river. Even though the banks were lined with ice and snow, the St. Croix was still flowing. It was beautiful, if not a little bleak and desolate.

Stacia made a show of looking around. "You know, this place is supposed to be haunted," she said in mock innocence.

"Aha. I knew you were up to something. That's why you picked this place."

"I was just curious if you would notice anything."

"I'll let you know if I see anything, but crowded restaurants don't usually attract ghosts." But even as I said it, a tingling began, launching my goosebumps quicker than the last space shuttle. I saw nothing abnormal, just ordinary people enjoying lunch. Several middle-aged women shared a table nearby, while the table across from us was a work group, judging by the lanyards they wore.

Our server, Chloe, took our lunch order. I asked for the French dip sandwich and salad; the others asked for soup, salad, and sandwiches. The tingling subsided while our server was at the table, but the moment she stepped away, the sensation began anew. This continued for several minutes before it faded. However, it started back up just as I thought it was gone. I found myself rubbing my arm, hoping the feeling would stop once and for all.

Staring out the window, I tried focusing on the river, but Stacia's laugh pulled me back. "Look, she's doing it again."

Kelly laughed. "There is something odd about her."

"What is she doing?" I asked, not wanting to stare. I was curious, but a girl should be discreet.

"She keeps swatting at nothing," Lexi said. "OMG, she did it again. She has to be drunk."

I could only be discreet for so long and turned to look for myself.

The woman in the red sweater waved a hand by her ear, getting more vigorous with every swat. My friends were trying to hold back their laughter.

"Maybe a fly is buzzing in her ear," Kelly offered.

Or maybe it was the man dressed in a Confederate soldier's uniform touching the woman's ear.

When she swatted again, the soldier took an unsteady step back and almost fell over. But he went right back and touched her ear again, letting out a loud belly laugh at her confusion. The woman turned in her seat, looking for the source of her torment.

As my friends cracked up, they clearly didn't see what I saw. If they did, they wouldn't be laughing. My gift, if that's what you want to call it, is the ability to see dead people. And I saw a drunken ghost tormenting a poor lady.

It made me angry.

Ignoring my friends, I marched right across the restaurant to the Confederate soldier. I was livid about what he was doing to the poor woman. Usually, I had to focus my mind first to enable my touch—but my anger accomplished the same goal, and I reached out and flicked his ear.

His reaction was priceless, and three things happened virtually simultaneously. He jumped like I'd touched him with a live wire. He shouted, "What in the Sam Hill?" And he farted.

It took everything I had to keep a straight face as I waved a disapproving finger at him. His face showed a range of emotions, everything from fear, anger, and hurt, before settling in on confusion.

Taking a step closer, I gestured for him to leave, pointing emphatically toward the door. He looked like he might say something, but ultimately dropped his head and shuffled away. His gait was unsteady as he swayed back and forth. Just as he reached the door, he took a swipe at a vase, knocking it off the shelf to crash to the floor.

The soldier faded away as he crossed the doorway.

Satisfied, I pulled back my shoulders, strode confidently back to our table, and took my seat as Chloe set my plate down. My sandwich looked wonderful, and I was so famished that I couldn't wait. Dipping my sandwich in the au jus, I took a big bite. Only then did I glance up. My friends stared at me, open-mouthed.

"What?" I asked with a mouthful of sandwich.

"Abbey," Kelly said. "That was," she paused, trying to come up with an adequate description of the unusual events. "That was crazy."

"It's been that kind of day, hasn't it? Hopefully, no one noticed." However, I don't know how they could have missed it.

"She definitely noticed," Lexi said, nodding across the room.

Trying to be subtle, I turned and recognized a face staring back at me.

It was the woman paramedic.

3

A STUFFED MOOSE HEAD FOR YOUR LOVED ONES

My father once told me that even though God probably shook his head the day I was made, he for sure smiled.

My mouth could use a filter. I've been known to speak my mind, especially when confronted by persons of dubious authority.

Case in point: we were leaving the restaurant when I decided I needed to visit the woman paramedic. She was at a nearby table—one that would have given her a fantastic view of the Confederate soldier incident. She may not have seen the soldier, but especially with the vase seemingly crashing on its own, she had to know something unusual was happening.

It didn't feel like a coincidence that she was here. There were too many questions. First, why didn't the other paramedics recognize her? Second, she wasn't using the usual tools of the paramedic trade —they don't usually carry a Geiger counter, do they? Third, what were the odds she'd end up at the same restaurant as us?

Highly unlikely.

So, what to do with the situation? I thought about ducking out, but my father taught me that being passive in life wouldn't make me happy. He said Apple founder Steve Jobs, speaking to graduates at

Stanford, said that you'll never be the same again after you realize that you can poke life and something will happen. Once you learn that you can change, improve, and make your mark on it, you'll be happier with your life.

"I'll meet you guys outside," I told my friends. "I need to poke life for a moment."

Even though she had a tablet in front of her, her expressionless eyes were tracking me. If she was surprised when I walked up, the woman didn't let on. She lowered her tablet and said, "Hello, Abbey."

"Hello, fake paramedic woman." I pulled out a chair and sat opposite her. An untouched bowl of soup was between us. Several breadsticks were in a basket, and I reached for one. "May I?" I asked.

"Go right ahead. I wasn't hungry, as it turned out." Her face didn't give away anything. Clearly a cool customer, I would have to heat things up.

I reached across the table and dipped my breadstick in her cream of wild rice soup, took a bite, and then, just to be obnoxious, went back for a double dip. She didn't acknowledge my poor manners, but I could tell I got to her all the same. The muscles of her jaw clenched.

Probably for the first time, I took a good look at her. She was in her mid-thirties, though there was a hint of gray at the part of her dark hair. Her form-fitting sweater showed off shoulders that an Olympic swimmer would be proud of. Her eyes were cool green, and she had a clear complexion. She could be pretty if she smiled or allowed an ounce of emotion out.

When I finished her breadstick, she pushed the basket towards me. I held up a palm. "I really couldn't." Leaning forward, I rested my chin on my hand. "But I could use some answers. And if you don't, I'm good at making a stink in public."

"We both know you won't be doing that," she said calmly. "Calling attention to yourself is not what you're about."

She picked up her cup of tea and took a long sip before continuing. "I haven't said I wouldn't answer your questions. You just haven't asked them yet."

The ball was clearly in my court. I decided to begin with an easy question.

"Who are you?"

"My name is Suzanna Neri," she replied.

"Okay, Suze, you're not actually a paramedic, are you?"

"No," she took another sip before continuing. "I am a doctor, however."

"Your parents must be proud. What was that device you used on me?" I held her gaze, searching for any sign of deceit. My father, the investigative reporter, had shared the "tells" he looked for when interviewing someone who may not be completely honest. When people feel uncomfortable about something, their eyes dart back and forth. Another tell is when someone who is right-handed looks up to their right, they are accessing their imagination. Up and to the left means they're accessing their memory.

Neri held her cup with both hands, making it difficult to tell if she was left or right-handed.

Another tell is the false smile. A genuine smile causes the skin around the eyes to bunch and wrinkle, while a false smile doesn't affect the eyes. However, I quickly realized she wasn't the smiling type.

Any or all of these tells will help determine if you're being told the truth.

That is unless the liar is a non-feeling psychopath, and then all the tells in the world go flying out the window.

Neri spoke evenly while she held my gaze. "The first device I used was a Geiger counter to assess the radiation risk. After all, Abbey, you were glowing."

"True," I admitted.

"The second device was an EMF meter. There is a school of thought that paranormal activity can influence electrical fields."

Ah, there it was—*paranormal activity*.

The woman had to mention paranormal activity. I steepled my fingers together, thinking. Who was this woman?

Was she one of those rabid ghost hunters from the cable shows? I dismissed that right away as her access was too good. No way would she have been allowed to cross police lines. A reporter? No, same access issues. Police? No. And if she were, I'd be downtown in a locked room, facing a two-way mirror and a ton of difficult questions.

"So, what did those devices tell you?" I asked.

"Radiation levels were consistent with environmental background sources. Natural sources, like the earth's crust, the atmosphere, cosmic rays, and radioisotopes."

Neri poked at her cuticles and continued.

"There were, however, elevated electromagnetic levels. An electromagnetic field, often called an EM field, is generated when charged particles, such as electrons, are accelerated. All electrically charged particles are surrounded by magnetic fields. Charged particles in motion produce magnetic fields."

I leaned back and folded my arms. "Thank you for that. I'm missing my science class right now. Maybe I can get partial credit if you go on about physics, too."

Neri nodded. "Fair enough. I didn't know your level of familiarity with the topic."

"There's one thing I want to know," I said, deciding to poke the hornet's nest to see what might happen. "Why are you interested in me?"

I was left waiting as Neri took a long sip from her tea. She swallowed and took a slow look around the room before answering.

"I picked up some chatter after your clown incident. I heard there was more going on than the story you told."

She was right, of course. There was more to the story. Considerably more. Shortly after starting Pine Ridge High School in the fall, a deranged clown followed me home from the circus. While it stalked me at school, the spirits of dead clowns came to warn me of the danger. That psychotic clown Rellik abducted several of my friends and held them in an abandoned warehouse. I did what was necessary to save my friends, and Rellik was killed in the process.

Like the classic eighties Go-Go's song, "Our lips are sealed," my friends and I kept the details to ourselves when the police and media arrived. Because that's what friends do for each other.

My raised eyebrows must have signaled my disbelief.

"You can't be naïve enough to think some of your friends wouldn't discuss what happened. Well, they did, and I flew in and canvassed the scene the next day. Residual levels portrayed elevated paranormal activity. And after looking into your background, I visited River Falls College. I believed there may have been more to the story there as well."

"And…" I said, although I wasn't sure I wanted to hear her reply.

"Nothing conclusive. But one thing got me curious. How did your attorney, Brian Thompson, provide actionable intelligence to a SEAL team thousands of miles away to rescue your mother? Of course, Mr. Thompson invoked client privilege and offered me nothing when I asked."

I know it's unusual for a fourteen-year-old to have an attorney, but I'm unusual. To say the least.

It was an exciting story. When I was abandoned over the summer at the wrong camp, I called a local attorney out of desperation to get away. Although Brian Thompson wasn't able to get me released from camp, he was able to help when I finally deciphered the ghostly clues that had been plaguing me. These clues pointed to a location in South America where my mom had disappeared the year before. I'm happy to report she was rescued and was back with my father and me. And I have an eternal debt to Brian Thompson for making it happen.

"He's the best attorney I've ever had," I told her. "You may consider calling him next time you get into trouble. Like when you get arrested for stalking an innocent teenage girl."

I pushed back my chair and got to my feet. "Thank you for the breadstick, Suzanna. Have a safe trip back to…" I paused, waiting for her to fill in the blank.

"Virginia. I'm from Virginia."

"I hope this hasn't been a complete waste of your time coming all this way. You should check out some of the antique shops. Stillwater is famous for them. Maybe you could bring home a stuffed moose head for your loved ones."

Suzanna Neri held up a finger to keep me from leaving. Clearly, she had more to say.

I wasn't willing to listen and shook my head. "I really must be running. My ride is waiting."

Neri lunged and grabbed my wrist, pulling me closer. "You have to see how things are changing. How much more power they have in our world." Her voice was barely a hiss. "You need the power of the three."

I was shocked to see the handle of a pistol at her side. Suddenly, all I could think about was getting away. I yanked back my hand and raced out of the Water Street Inn. Maybe I should have heard her out, but she had a dangerous edge.

And I didn't need her digging into my business—especially my ghostly business.

4

SHANGHAI SURPRISE

Half asleep, there were sounds of movement directly behind me. It wasn't loud, but it was enough to register that someone was getting closer. I lifted my head.

"Thank God," I exclaimed when my mom reached around and placed a plate of steaming French toast in front of me. "I'm starving."

"Glad you woke up early enough to have breakfast with us," she said.

"Have trouble sleeping?" my father asked from across the kitchen table. "There's definitely a disturbance in the universe when you need to ask a teenager on a school morning if she had trouble sleeping."

"Funny, Dad."

My mother joined us with plates of French toast for her and my father. With just the three of us in our household, the family dynamics were relatively simple. My mother worked as a doctor at the University of Minnesota hospitals. In the past, she traveled the world with the Doctors Without Borders organization. Now, she stays close to home and does dual duty on the emergency room staff and the school's teaching faculty.

My father, the magazine writer, has a naturally curious mind that has led him around the globe to research the mysteries of our world. It could be a UFO crash, a sighting of some strange new beast, or a haunted cruise ship. My father loves mysteries.

"I woke up early and couldn't sleep," I said between bites. French toast was my favorite, especially when floating in a sea of syrup. "You know how it is when something is running through your head? Your brain works overtime trying to figure it out."

My father nodded. "I most certainly do. That sums up my life."

Mom laughed. "That's your father. What's got your mind running in circles?"

"There's this phrase, but I don't know what it means. I think it ties into the..." I paused, looking at both parents. They know some, but not all, of the paranormal events I've dealt with on a regular basis. "I think it ties into the ghostly stuff."

My father gave me the look. It was a combination of curiosity and "oh crap, not again." I have to be his greatest conundrum: a walking, talking paranormal magnet and the daughter he wants to protect.

My mom lowered her fork. "Oh, dear." As a doctor, ghosts don't fit the scientific realm she lives in. "Have things been happening to you again?"

"I chased away a drunken Confederate soldier at the Water Street Inn. He was bullying a defenseless senior citizen." I left out the rest of my day.

"Good food there," my father said. "You should try their French dip sandwich."

"That's what I had," I said with enthusiasm. Like father, like daughter.

"Then you know," he said. "Simple, but amazing." He smiled a smile of pleasant sandwich memories.

"So, what is the phrase that's keeping you awake?" Mom asked.

"The power of the three."

Dad leaned back in his chair, stroking his chin. "Three has been used throughout history." It may come with his profession, but my father knows his history.

"The pyramids, for instance."

"There's the trinity," my mom offered. "The Father, Son, and Holy Spirit."

We brainstormed as a family over the French toast, throwing out ideas.

"Three dimensions."

"Trimester for a pregnant woman."

"Time. Past, present, and future."

"Thought, word, and deed."

"Heaven, hell, and earth."

"Earth, Wind & Fire, one of my favorite bands," my father said.

"On the third day."

"Listen to this," my father said as he read from his phone. "Three is the first number to which 'all' was given. It is the triad, the number of the whole, as it contains the beginning, a middle, and an end. The power of the three is universal and is the tripartite nature of our world as heaven, earth, and waters. It is human as body, soul, and spirit."

"Tripartite," I repeated. "Now, that's a word you don't hear very often. I'll try to use it in a sentence today."

My father laughed. "Bet you can't."

"Bet I can. Hey Mom. I like your hairstyle, but you should tripartite it on the other side."

This brought a groan from both my parents. "You should go to school. That was almost a dad joke," my mother said with a smile.

"C'mon, it wasn't that bad." I laughed, and my father gave me a pretend hurt look.

Getting up, I carried my plate to the sink. "Thanks for the breakfast and the brainstorming session."

"Such as it was," my father said. "There's always been power in threes. Just not sure how it fits in with ghostly things."

"Me neither," I said, grabbing my backpack and heading out into the cold morning air.

◊◊

I was in my third-hour class when the classroom wall phone rang. The room instantly quieted. We all knew it meant one of us was needed somewhere else. Mr. Cheng answered, listened, and said, "Okay, I'll send her down."

My feeling of dread was affirmed when he announced, "Miss Hill, you're wanted at the office."

Gathering my things to a backdrop of whispers, I shoved my notebook and pen into my backpack. I had no idea why I'd be called to the office. I've managed to keep a low profile since the clown apocalypse.

The secretary gestured for me to go behind the counter and directed me into the vice principal's office. Mr. Fischer stood in the doorway. Someone waited in his office—and unfortunately, that someone looked familiar.

"My name is Special Agent Suzanna Neri," she said, holding a badge case with a shield and FBI credentials. "Come have a seat. I'd like to speak with you."

Mr. Fischer followed me into his office. "It's policy that a school representative be in attendance in cases like this."

Special Agent Neri looked up sharply. "Not this time."

"Not this time," Mr. Fischer repeated and hesitated. "Okay, then." I was pretty sure his shoulders sagged as he shuffled out of his office. I felt terrible for him. This was probably going to be the most exciting part of his day.

Taking a seat across from Neri, I thought that this was probably the first time this office had been used by the FBI to discuss ghosts with a student.

Special Agent Neri closed the door. The latch clicked as it

engaged, sounding utterly final as it echoed in the room. Neri turned around and proceeded to surprise me once again.

"I'm not really with the FBI," she said, holding up her badge case. "These things are remarkably easy to come by, and they fool most people." She tossed her fake credentials into her purse.

Mind officially blown, I studied Neri, wanting to get a read on her as I weighed my options. Professionally dressed in a navy blue pantsuit, she wore black heels and probably a matching holster under her jacket. Her dark eyes held mine in a comfortable gaze. Neri was 100 percent the alpha woman. Even Vice Principal Fischer had cowered as he slunk out.

"I appreciate the trouble you've taken to visit me. I don't get many visitors here at school." I needed to keep up a strong front with her. The queen of the jungle don't keep no prisoners.

Neri laughed. "I suppose not." She folded her arms and leaned on Mr. Fischer's desk. "Let's cut to the chase. I need you to do something for me. Something dangerous."

"That's not exactly enticing, is it? I see why you had to give up your career in sales." I held up a hand. "But, hold on for a moment." I wanted to break up her rhythm and regain control from this woman.

Neri brushed her hair back and gestured for me to continue.

"I'm not saying I wouldn't help you, but let me play devil's advocate for a second."

"I'm listening."

"I'm sure you must have at least one reason why I can't just walk out of here." I looked up at Neri. She said nothing.

"Well," I prompted her.

"Several reasons come to mind," she said, holding up a finger. "One, I have a gun."

"Do You Really Want to Hurt Me" by Culture Club briefly ran into my eighties-wired brain, took a hasty look around and beat it.

"Two," she continued, now holding up a pair of fingers. "I could expose you to the world. From what I've seen, you've made considerable effort to fly under the radar. Having me announce that there's someone with the ability to talk to the earthbound spirits of the dead would not only complicate your life but your parents."

She's right. I don't want that.

"And three," she said with another finger held up. "I wouldn't be asking if it wasn't vitally important."

Whatever. "So, just the three reasons, then?"

"That should be enough. I wouldn't be bothering you if I could do it myself." She turned and lifted her hair, exposing a vicious-looking groove. "I used to have your gift until a bullet took it away."

Gift?

"I'm not sure I'd call it a gift," I told her.

Gift feels like a strong word for something that brings so much fear and heartache into my life. Let alone the sleepless nights enduring flickering lights or the pacing of a ghost with possibly the most enormous feet ever. Life hasn't always gone smoothly when dead people come into my life.

Once, on a school field trip to the Minneapolis Institute of Arts, an old woman scolded me. We were in the museum's period rooms section. Our guide said the period rooms were meant to show how people lived. Siena and I had been playing a game of tag. We would poke each other and run and hide behind something. I don't think our chaperone was being attentive, but someone else was. I had just hidden behind a large chest and looked up and saw a wrinkled old woman. She was decked out in a cream-colored gown. Scowling, she shook her finger at me as if scolding me and then floated right through a wall.

I was done with museum tag after that.

Neri shook her head. "It can be a gift if you use it correctly."

Stroking her chin, Neri leaned forward. "Let me tell you a story before we get any further. Back in the early 1900s, there lived a man named Manfred Krug. A world traveler, a fabled trader, a roguish fellow, and a chef to only the most well-to-do, Manfred was a lot of things. But it was Manfred's culinary magic that brought him fame, accolades, and audiences with the most wealthy and powerful.

"In his search for spices and rare ingredients, Manfred combed the Far East—a considerably wilder place back in his day. It was in these far-flung places that he learned the value of trading. He discovered that in exchange for the right item, Manfred was able to acquire the spices he sought. Money wasn't always important to the people there, and some items were worth more than any amount he could offer. At times, he would have an entire string of trades in the works to get the one ingredient he sought.

"As you can imagine, Manfred came across some unusual items in his travels and would gift them to his wealthy benefactors when he returned home. Which was Saint Paul, here in Minnesota. Considering the large number of wealthy families in the area, it made sense. It turns out mining and grains could make for some seriously wealthy families. Since these benefactors funded his globe-hopping adventures, he wanted them to know how appreciative he was—it helped keep the money flowing.

"But Manfred disappeared shortly after his return from Shanghai. He completely vanished off the face of the earth. And for someone who enjoyed the limelight as much as Manfred did, it must have been something terrible that happened to him."

"If he vanished, how do you know so much about him?"

"As it turns out, he kept a diary of his adventures and discoveries." Neri paused, whether for drama or to catch her breath, and then continued. "I have that diary."

I admit it. I was intrigued.

"Go on," I urged her. Neri showed just the hint of a smile. There was a twinkle in her eye.

"Manfred wrote about his trip to Shanghai. In the early 1900s, Shanghai wasn't like the rest of China, or really, like anywhere else in the world. Shanghai was an amazing city at the most amazing time in its history. Shanghai was a frenzy of development as business people, thrill-seekers and refugees poured in from all corners of the globe. The Far East's most cosmopolitan city exuded luxury, style, and excitement. Shanghai had the best art, the greatest architecture, and the strongest trade in all of Asia. If you had money, you could get anything. And thanks to his many benefactors, Manfred Krug had plenty of money.

"Manfred wrote about traversing the city in a rickshaw carriage. He described the sights, smells, and sounds as unlike anything he'd ever experienced. His rickshaw driver told him about a man only described as the uncle of the Li family. This man was known as a collector of rare items.

"Manfred's plan was to trade these rare and valuable items to the spice king, Kwan Huk Fat. He was notorious for keeping his best offerings only for his best clientele. The average customer got the average spices. But, if anything could be said about him with certainty, Manfred was anything but average.

"According to the diary, it was twilight when Manfred arrived at the Li family shop. The door opened with a creak that Manfred described as 'A creak worthy of a centuries-old demon's tomb gate.' He was led by a young girl through a maze of crowded rooms into a dining area. She introduced the man at the table as Sinmay Zau. As it turned out, Zau was a deeply superstitious man who recognized the opportunity to clean his shop of negative spirits by sending the unclean items off to America with Manfred.

"Zau pulled out an intricate wood box with gold inlays made generations ago. Designed to gather and focus otherworldly energy, Zau was convinced the box had led to the death of his son and wanted it far, far away. Manfred was intrigued and agreed to take it back to America with him. Zau was adamant it had to go home with Manfred. In all, he left with a half dozen artifacts rumored to have similar spiritual capabilities.

After meeting with the spice king, Manfred returned home with a treasure trove of spices. According to his diary, Manfred gifted one of these spirit boxes to his benefactors, Chester and Clara Congdon.

"I've heard the name Congdon," I said. "They have that massive mansion up in Duluth."

"Yes, the Glensheen Mansion. Twelve acres, 39 rooms, 27,000

square feet of living space. And the spirit box from Shanghai is tucked away somewhere there. Efforts to locate it have not been successful."

I found myself nodding. "I could see why. I have trouble finding my other shoe in my bedroom. Okay, my room might not be the neatest one in our house. But sometimes, it's just easier to have floor stuff. Just because it's in a drawer or hung up in the closet doesn't make it easier to find. In fact..."

Neri's serious expression halted my stream-of-consciousness rambling. "Abbey, I'd like you to retrieve the spirit box from Manfred Krug's benefactor," she said.

"Wait, how am I supposed to find it when everyone else couldn't?"

"Everyone else doesn't have your abilities." She paused, letting her words hang.

I didn't like how she stared at me while waiting for me to react. Not wanting her to have all the power, I tried not to be the first one to speak.

It wasn't easy.

I took a deep breath and tried counting to ten.

By the time I got to seven, I was frustrated. "Look, I don't know what you think you know about me, but—."

"I know you can see and communicate with dead people. I believe you may have the ability to cross over and back from the other side."

Oh, crap. Nobody should know this. Especially this woman. She has clearly shown she couldn't be trusted.

After studying Neri for a moment, I sighed. "My communication with spirits could best be described as a blunt instrument. I'm not exactly having conversations with ghosts. 'Hey, how's the weather on your side? How's Elvis these days?' I'm no ghost whisperer."

Neri laughed. "I'm sure you're not. That's where the power of the three comes in."

I sat up. "You mentioned that yesterday."

"Yes. Right before your dramatic exit." She gave me a look that I can only describe as distasteful. Like when the milk goes bad or when someone around you farts.

I chose not to acknowledge her display of distaste. "What is the power of the three?" This question had been eating at me all day.

"It's a way to enhance your abilities by looping in two other people. Physical contact between the three of you is essential for it to work. But when it does, it amplifies your ability to connect to ghosts."

Nodding, I understood. "I've done that with just a single person before. Several times, in fact. But it was always so they could share in what I experienced. So they could see the ghost, too."

Neri stood up and began to pace while she talked. "The power of the three closes the loop and takes your abilities to an entirely new level. Bring two others to the Glensheen Mansion, and you'll elevate your capabilities. But for this—for lack of a better term—performance enhancer of yours to work, the two people you bring must trust your abilities completely."

I nodded. "I've got several friends who fit those criteria."

"I assumed you would be bringing Lexi and Kelly," she said with an even expression.

I stared at her. She had resources, I'll give her that. But the intrusion into my privacy...well, I'd have to do something about that.

"What about you? Will you be there with us?"

Neri shook her head. "I'll be in Duluth, but not right with you. Things will work better if I leave you three to do your thing. I would be a distraction."

This was actually good news. Having her along would make things awkward. Now, I just had to convince Kelly and Lexi that we needed to break into the most famous mansion in the state. And if that wasn't bad enough, we'd be there to steal an ancient artifact—one with the power to gather and focus otherworldly energy.

What could be easier?

Handing over a folder with the University of Minnesota Duluth logo, Neri said, "I've got your alibi covered for this weekend. You're going on a college visit." Inside the folder was a letter from the school's admissions office. "There are copies for both Lexi and Kelly as well. You can use this as a perfectly plausible explanation for your Duluth visit."

Along with the letter, I found literature on the admissions process, the campus, and the programs they offer. And just for fun, another brochure was tucked in, "Historic Glensheen Mansion Tours."

"I've also included pages from Manfred's journal so you can learn about the spirit box. There's also an illustration of the box." There were photocopies of several handwritten pages tucked in the folder.

"I have to say, the school letters look legit. You must have used the same service as the one that made your FBI credentials." I gave her my most disarming smile.

She laughed. "Don't worry, they'll pass anyone's inspection."

Gesturing toward the door, Neri said, "You'd better get back to class. Can't have you getting behind in your schoolwork."

"I appreciate your thoughtfulness."

Neri leaned in close. "You best take this matter seriously. It could be dangerous."

There it is.

"Dangerous? You mentioned that earlier. Please explain."

"There's someone else after Manfred Krug's artifacts. And that someone is dangerous."

I looked at her, stunned. "Someone?"

"Who do you think shot me?"

But before I could say anything, she opened the door and said, "I'll be in touch."

She strode out of the vice principal's office and pushed past the school staff.

I was rooted in place as Mr. Fischer stuck his head in the office. He looked at me curiously while I wondered what rabbit hole I'd just been pushed into.

5

THE PHOTOGENIC PSYCHIC

Some of my earliest memories were of playing with our cat, Bojangles.

Cute, playful, and entitled, he was always at my side, demanding attention. I was seven years old before discovering we didn't have a cat.

Yeah, ghosts.

The thing is, I didn't always realize I saw what other people couldn't. I mean, when you're a child, how could you? My parents accepted these friends as a normal part of childhood. A lot of kids have invisible friends. The only difference between all the other kids and me was that my invisible friends just happened to be people who used to be living.

Being nearly 15 years old now, I can usually tell the difference between the living and the dead. I should, the dead have been coming to me pretty much all my life. For some reason, they're attracted to me like my dad's golf balls are to sand and water.

I'm unsure why I walked into Maynard's Emporium of Mystical Minds (formally Dearly Departed Connectors). Located in Uptown Minneapolis—the San Francisco of Minneapolis—the psychic readings shop hid in an ancient Victorian that looked years past its use-by date. Set well back from the busy Hennepin Avenue, the house blended in with its surroundings. In the ongoing fight between man and nature, the shrubs were winning the war and obscured much of the house. I wouldn't have known the place was occupied if it wasn't for the hand-painted sign out front.

As the door groaned shut, the crowd noise of the Uptown Art Fair disappeared behind me. The house was still; the only sounds were of the creaky wooden floor and a wobbly ceiling fan that had me scampering across the room rather than risk certain decapitation. The air smelled of dust, bacon grease, and, oddly, men's cologne. It's not a combination I would recommend.

Unsure of what to do, I waited.

As they often do in such moments, a song from the eighties bubbled up from the depths of my mind. "Money for Nothing" is a Dire Straits song that my mom liked to play. From the iconic *I Want My MTV* intro to the legendary guitar opening riffs, it was the kind of song that always had us singing along, which probably wasn't that uncommon for a song that catchy.

"Hello, young lady," a deep voice said from the shadows. Stepping into the light, that voice belonged to a large black man dressed in a reggae green and yellow robe. He glided into the room with a grace that contradicted his robust build. But even with his eyes that sparkled and danced and hair that would frustrate almost any hat or helmet looking to contain it, it was his smile that got me. You know those smiles that light up a room? Well, his was a smile that also made you feel a mix of happiness and gratitude. I liked him immediately.

"Hello, sir." I reached out my hand. My father taught me to make eye contact as I shook their hand firmly. I had the eye contact part down, but since my hand was utterly swallowed up by his, there was nothing for me to squeeze. There was a tingle in my fingers, possibly from being on the receiving end of his firm grip.

He must have sensed my discomfort because he broke into a belly laugh. "Just call me Maynard. If it's good enough for my relations, it's good enough for a nice suburban girl like you."

"Wait, how did you—I mean—what makes you think I'm from the suburbs?" I felt my cheeks flush. I don't like being profiled and put in a box.

There was that laugh again. "Please. It's the Art Fair. Our neighborhood is swarming with suburban teenagers named Brittany, Emma, and—." He paused, waiting for my answer.

I swallowed. "Abbey."

"Abbey? I was sure you were going to say, Sophia." This got him laughing again.

"I do know three Sophias."

"I'm sure you do," he said with a grin, his gaze holding mine. "So, you're here for a reading?"

I nodded.

"Why don't you have a seat?" Maynard gestured to a weathered wooden table that reminded me of one of my grandpa's furniture projects. Sturdy but slightly off-kilter. The chairs on either side of the table made the whole setup feel like a police interrogation. I hesitantly pulled out a chair.

"Hey, that's mine," Maynard barked at me. "The spiritual energy in this place is centered around that specific chair. When I sit there, the energy is drawn in and flows right to me, allowing me to make psychic connections, the likes of which are rarely seen. Girl, you can't mess with a man's flow."

I sheepishly pushed the chair back in. "Sorry."

His laugh told me I was being messed with. "It doesn't matter at all which chair I'm in. Sit where you like."

My finely tuned sense of danger wasn't raising flags of any color, but still.

I didn't sit in his chair.

Twenty minutes ago, getting a psychic reading was the furthest thing from being on my radar.

My father and I had strolled leisurely, taking in the art fair's paintings, photography, sculptures, and decorative furniture, when we saw Maynard's Emporium. As we passed, I got an idea so simple that I knew I had to try. If a psychic could summon spirits, maybe I could learn how to summon someone who can help me locate the Glensheen's artifact. Usually, ghosts come to me and not the other way around.

So, as soon as my father got rolling on a discussion about depth of field with a nature photographer, I excused myself, saying I wanted to go back and look at something. My father waved for me to go. I wasn't sure what to expect with a psychic reading as I stood on the sidewalk looking at the old house.

Now, looking across at the smiling giant, whatever I could've imagined a meeting with a psychic would be like was nothing compared to this.

"Grab on," Maynard said as he reached his hands across the table. Tentatively stretching out my arms, I held onto two of his ginormous fingers. There was another tingle of electricity that lasted just a moment. Maynard closed his eyes and said, "Bitter elephants. Bitter elephants."

Bitter elephants? Whatever, I rolled with it.

As his voice grew in volume, there was a growing energy. I expected to see a gaggle of ghosts, but we were alone in the room. Not a ghoul, spirit, or poltergeist to be found.

"Grumpy cats. Angry dogs. Grumpy cats. Angry dogs."

Maynard moaned, his head rolling from side to side and his eyes squeezed shut. As his voice got louder, his arms trembled as he stomped his feet on the old wood floors. A picture frame fell from the table behind him and crashed to the floor. I wanted to tell him this is why you can't have nice stuff, but I kept my mouth shut.

Maynard's breathing came out in big bursts that had me debating if he was having a stroke or simply practicing his Lamaze breathing techniques. Just when I thought things couldn't get any stranger, they didn't.

Maynard went still, and his eyes popped open. "Dead elephants," he said breathlessly, staring right into my soul. "Dead. Elephants."

I let go of his fingers.

Pulling back his arms, Maynard leaned forward and said, "You're searching for something—or someone."

I nodded. But wasn't everyone that came here searching for something? Guidance? Certainly. Answers or advice? Probably. Missing people? Maybe. Grandma's missing teeth? Hope not.

"The spirit world holds the answers. You may not realize it, but life is often impacted by the dead."

Believe me, I know it.

"The dead can come back to help the living. And someone is here with us right now," Maynard said. "Someone that you've lost. Someone that has the answers to all your questions." He said this with the passion of a preacher on Easter Sunday.

I looked around, but we were alone. It was just us. Confused, I turned back to the man in front of me.

Maynard laughed as he shook his head. "Child, you won't be able to see them. Only the anointed have the gift to see the dead."

I must be anointed then because I can see the dead. But glancing around the room again, I didn't see anyone. This felt wrong. "So, there's someone with us right now? Here in this room?"

Maynard nodded and gestured to his right, my left. "Right there. Here to help you."

I looked where he pointed. I looked high. I looked low. I even tried squinting. There wasn't anyone there.

Sigh.

Pulling out a crumpled twenty, I tossed it on the table. "You've been a peach. Thanks for the enlightenment." The weight of frustration made it difficult to stand, but anger fueled my movement. I felt stupid, and I just wanted to get out of there. I headed for the door.

"Wait, we haven't even started." Confusion colored Maynard's face.

Anger colored mine. "I'm finished."

"Okay, then. Bye-bye." The slightest hint of a smirk was on his face, and the twenty was no longer on the table.

I took several steps towards the door, but anger made me turn back.

Narrowing my eyes at the psychic, I cracked my knuckles. As much as I wish I weren't one of those people who made a scene, I was one of those. Some people can take their anger and stuff it down, only to have stomach problems later. But I have enough problems without adding stomach ones to the list. I marched back to the table where Maynard sat back in his chair with a bemused expression.

The pounding in my ears was loud. "Look, we both know there wasn't anyone in the room with us. No ghosts, no spirits, and no dearly departed. Just me and a big fat fraud."

Maynard frowned and looked hurt. "But I've been losing weight."

Wait, what?

"No, I didn't mean you were fat. I meant that fraud-wise, you are ginormous. Larger than life. Bigger than a building. If you were a lake, you'd be Lake Superior. If you were a liar, you'd be a former president. If you—"

Maynard held up his hands. "Okay, okay, I get it. You're upset. My bad."

I pointed my finger at him, which usually helps get my point across, and said, "I'm not sure you do. You say you help people, yet you make up ghosts." I studied him for a long moment. He looked at me uncomfortably as he sat there blinking, twitching. But something in his expression bothered me. "Wait. You don't even believe in ghosts, do you?"

"Um." He looked like someone who had just been asked if they had enough life insurance.

"Just answer the question, you big goof." I already knew the answer, though.

He shook his head. "But I find the idea of them useful."

"To con people, you mean." I jabbed my finger at him, enjoying the feeling of power as I challenged him. This must be how trial lawyers feel as they break down the opposing witness.

He shook his head and looked down at his hands. "Not in the way you're thinking. I have a talent for reading people, and I sometimes get impressions and words that come to me. Often, it's just what people need to hear. These words have helped many, many people, but I don't know where they come from. So, it's far easier for people to understand that the ghost of a relative is there giving me information." He looked up at me. "See? No harm, no foul."

"You're one smooth criminal."

His eyes lit up. "Hey, 'Smooth Criminal.' I love that song. Michael Jackson, right?"

I nodded.

"The eighties sure made some great music." He smiled wistfully. "So much better than today's crapola."

Today's crapola. I couldn't help but grin. Maybe there could be a basis for at least an understanding. Perhaps even a second chance.

"Okay, Maynard. I'll give you another try. But you're wrong; there are ghosts. Plenty of them." If anyone knows this, it's me.

Shaking his head with a smile, he said, "Naw, you're just messing with me. If there were actual ghosts, I would know."

"Really?" Interested, I sat back down.

With the confidence of someone holding four aces, he nodded. "I would. I'm a psychic, after all."

Apparently, not a good one.

"Okay, Maynard, let me tell you about something that happened when I was in grade school. I went to a friend's house, and as I walked up the driveway, I saw a man sitting in a car. He waved at me, then just disappeared. It was like flipping a switch. Confused, I described the man when I went inside, and my friend's mom broke down crying. Evidently, I'd described her recently passed father, who left her the car."

I remember my friend's expression as she looked between me and her crying mother. She looked amazed but also a little scared of me.

Maynard stroked his chin. "That didn't really happen, did it?"

I nodded. "Yes, sir, it did."

Leaning forward, I continued. "But that's not the only time. When we were staying at my aunt's, I saw a man in blue overalls the night we arrived. He waved and walked into the guest room, but when I followed him, he wasn't there. The only other door in the room led to a closet. But when I opened it, there wasn't a man there—just a set of blue overalls on a hanger."

Eyes wide, Maynard said, "For real?" Again, I nodded.

"There's more, plenty more. When I was young, we rented a cabin on the north shore of Lake Superior. I woke up in the middle of the night to see a long-haired woman in a nightgown rocking in a chair that creaked as it moved. I tried talking to her, but she only smiled. I told my parents in the morning, but they didn't believe me. So, when we were checking out, I insisted on telling the clerk at the front desk about the woman. The clerk said it sounded like the previous owner, who'd died there a decade before. I remember my parents being speechless, which, if you know my parents, is quite unusual."

Maynard laughed. "The woman sounds like some of my relatives. They never know when to leave. I had an uncle who came to stay with us for two weeks and ended up staying for two years." There was that belly laugh again. I couldn't help but smile.

When he settled down, he fixed me with a look that should have been accompanied by a light bulb appearing over his head. "Speaking of relatives, I'm guessing that's what brought you here."

I gave him nothing.

"So now you're quiet?" He studied me for a long moment. "Let me ask, have you ever seen a relative come to you as a ghost?"

I thought for a moment about how best to answer. "Apparently, when I was a baby, I would start waving and talking, like kids do. My mom said I'd babble, pause, then laugh. Eventually, I'd wave goodbye and return to what I'd been doing. But the thing was, every time I had one of those one-sided conversations, my mom noticed that my deceased grandmother's scent would unmistakably show up."

Maynard's eyes widened and then just stayed that way. It looked like he'd forgotten to blink. "Really?" he asked after a long moment.

I nodded. "Do you believe me?"

Clearing his throat, Maynard reached out across the table. "I believe you believe it, but let's try this again. Maybe I can help. Grab hold."

Grabbing onto his large fingers, I felt the tingle once again. Maynard closed his eyes. I kept mine open.

"Bitter elephants," he said with the panache of a second-year drama student. "Bitter. Elephants."

When I loudly cleared my throat, he opened one eye.

"Do you have to go through the entire animal thing again?" I asked. "It's a little theatrical for my taste."

With a wounded look, he said, "It helps me focus, but I can skip the other parts if you like."

"That would be nice."

"Okay, here we go." He gave me a wink. "Bitter elephants. Bitter elephants."

I couldn't help but wince when Maynard started to moan, but then he chuckled and said, "Just kidding."

"This is why you don't have friends, Maynard," I said sternly, but I couldn't help but giggle. "Please continue, I don't have the entire evening." And my dad was probably wondering about my whereabouts. He couldn't talk to the photographer forever, could he?

"Okay, okay," he said, but a grin was on his face. After a moment, he relaxed his smile and closed his eyes. "Grumpy cats. Angry dogs," he said, pausing before finishing with, "Grumpy cats."

Meow.

Maynard paused dramatically. "Dead elephants," he said finally, and his eyes fluttered open. "Young lady, you're here because you're missing someone. But don't worry, everything will be okay."

He must have seen my face because he quickly added, "Really.

Everything is going to be fine. I can see it in your future." He smiled. It was a smug smile.

I absolutely hate smug smiles, but something behind Maynard caught my eye before I could address my feelings. Where there was space a moment before, a woman now stood. I watched her shimmer into being by the large bay window, beams of light sparkling right through her. The woman was older with a lined face that showed many years of smiles. Her hair was piled on her head, and she wore a long, colorful gown. She smiled at me with a dazzling grin, and I suspected I might know who she was.

Maynard noticed my gaze and looked over his shoulder. I pointed to where the woman stood. She looked back at me over her glasses with an amused expression. He turned around, evidently not seeing anything. His loss.

Maynard wore his confusion the way most people wore their joy. It was all over his face.

"Maynard, are you telling me you can't see her?" I pointed toward the woman again.

"See who?" he asked with growing frustration. "Don't tell me it's a ghost because there aren't ghosts. They're a product of simple minds. People only see what they want to see." His exasperation with me wasn't unusual, but it was understandable.

"Look, Maynard. Maybe I'm abnormal, but I see ghosts all the time. I'm not saying this to brag but to open your eyes. Seeing ghosts isn't nearly as glamorous as it sounds." I flipped my hair back. "It's made for a really tough life at times."

Maynard flicked his eyes up at me. "Really?"

"Really. Let me tell you a story. We went to the Minneapolis Institute of Arts for a field trip in third grade. I was so excited to see all the paintings and statues, but I saw something else, too."

Maynard looked intrigued, so I kept talking.

"We sat on the benches listening to the docent lady. She talked about the Impressionist artists—I still remember that because I love Monet—when I noticed a woman who had glided into the room. She had red hair and bright red lips, which I thought was so beautiful. Her clothes were different from anything I was used to seeing. Her colorfully patterned dress went to her knees, and she wore heels with a strap like my dance shoes. She had a hat, gloves, and a small handbag."

I leaned forward.

"Something about her captivated me, so I followed her when she left the room. I almost bumped into the woman when I came around the corner; she'd paused by a humongous painting of a house. She seemed to be studying it, so I asked her if she liked that house. Without saying a word, she turned and looked at me tenderly. Since she looked kind, I told her my house was white with green around the windows. When I asked what color her house was, she paused and touched her cheek like she had to think about it. I started laughing because I thought it was funny that she didn't know what color her own house was."

I shook my head at the memory.

"My friend, Jenny, asked why I was laughing. I turned around and saw my whole class staring at me, even my teacher, Mrs. Olson. I pointed to the red-haired lady and said she was being funny. The woman smiled at me. Jenny said there wasn't anyone there and that I should stop. I told her it was the red-haired lady in the pretty dress and fancy shoes standing next to me. Jenny said I wasn't being funny."

I pushed back my hair and sighed. "Sometimes I can't tell if the person I see is alive or dead. I'm better at it now, but some ghosts are closer to our plane, and it's nearly impossible to tell the difference. I moved over so Jenny could see the red-haired lady, too, but she couldn't—I was the only one. That's when things went from bad to worse."

Maynard looked at me with wide eyes.

"When I went to grab the lady's hand to bring her over to Jenny, something happened. The woman's smile faded. Her skin seemed to melt away, and I could see the tendons and bones underneath. I smelled something that reminded me of when my dad's grilling went wrong. As I watched, one of her eyes sort of rolled and fell out of its socket. I screamed as loud as I could, and it echoed in the quiet art gallery. I couldn't stop screaming, and when the woman fell to her knees in front of me with her single eye pleading for help, I completely lost it. I was still sobbing when my parents came to take me home."

Tears ran down my cheeks. This story has always stuck with me, and not for good reasons.

"I lost my school friends that day. I sat by myself for the rest of the school year. But that wasn't the only time my friends became scared of me and didn't want to be near me. Life—and death—aren't always fair."

The woman in the room with us had moved closer to Maynard while I told my sad tale. "Still can't see her? This woman right here?" I asked as I gestured like a frustrated traffic cop to a driver who wasn't moving when it was their turn.

Maynard wisely didn't say anything, just shook his head. The woman shook her own head but wore a tender expression as she gazed at Maynard.

Clearing my throat, I looked him in the eyes. "Do me a favor and just this once, believe there's another world alongside ours. Just because you haven't been able to see, hear, or feel it doesn't mean it isn't there. You can't see electricity, but it's there. You need to open your mind to the possibilities around you," I urged him. This got me thinking, and I blurted out, "Let me lead this reading."

He looked as skeptical as my father when I suggested raising llamas would be an excellent way to keep our lawn trimmed without having to push around our old mower.

"When I meditate, there are times I've crossed over and left our plane of existence. I've gone somewhere where there are more shadows than light. I still see the room where I started, but it's like looking through a foggy mirror. I know I'm not alone there, but it's difficult to see anyone—or anything—directly. If I look out of the corner of my eye, I sometimes see the inhabitants of this shadowy place. There's been children, grandmothers, and things that aren't human."

Maynard shuddered.

"It's a place I visit when I'm curious or need a reminder that living in the present is how I should be living. It's a place of wonder and terror, but there's nowhere else like it. The thing about being surrounded by the dead is it makes you feel alive. Let me take you there."

Maynard didn't look convinced. "I don't think you've got a career in writing travel brochures, but sure."

I reached across the table and said, "Grab on, big guy. It's time you started believing in ghosts and the paranormal. I need you to experience my world."

With a bemused look, Maynard swallowed my hands inside his, and there was that tingle again. It felt like a low-level electrical charge ran through his fingers into my hands and up my arms. The hairs on my forearms stood at attention.

"Okay, picture a place—"

"Do the animal thing," Maynard urged.

"Really?"

He nodded, and there was a hint of a smile. "For me?"

Various comebacks ran through my mind, but I decided it couldn't hurt to oblige his request. "Fine, but I get to do my own version."

"Fine," he said, but he grinned.

I closed my eyes. "Cooked goose. Cooked. Goose."

Maynard made a noise that sounded like a snort.

Because I meditate nearly every day, I've gotten speedy with phasing out of my everyday conscious thoughts and leaving all anxiety, drama, and social media behind. The very process of moving to this other plane has never failed to surround me with inner calm and blanket me with warm feelings of love and acceptance.

I could so write travel brochures.

"Picture a place with swirling mists, dancing shadows, and warm, humid air. Picture a place where the dead can feel at home, where the living don't belong but are still welcome. Picture a place where you see a woman who may be familiar. She's older with a face that has known many years of smiles. She has those stylish half-frame glasses and hair that's piled on top of her head. She's wearing a long gown with many bright colors." Maynard made a slight noise.

"Hang on, Maynard, we're almost there. When I say my next animal phrase, open your eyes to this new place."

Taking a deep breath, I said, "Hog wild."

I opened my eyes just in time to see Maynard's pop open.

"Sweet mother of Jesus." His eyes were wide with surprise and recognition. Maynard stood and took a step toward the woman.

"Momma?"

"Mighty," she replied with obvious affection. "My mighty boy."

I had to agree as I looked at the giant in front of me. Although, for such a large man, he sure had a tender side. The way he looked at her and the way she looked back at him made my heart melt.

But then—

It was the smell at first.

An odor of sulfur wafted in while I watched mother and son. Initially, it was just a hint of the pungent smell. But soon, the air grew thick and foul from the stench.

"I gotta go," Maynard's mother said abruptly. "This isn't right." And she was gone in a shimmer.

Maynard turned to look at me, but I was too fascinated with the black tentacle that had slithered from the shadows behind Maynard. He didn't seem to notice when it wrapped itself around his ankle.

I frantically pointed at his foot the way a cameraperson would point at an oncoming tornado behind a storm-chasing reporter.

But rather than noticing, Maynard stared at me with his soft eyes. "Why?" he asked. "Why?"

Before I could even think of a reply, a picture fell off the wall behind me, shards of glass skittering across the wooden floors. I flinched but didn't turn around. This was a new development—and not a good one. In theory, the place we are in shouldn't be able to affect our world. We were the ones visiting, not the other way around. Unfortunately, no one seemed to have told this to the shadow place.

An antique couch with artsy pastel flowers slid across the floor, bunching up the rug in front of it. I stared.

The ornate crystal chandelier took that moment to light up and pop every bulb. I gaped.

The table where we sat sunk into the floor as if sinking into a swamp. I gawked.

The nails on the weathered wood floor started to pop up one by one. I swore.

A surge of warm, moist air came and went like the entire house was breathing. I stood up.

Maynard was rooted in place. He looked like a kid experiencing the State Fair Midway for the first time, totally in awe of all around him. The tentacle was now wrapped up to his thigh.

From out of the shadows, a strange thing came into view. A solid oak table levitated three feet off the ground and moved toward me at the speed of a basset hound on a Sunday stroll. I took a step backward. There's something decidedly unsettling seeing such a familiar object acting so unnaturally.

Even though the table moved with the speed of a basset hound, it occurred to me that some dogs bite. I took another step back.

The table stopped and shuddered as it rotated. The legs turned upwards towards me, and I couldn't help but picture myself getting run through like knights jousting in the movies.

Suddenly, from the same direction the table came from, half a dozen knives streaked through the air and slammed into the tabletop. They must have been moving fast because the blade tips burst through the bottom. If the table hadn't been there...

As with much of my life, the music of the eighties was my soundtrack. Another Michael Jackson song popped into my mind with its synthesizer opening, followed by the dirty sneer of one of the world's most recognizable guitar riffs. "Beat It" was there telling me my next move.

Time to leave.

I was so out of there but stopped immediately as I couldn't leave Maynard behind.

The tentacle had continued its upward climb and was now around his waist. Glistening with a wet, slimy oil, it pulsed with evil intent as the thick cable-like tentacle squeezed his mid-section. A second one was now going after Maynard's other leg. His eyes were squeezed shut, and there was a tremble in Maynard's cheek, but otherwise, he remained still.

The thought of getting near those tentacles made my stomach churn, but there are times when you have to face your fears. This was one of those times.

Moving in front of Maynard, I grabbed his hands. The tingle returned and flowed up my arms.

"Maynard. Look at me." I needed his help.

Maynard's eyes popped open, and we held each other's gaze. A tentacle bumped into my leg, and I fought the urge to run.

"I'm going to get us back home. Shut your eyes and hang on. The ride may be a bit bumpy."

Closing my eyes, I tried to moderate my breathing. I knew I needed to slow my heart rate and racing mind to get us back. It wasn't going to be easy, especially when I could now feel something wet and slimy wrapping around my calf.

Got to relax. Got. To. Relax.

A strong gust of wind swirled my hair—unusual since we were inside—and the floor began to heave and tilt. I hung onto my giant for support and willed myself to slow down my ragged breathing. I took a long breath in through my nose. The sulfur burned. I briefly held it before pushing it out slowly through my mouth. Again. And again.

Shoving the fear away, I focused on the image of the large room where we started. Wooden floors, paisley wallpaper, chair rails, and crown molding. The large, wooden table where we sat across from each other when this began. Time to return.

"Maynard, keep your eyes closed. Picture the room as it was, with us in our chairs at the table. We're holding hands across the table, just two friends offering support for one another."

There was silence from across the table. Even his hands felt slack on mine.

"Maynard," I said evenly. "Are you still with me?"

A moan came from my large friend.

"We're going to open our eyes when I say three. Ready?"

"Uh, huh."

"One." The wind picked up and rose to a roar. My hair swirled around my face. I felt like I was riding a motorcycle.

"Two." The sensation of my leg being squeezed moved up to my thigh. It felt like one of those blood pressure cuffs on steroids.

"Three." I opened my eyes, stunned at what was in front of me.

Everything was back to normal, the shadow plane gone, but definitely not forgotten. Maynard sat across from me with a dazed expression. We were still holding hands.

"Well, this is awkward," he said after a moment and let go.

There was no sign of the earlier damage. The table was back, the kitchen table was gone, and there was not a single tentacle in sight.

"Is it always that chaotic, that scary in your world?" he asked with a shake of his head.

I shook mine. "No, I've visited that shadow plane a dozen times, and nothing like that has ever happened. And nothing like that has ever intruded into our world. I have no idea what was different or why it happened this time."

"Girl, that was a freak parade if I've ever seen one. You're welcome here anytime, but for heaven's sake, leave the ghostly folk home. Lord have mercy." And I got his belly laugh again before leaving to find my father.

◁▷

"There you are. I wondered what happened to you," my father said as he sat on a curb with several matted photographs at his feet. The one facing me was of a star-filled night sky over a wooded shoreline. It looked like the Boundary Waters in northern Minnesota, one of our favorite places.

"That photographer found a new patron," I remarked. "Did you spend your entire allowance on him?"

My father laughed, which sounded like an out-of-control goat. I loved him for that. "Maybe. But I have enough left for those mini donuts we saw near the parking lot." He pointed down the avenue.

"Sweet." They smelled amazing when we passed the donut truck. "I love mini donuts. They should be their own food group. Seriously."

My father stood and gave me a once-over. "Everything okay? I'm surprised you didn't find anything."

I wrapped an arm around his waist. "I have everything I need right here. That is, except for the mini donuts."

We walked together toward the donut stand. "Your mother mentioned you're visiting Duluth tomorrow," my father said after a moment. "I'm happy you're thinking ahead and visiting a college. Though I suspect the weekend may be more about chasing adventure than chasing a higher education." His eyes had a twinkle.

"Well, there's no reason both can't happen, right?" I gave him my most angelic smile.

He laughed. "Nope. No reason at all. But you should visit the Congdon mansion while you're up there."

Little did he know that's why we were going to Duluth.

"It's supposed to be haunted, you know. The Glensheen was built by Chester and Clara Congdon in the early 1900s. The large mansion went from noteworthy to notorious when the Congdon's youngest daughter, Elizabeth, was murdered, along with her nurse, in 1977. They were killed by Elizabeth's adopted daughter, Marjorie, and her husband. Those old homes hang onto a lot of energy, both good and bad, due to the life and death moments that occurred."

He laughed when I told him that he'd talked me into it.

"Knowing you, it probably didn't take much to convince you," he said.

He was right, of course.

We walked in silence for a block as we navigated through the crowds. Across the street was the sign for Maynard's Emporium of Mystical Minds (formally Dearly Departed Connectors). The house sat far back from the busy street and looked utterly lifeless.

My father saw my gaze and nodded toward the old house. "Such a sad story."

"Wait, what?" I turned to my father. "What's a sad story?"

We paused as he gestured toward Maynard's home. "This place was a neighborhood icon. The owner was such a character, and people used to come from all over to have readings done."

"Wait, Dad. You said the owner was such a character? Did something happen to him?" Was he talking about Maynard?

My father set his photographs at his feet and ran a hand through his hair. "You never read the news, do you?"

I shook my head. The news is primarily politics and murder. In both cases, it's people doing wrong things because they thought they were right.

"Well," he said with a nod, "there's a lot of history in that house. The business and the home were passed down through generations. Most recently, it passed from mother to son. When the son took over, he quickly became immensely popular and loved to entertain with his flamboyant readings."

He looked at me, a weariness in his eyes. "But sometimes life isn't fair. One day, he was giving a reading to a woman who had flown all the way in from Virginia. Just after he started, Maynard Devellioux put a hand up to his temple, moaned, and said one word. Then he fell over. Dead from a brain aneurism."

"Lord have mercy. What was his last word?" My stomach felt queasy.

With a grim nod, my father answered. "His one word was the question of many over the ages."

"Why?" I answered for him, thinking of when Maynard stared at me with his dead eyes, asking the very same thing.

"Exactly. Maynard asked that final question and passed away, never to speak again." My father picked up his art fair purchases and gestured for us to continue. I hesitated.

But he spoke to me. Maynard spoke to me.

In our short time together, I'd grown to like Maynard immensely and planned on stopping by whenever I returned to Uptown. But now, after hearing my dad's story, I guess it'll be Maynard's ghost I'll visit.

One sure thing about ghosts is that there isn't any certainty. Each one is different, and each one is unpredictable. Some are more like faded shadows, and some are so close to our world that I can't readily tell they are ghosts. Maynard definitely belonged in the second camp, which could explain why things went so haywire when I brought him to the other plane.

As I turned away from Maynard's house, I shook my head. Honestly, I don't think he knew he was dead. Breaking the news to Maynard wouldn't be easy, but it was something he needed to hear.

It felt like the dead were always going to complicate my life. That's just the way it is when you're a spook magnet.

But I'm okay with that. It keeps life interesting.

I hurried to catch up to my father and the promise of mini donuts.

Mmm.

6

NOOKS, CRANNIES, AND SECRETS

Duluth sits at the lowest tip of Lake Superior in Minnesota. From the lakeside, its sweeping hills are dotted with Victorian homes built by wealthy shipping and mining families a century ago. Except for a few ice-bound months, massive ore ships regularly come and go across the harbor. I've always loved visiting Duluth, where even the air smells sweet.

It was a sunny Saturday morning as we crested the hill and got our first view of Lake Superior—and it was stunning. Kelly let out a loud whoop, "We're here."

Kelly's confidence had always been off the charts high, and she didn't hold things in because she was worried about what others might think.

This brings me to Abbey's key to happiness: Why go through life acting like you don't care about things? It's not only okay to show your passions, it's encouraged. You'll have more fun simply being yourself. It's okay to let loose when the spirit moves you.

After leaving Mr. Fischer's office, I'd found Kelly and Lexi. When I filled them in on my strange meeting with Neri, they were super excited about the idea of a road trip. And as Neri predicted, convincing our parents that this trip would be a good thing wasn't tricky. Only two and a half hours straight north, driving to Duluth would be an easy trip. Lexi offered to drive—she's older than Kelly and me—and said her parents loved the idea that she's looking at schools.

As we turned into the mansion's parking lot, Kelly read from her phone. "The Glensheen, a posh mansion perched on the Lake Superior coast, has a deserved reputation here in Minnesota. In 1977, the aged heiress to a vast mining fortune was killed along with her night nurse. The mystery has been a media sensation ever since."

And here we were at the Glensheen Mansion for the last tour of the day.

We'd just parked when a small gray sedan raced into the parking lot. Driving way too fast, it swerved around a group of older women. They scrambled out of the way as the car roared on by. It skidded to a stop in the accessible parking spot closest to the entrance. A woman threw open her door, slamming it into the door of the neighboring car.

If it bothered her at all, she didn't let on.

Her long-braided hair was as gray as the overcast sky, and she wore a cranberry-colored knit cap. She was tall and thin but not in a frail sort of way. Her face was angular, with the palest blue eyes I'd ever seen. She glared at us like we were the ones who had just done something wrong and stormed off.

"That Cruella de Vil can be a mean bitch," Kelly said as she looked after the woman.

I couldn't help but laugh. Some people will always tell it like it is. That's Kelly.

ᗡᗞ

At the stables, we met up with our Glensheen Mansion tour guide, Sarah. With a bright smile, Sarah introduced herself as a University of Minnesota Duluth student. She said the mansion had been gifted to the University by the Congdon family years back with the provision that Marjorie was allowed to live there. After her untimely death, tours were started, and hundreds of thousands went through the mansion and its grounds every year. She asked if it was our first time visiting the Glensheen. When all three of us said it was, she beamed and said, "Wonderful. You're in for a real treat."

Turning to the rest of our group, Sarah started her tour talk. "The Glensheen was built over a century ago by iron ore baron Chester Congdon for his wife, Clara. Construction took three years and nine months to complete the entire estate. Sitting on seven acres, the grounds include a private beach, boathouse, gardener's house, greenhouse, tennis court, cow barn, and vegetable garden where the family grew their produce. Along with all those amenities, there is the 39-room mansion itself. It overlooks a formal English-style landscape, giving way to Lake Superior's rugged shoreline. It is hauntingly beautiful."

"I'm getting shivers," Lexi whispered.

"We're standing in the Carriage House," Sarah continued. "This two-story building includes apartments, a horse stable, and a carriage room. Today, this building is home to the Glensheen administrative offices." Sarah led us down a hallway past the large stable enclosures. We stepped out into the cool November air, and I wished I'd dressed warmer. Don't get me wrong, other than the frigid temperatures, Minnesota was beautiful in the winter. And to make my point, the sun peeked out from the gray clouds and illuminated the frosted trees.

"At the turn of the previous century, Duluth had more millionaires per capita than any other American city. And these millionaires waged a contest to see who could build the biggest, finest mansion on the north shore."

"Clearly, old man Congdon won," Lexi blurted out, cracking up the tour group. Even our guide was laughing hard enough that she had to take a moment to compose herself before continuing.

She pointed to a small brick building that reminded me of the English cottages that dot the countryside in rural England. "That's the gardener's cottage," Sarah said. "As you may imagine, maintaining the grounds was a full-time job. There are over 30 varieties of trees alone. And aren't they looking spectacular today?"

I had my phone's camera on as I took a picture of the tree line leading up to the mansion. Most everyone was doing the same, but I noticed one woman wasn't taking pictures. It was the mean woman from the parking lot. When she saw me looking, she nodded. I turned away to take another photo.

Our guide brought us to the front entrance, where a massive door awaited us. Sarah pushed it open, and we all paused in wonder at the splendor inside. It was as if we had been transported back a century.

"Wow," Lexi said. "So, this is how the other half lives."

"I don't know about half of people living like this," Kelly said. "Maybe the other two percent. Bill Gates and the King of England. But that's about it."

The stairway had massive columns leading up to ornamental carved wood adorning the walls. The railing and spindles were museum-worthy, let alone the intricate woodwork surrounding the windows at the top of the landing.

The effect was not over the top, but the timeless beauty of the centuries-old craftsmanship was impressive. I couldn't imagine what it was like growing up in a place like this. Would it even be possible to take these surroundings for granted? I doubted it.

Sarah led us through a reception room and into several other rooms, each more stunning than the last. But it was the library that took my breath away. Maybe it was my love of books or my appreciation for exotic souvenirs, but I was lost in this world of yesteryear. I found myself only half listening as our guide talked about the collection of books. She said the library included the complete works of one of my favorite authors, Edgar Allan Poe. Sarah pointed out the finely detailed mahogany wood and the beautiful grand piano. I felt transported back to the days when the Congdon family lived there.

It wasn't until she mentioned the collection of rare artifacts from around the world that I perked up, remembering why we were there.

"The *Paris by day, Paris by night* lamp is a fine example of the mansion's unique décor from around the world. This epitomizes the Congdon's interest in the world around them. They may have lived here in Duluth, but they traveled the world and were connoisseurs of the finest art and collectibles the world had to offer. And a century later, we still get to enjoy them." Sarah smiled. "Can you tell that I like my job?" she asked.

"How could you not?" I said. "What beautiful surroundings."

"Better than working fast food," Lexi added.

I leaned in close and whispered, "Maybe she'll mention the spirit box and save us the trouble of searching the entire place."

Kelly shook her head. "We can't get that lucky."

Sarah continued. "There are five levels in the mansion, three of which are included in the standard tour you're on. You'll find that every room has treasures from around the world. Even the attic is filled with cast-off furniture that would easily find a place of prominence in most homes. The living spaces have an endless array of dazzling art, woodwork, fireplaces, libraries, and influences of Victorian, Art Nouveau, and Arts and Crafts styles."

Sarah led us up the grand staircase and through one bedroom after another. "Holy cow," Lexi exclaimed. "How many kids did the Congdons have? There's a ton of bedrooms here." Lexi giggled, the surest sign of more silliness to come. And Lexi never disappointed.

"Um, excuse me, Sarah. How many children did they have?" Lexi asked. "Did old man Chester rent out all these spare rooms for some extra spending money?"

Sarah had a grin on her face. "That's the first time I've been asked that question. With seven children—and an orphaned nephew—there weren't extra bedrooms. And I'm sure that *old man* Chester already had plenty of spending money."

The shower in the master bath was over the top, even by today's standards. Full body sprays were in each corner, with an overhead rain showerhead. Sarah said that when the Congdons wanted to use it back in the day, they had to call down to have the boiler started to make hot water. The shower experience was said to be painful, as the intent was to remove dead skin cells by blasting them off.

After touring the third-floor boy's bedrooms, we were led down to the kitchen back on the first floor. Sarah brought us to a control panel of sorts. "Every room was connected by intercom, technology that had just been introduced. Surprisingly, it's mostly still working today. There's also a system to summon the servants. The bell would ring, and the arrow would flip to show where they were needed. Way ahead of their time."

We were brought through a gorgeous breakfast room with green tiles and stained-glass views of the lake. The tour ended in the basement laundry room. "As you may have guessed, the Congdon family didn't do their own laundry. They had a staff that took care of it. It was unheard of in their day to have a setup like this. But, as you've seen, the mansion was ahead of its time."

Sarah looked around our little group. "Well, that's the end of our tour. Does anyone have any questions before I let you go?"

"Umm," said a voice behind me. I turned, and it was the woman who roared into the parking lot.

"Yes?" Sarah said with the nod of someone expecting the question.

"Wasn't there a murder here? One of the Congdons?" The woman had an accent.

"There were two, actually. Both happened the same night. Back in 1977, Elizabeth Congdon lived here. Elizabeth was 83 years old and somewhat of an invalid. She was murdered in her sleep. It's an interesting story." Sarah's eyes sparkled, and judging by her dramatic pause, this was the part of her job she looked forward to. "Let me tell you what happened."

I stepped closer, not wanting to miss a single word, and noticed the entire group had done the same. Sarah glanced around like she wanted to keep this just between us. "On the night of June 26, 1977, an intruder entered the Glensheen Mansion through a window in the billiards room."

"What's billiards?" Lexi whispered.

"It's another name for pool," I whispered back.

"The first murder was Elizabeth's night nurse, Velma Pietila. The intruder encountered her on the way to Elizabeth's bedroom. The surprised nurse was thrown down the stairs and then clubbed to death with a brass candlestick."

"Harsh," Lexi said to no one in particular.

"Exactly," our guide said. "But the intruder had a larger target in mind. Elizabeth was in her bed, and using a pink satin pillow, the killer suffocated Elizabeth."

"Death by a pink satin pillow. Really harsh." Lexi again.

Sarah continued. "Initially, without a single suspect, the police considered the possibility that the crime was a robbery gone awry. An empty jewelry box was found on the main bedroom floor, and the house had been ransacked. Additionally, a car was stolen from the estate and found at the Minneapolis-St. Paul airport."

Pausing to glance around at our group, Sarah continued. "But in cases like this, police looked at the family members. Greed can be a powerful motivator. Marjorie stood to inherit the Congdon fortune upon her mother's death. Three days before the murder, Marjorie had authorized her husband, Roger, to receive roughly $2.5 million of her share of the inheritance. Marjorie was acquitted. Roger was convicted and later confessed to both murders before committing suicide a few years later. He never got any of the promised money from Marjorie."

"Wow," someone said behind me.

"That's the sordid story, but you shouldn't judge the mansion based solely on one event that happened many years ago," Sarah said. "The Glensheen is a remarkable place with many nooks, crannies, and secrets. Come back and see us again."

Our group broke up, some lingering, some headed for the stairs and presumably the exit. Another group headed for the boiler room to hide. That would be us.

We booked down the hall to the boiler room. Inside, we hid behind the large heating equipment. Unless someone specifically came looking for us, we would remain undiscovered. At least, that was our plan.

Fingers crossed, I slid to the floor and looked at my two brave friends. Not many would follow me on such an adventure. Smiling, I told them to sit with me. "We're going to be here for a while."

Kelly and Lexi sat on either side of me. We looked at each other in the dim light, no one saying anything. The weight of what we're there to do sank in. Judging by the severe expressions that looked back at me, they felt it, too.

Kelly pulled out her cell phone. "No signal," she said. "Looks like we're completely on our own."

"Just the way I like it," I said, trying to sound braver than I felt. At that moment, the lights shut off with an echoing click. We were plunged into darkness.

I've said it before, and I'm saying it now: The eighties are my soundtrack, which must be why R.E.M.'s "It's the End of the World as We Know It (And I Feel Fine)" started playing so loudly in my head. Not many songs capture a sense of apocalyptic foreboding alongside a resilient, carefree attitude that you can dance to. Music is what my feelings sound like.

I couldn't help but shrug at the absurdity of my life while quietly singing along in the darkness.

7

WHAT EVEN MAKES YOU THINK I
HAVE A BICYCLE?

"Breathe deep the gathering gloom," Lexi said as she switched on her flashlight. The eerie light from below effect had us all looking more than a little creepy. She made a scary face that lightened the mood.

Just because these lights had gone out didn't mean everyone had left the building. We needed to wait a while here, and it was already beginning to feel like we'd been there for hours. "All Night Long," by Lionel Ritchie, came to mind, and I perked up thinking of its positive, feel-good energy. Maybe we could make this fun. I pulled out the photocopied journal pages that Neri included in the packet.

"Let's see what Manfred Krug had to say," I whispered. "Shine the light over here."

Written a century ago by a strong hand, the letters were written in heavy block handwriting.

Shanghai is a city like no other I've visited so far on this journey. The streets bustle with constant activity. There are people everywhere. And they are not all Chinese, as I would have thought. A true melting pot, British, American, and French all have settlements here, utterly independent of Chinese law. Each country's colonial presence has its own culture, architecture, and society. The mixing of cultures is unique and, by all accounts, is what shaped Shanghai's openness to Western influence.

My first night here was a remarkable experience. My British hosts demonstrated the resolve that her majesty's men have with their ability to drink. Although I am no slouch in that department, as I've written in previous entries, I found it challenging to maintain their pace. Beyond the drink, I've enjoyed the view. The women here are hauntingly beautiful. There was one in particular who I'd like to get to know better.

"Way to go, Manny," Lexi interrupted with enthusiasm. Kelly and I broke up, and we shushed each other right away. The last thing we wanted was to be discovered hiding in the boiler room.

I went back to Manfred's journal pages.

There's one in particular who I'd like to get to know better. I'm picturing walking the Bund, as the locals call the waterfront promenade, with this exotic woman showing me around. Perhaps after my acquisitions are complete.

My adventure today began when the old man in the rickshaw left us at the alley's entrance. My guide was Ling, the teenage daughter of my hotel's manager. The Western influence that is so pervasive here showed itself with her first words after leaving the Cathay Hotel.

"Call me Gigi," she had said. "That's what my friends call me."

"It sounds rather American," I had replied.

"Exactly," she said with a grin.

Ling—Gigi—had insisted we take a rickshaw to our destination, even though it was just a short walk. She said I would love the experience, telling me life was all about experiencing as much as possible. And she was correct. Once I became used to the driver taking corners at speed, I found myself laughing out loud the entire way.

Life in Shanghai goes from good to great when you enter the alleys. This is where the real living happens. The tightly packed alleyways in Shanghai are called Longtangs, translated as community lanes. The living quarters are tall, two or three stories, of stacked wood buildings that tower over the mazes within. Due to their small dimensions—often no wider than 15 to 20 feet—these interior lanes are designed for pedestrians rather than vehicles.

The smells, the sounds, and the interaction of the Longtang's residents are unlike anything I've experienced anywhere else. There are small stands selling food and other items, as well as haircuts and various services. The alleys branching off the main lane become even more intimate, with residents cooking, washing clothes, or talking with neighbors.

Gigi told me that the pace moves slower in Longtangs than in the hustle and bustle of the surrounding city. Residents sit outside watching the world go by. Children play while elders gossip. Passersby greet one another. Street vendors tout their goods. Neighbors cook together and usually eat their dinners outside, where they can see what other families are having. Toilets are shared.

Gigi informed me that over half the city's residents live in alleys like this one. And that for good and for bad, there's no privacy in the Longtangs, and you get to know everything about your neighbors. If there are quarrels between families, everyone in the neighborhood gets involved. She said that windows look into other windows, barriers between one rooftop laundry space and the next are insignificant or non-existent, and the sounds and smells of the city waft easily in, even through closed shutters.

As I said, it was life unlike anything I've experienced.

A blind man played a fiddle while a young girl sang at the alley's entrance, her soft voice winding around the Longtang alleyway as Gigi led me into this new world. We were stopped by a young man of Chinese origin, who spoke to me in rapid-fire

Shanghainese. He ignored Gigi and looked at me as if waiting for my reply.

I turned to my guide, telling her that since I didn't speak Shanghainese, I had no idea what was just said. She laughed and said that he wanted to fix my bicycle.

She said something to him in his language, which made him laugh. He turned to me, speaking in stilted English this time. "I will fix your bicycle."

I remember this had seemed absurd to me, and I had to know. I held up two fingers and said, "One, what makes you think I even have a bicycle? And two, what could possibly make you think it's broken?"

The man folded his arms across his chest and stared at me for a moment. I couldn't tell if he was angry or not. Then he suddenly spoke rapid-fire as he held up a finger. "One, everyone has a bicycle in Shanghai. Two, you're not riding it, so it must be broken. I can fix your bike for you, Joe."

I'll give the man credit. He made me laugh. I shook his hand and told him no thank you. I had taken several steps and turned back. The man was still looking at me. I told him that my name wasn't Joe. This greatly amused my guide as she covered her smile with her hand. When I quizzed her, Gigi said that Joe is simply a Shanghai expression for someone you don't know. Live and learn.

I lowered the pages and said, "I'm starting to like this guy."

"Me too," Kelly said.

"He's a character for sure," Lexi said. "Keep reading."

Back to the pages, I picked up where I left off.

Gigi led me to a doorway where several men sat outside the entrance. They played a board game of sorts. One moved his piece and laughed, while the other spat out a series of phrases that had to be curses. Gigi leaned over and whispered, "He is taking exception to the other man's gameplay. He is swearing."

I laughed and told her I had guessed as much. "You don't always have to know the language to understand the meaning."

When Gigi asked for Sinmay Zau, the men pointed through the doorway and said something I didn't catch. The man ever-so-subtly slid the game board aside to show a pistol underneath. He didn't have to say anything for me to catch his warning. I will clearly need to respect my host when I'm visiting his establishment.

Gigi said Sinmay Zau was in the rear, and I followed her into the murky shop. Through the twists and turns, the light became progressively dimmer. An occasional beam of light found its way through some hole in the structure, giving enough light to see our way through the clutter. There was stuff everywhere.

We stepped into a larger room and found an immense man behind a table with food of every kind, enough for ten men. However, there was just the solitary man sampling from the different dishes. Sampling was not nearly a strong enough word. He attacked the food with the same vengeance a hungry tiger might devour his prey. The man was older with a sizable but graying mustache. His eyes had flicked up momentarily when we entered. He said nothing. Maybe he didn't want to talk with his mouth full.

"Are you Sinmay Zau?" I asked.

He simply nodded. Without waiting for an invitation, I sat across from him and explained that I was seeking rare items that could grant me access to Shanghai's spice king.

"Kwan Huk Fat," Zau had said immediately. "I know of him—and his tastes. They can be rather expensive."

I wanted this man to know I meant business and told him I was prepared for that. I heard the slightest sound from my guide, who stood behind me. When I glanced in her direction, she ever-so-slightly shook her head. Turning back to Zau, I caught a gleam in his eye that hadn't been there before. In poker—like life—showing your cards is considered a mistake. And I just showed this man mine. Stupid.

Zau got up, a painful sight to behold, as it looked a Herculean feat to rise out of his well-worn seat. After a moment, he returned with several items and pushed them across the table. He swore that Kwan Huk Fat would desire them and open his willingness to trade. I made a show of studying the intricately carved bowls. They were beautiful. Examining each one closely, I understood the value someone would see in them. When I asked Zau about the cost, he made a show of looking up and pondering the item's value. He stroked his mustache and offered me a figure.

Again, I heard the slightest of sounds from behind me. Apparently, my guide was continuing to guide me.

I pride myself on being a pretty good poker player, and it's the eyes that give away someone's intentions. I studied the fat man's eyes, trying to get a read on him. He didn't give away much as he dipped his sausage-like fingers into a bowl of greasy noodles and fish, dropping the greasy morsels into his mouth. I caught him glancing at me. Continuing with my poker analogy, I decided to bluff.

I pushed the bowl back across the table. And waited.

Zau paused with a mouthful of food in mid-chew, the scales of a fish just inside his mouth. I told Zau that his price was not what I had been expecting and there were other shops I could visit before I traveled back home to America. Glancing at Gigi, I told her we should visit those other shops and stood up.

Zau had laughed, a barking sort of laugh. He told me to wait. Pushing himself back from the table—and his food—Zau moved his immense bulk across the room. Something about the way he moved, touching everything along the way, made me suspect his eyesight might be severely impaired. He stopped at a sizeable ornamental chest, removed several heavy objects sitting on the lid, and opened it. The top lifted with the creak of hinges that hadn't been opened in decades. Zau pulled out a woven basket. Numerous black ribbons held the basket securely shut.

Holding it at arm's length, as one might carry something with a particularly rotten odor, he lumbered back to our shared table. Once again seated, Zau began the process of untying the black ribbons. I could hear him chanting something under his breath as he pulled off each ribbon from the basket. When he removed the last of the ribbons, Zau carefully opened the basket's lid. His body language showed me a man on edge, almost as if he expected something to fly out of the basket. This was a man afraid.

He pushed the basket across the table so it rested in front of me. I glanced at Zau as he sat back down.

Looking into the basket, I was drawn to a large wooden box. I couldn't help but take the box out to examine it. Made of wood with inlaid gold strips, the quality of the craftsmanship was genuinely remarkable, I had never seen such a work of art. It was beautiful. Running my index finger along the edge, it felt so refined and smooth that the wood almost hummed with the vibration of my touch. I'd imagine getting the same feeling from examining a Stradivarius violin.

He gestured for me to open the lid. Inside was a smaller version of the box.

"There is a third, smaller box inside," he said. I closed the lids quietly, not wanting to show excitement at finding such beauty. I looked up at Zau, careful not to show my hand again.

"I'm sure Kwan Huk Fat will like these. But I'm also sure you want double for them."

Behind me, Gigi said something quietly in Shanghainese. Zau shook his head and looked up at my guide. "No," he said before turning towards me. "They are not for Fat. Not his taste. You take them, bring them home with you." And then he added several surprising words. "No extra charge."

Again, Gigi spoke to Zau.

Again, he replied to me. "They go back to America with you. Make gifts to people back home."

Zau asked if we had a deal. The bowls for Kwan Huk Fat, plus the free boxes to take home. And as calmly as I could muster, I told him we did.

Gigi helped with the transaction, smoothing things over with Zau. The immense man appeared to be in a rush for us to leave. For my part, I was anxious as I had concerns that he would come to his senses and ask for more money. But he didn't.

The men were still at their board game when we stepped back into the alley. When we were away from the entrance, I thanked Gigi for her expert guidance, telling her I couldn't have done it without her help. I offered her one of the small boxes to thank her. Gigi shook her head and gestured toward my money. I held out my clip of bills, and she plucked a small amount. "This will be fine."

"I am still baffled why Zau gave away these treasures," I said as I tucked away my money. "He doesn't seem the sort to give away anything to anyone. Did he indicate why he would have done this?"

"Zau believes the three boxes to have power. They supposedly gather and amplify spiritual energy." Gigi's expression didn't give away her thoughts on the subject.

"They can?" I asked out of disbelief.

"That's what Zau believes. He's a superstitious old man who thinks the death of his son was caused by the negative energy gathered by the boxes."

I nodded, and a thought came to me. "Is that why you didn't want one of the boxes?" I asked.

She shook her head. "Boxes do not pay for Western clothes," she had said with a hint of a smile.

I lowered the pages and sat upright. "That's where the pages end."

"Manny is my new hero," Lexi said.

"Mine too," I agreed as I got to my feet and stretched. "The mansion should be empty by now. Let's go find that box."

8

GHOSTS, SPIDERS, AND BASEBALL CARDS

I hate this part.

Poking my head around the corner, I half expected to find a heavily armed posse of law enforcement professionals. There would be no plausible explanation we could offer for why were still here. But the coast was clear, not even an overweight rent-a-cop on a Segway.

"It's clear," I whispered. "Let's go. Flashlights on." We'd bought small LED flashlights at our Hinckley gas station stop.

From the basement, we took the stairs up to the main floor. Since this floor was filled with artifacts and souvenirs from around the world, it felt like the most obvious spot to find the box. As we toured the mansion earlier, we'd kept an eagle eye out for the box, but no luck. It couldn't be that easy, or the Neri woman wouldn't have needed my help. No, the box would be tucked away someplace out of direct sight.

We started in the library first. We checked shelves, opened cabinets, looked high, looked low, but no box. After nearly 45 minutes of searching, the monumental task of finding one small box in this humongous building hit us. "Well, that was fun," I said. "Only 38 more rooms to search."

"37. We can cross the boiler room off the list, too," Kelly said.

"Good point," Lexi said. "I'll go search the hot tub next."

"There's no hot tub, goofball." Kelly grinned.

"Shhh," I hissed. "I hear something." As one, we clicked off our lights and listened. There was a distant sound of someone moving around. Lexi had a look of panic, but Kelly grabbed her sleeve and pulled her underneath the piano. After venturing a glance down the hall, I joined them. I shook my head to tell them I hadn't seen anyone in the hallway. We huddled under the grand piano, listening, waiting, and worrying.

It wasn't long before we heard the sound of approaching footsteps.

The way Lexi and Kelly looked at me, I knew my friends were scared. I was too, but that was okay. The purpose of fear is to raise awareness, not to stop progress. Hyper alert, we waited in the shadows underneath the grandest piano I had ever encountered.

A shadow fell on the rug in front of the library's entrance. The trouble with a shadow is you can't tell anything about the person who casts it. Male, female? Large, small? Unarmed, armed? Human or ghost? Probably not a ghost, though, thinking it through.

I was transported back to a childhood memory of playing hide and seek with my cousins. I don't recall how old I was, but I was probably in grade school because I was playing hide and seek. My aunt's house in south Minneapolis was ancient, and I vividly remembered its musty smell. I had found the perfect hiding place: a linen closet on the second floor. The door wouldn't shut all the way, so I covered myself as best I could with towels. No way would someone have spotted me unless they removed the camouflaging towels. So I waited.

At one point, I heard the sound of Addy, my cousin—and the seeker for this round—run right by. The thing about the game is it feels like forever while you're hiding. Impatient, crouched under the towels in the smelly closet, I adjusted my cover to peek into the hallway. Right away, the shadow of someone's legs was outside the door. I tried not to giggle as I was so close but so cleverly hidden. It took a second as I stared at the shadow, waiting for it to move, before the realization sunk in. It wasn't a shadow at all. I was actually looking right through someone. There was a ghost standing right outside the closet. I hadn't wanted to face it, so I hunkered down under the towel and waited. I couldn't help but cry. I was so scared. Eventually, Addy came and found me, and like much of my life, I pretended nothing out of the ordinary had happened.

Now, here in the Glensheen Mansion, I wondered who was waiting for us out in the hall. Whoever—or whatever— paused at the entrance for a long moment before receding down the hallway. I waited until the sound was gone before whispering, "Who do you suppose that was?"

"Security guard? Possibly one of the guides taking a final walk through," Kelly offered.

Shaking my head, I said, "But why would they do it in the dark? The guides would do it before turning off the lights. A security guard would have a flashlight."

Both of my friends shrugged.

Sliding out from under the piano, I motioned for Lexi and Kelly to follow. "Let's go. We need to find the box first."

Kelly held up her palm. "Hold on, I need you to clarify something. You said we need to find it first. Do you mean before we leave? Or do you mean find it before someone else?" Kelly was never the one to avoid asking the difficult question.

"Both," I said after a moment's hesitation. "The Neri woman made it clear we needed to get the box. But she also said that someone else may also be after it."

"Really?" Lexi said, shaking her head. "And this is the first you've mentioned it?"

"You have to be straight with us, Abbey," Kelly said. "We're putting a lot on the line here to help you. You can't be holding anything back. What else did she say about someone coming after the box?"

I take a deep breath. "Only that whoever it was had shot her."

"Oh, shit," Lexi said softly.

"I don't see how it changes anything," Kelly said. "We're still being careful, still hiding from anyone, still being total ninjas." That a girl. Kelly would make a great cop someday, that is, if she didn't get arrested for removing an antique from the Glensheen Mansion.

"So, let's be careful." I looked the other two in the eye.

"Got it, careful." Kelly was all business.

"Careful. Like the fox sneaking into the henhouse," Lexi said.

"More like the hen sneaking out the back door when she sees the fox coming in the front door," I replied. "But you have the right idea."

We moved down the hall to the main staircase, heading for the second floor. For some reason, I paused on the landing. Glancing at the bench seat beneath the landing window, I started getting a vibe. There was an energy lingering here. Something happened at this very spot. Something bad. I held my breath as I felt a little woozy. The edges of my vision blurred.

"Abbey." I heard my name being called, but I was in a place where I couldn't respond. I had slid into...somewhere else. Somewhere where living things didn't exist, and dead people and long-forgotten murder weapons do.

My eyes were drawn to the floor near the bench. There was something there. Unable to help myself, I knelt to examine the object. It was a brass candle holder. A bloodied brass candle holder. There was a hyper-realistic quality to what I saw, which told me that the candlestick holder wasn't really there.

I glanced at my friends, their concern evident. "This is where the night nurse died," I explained. "But we need to keep moving."

At the top of the stairs, I put a finger to my lips. After waiting for several long moments, I was confident that no one was moving on this floor.

As I turned the corner, I realized my mistake. While there was no one alive here, there was someone here. A woman dressed in all white was moving down the hallway in our direction. She radiated a diffused glow, like looking at someone in the bright sunshine through wet window glass. She didn't notice us as she glided ever closer. It was like she was on one of those moving walkways at the airport.

An older woman, she had glasses and the style of hair you pretty much find on everyone's grandmother. She looked peaceful and content, carefree in her movement, as she adjusted a book on a table. The thing was, the book didn't actually move when she touched it.

It felt like I was watching a video of her from decades ago, back in her happier days. Back before someone brutally ended her life with a candlestick holder.

She walked right toward us, and I stepped aside to let the nurse continue her never-ending journey. But that wasn't what happened. Instead, the nurse paused and looked directly at me. Her dark eyes stared at me unblinkingly.

"There's someone here with us," I announced, keeping my eyes on the nurse.

"Where?" Kelly asked. She glanced around.

"Directly in front of me. It's the nurse who was murdered," I replied.

"How does she look?" Lexi asked. "Bloody? Hole in her noggin?"

"No, she's looking no worse for the wear." The way she stared at me would be incredibly awkward if she were alive. But since she'd been dead for over 40 years, it's just part of how this spirit stuff worked. For example...

I went to a sample sale in a loft studio last year. The warehouse building was decades past its prime, and the freight elevator made too many noises for my comfort. The dozen people who joined me for the two-story elevator ride crowded me into the corner.

After the heavy doors closed, I noticed someone was facing me as I stood in the back of the elevator car. This was a clear violation of elevator etiquette, which demanded that all riders should face the front. A man just stood there—and to make the moment more awkward, his eyes were locked on mine like a cocker spaniel waiting for his dog biscuit to be handed over.

In his early thirties, he had messy dark hair, a week's worth of stubble, a black leather jacket over his white shirt, and a skinny black tie worn loosely. He was a good foot taller than me.

The elevator had started its upward progress with a jerk and stopped at our destination floor with a similar jerk. The elevator operator opened the doors by shoving up the top portion while the bottom receded. He announced that the studio was to the right, and people began filing out. The staring man stood in front of me, blocking my exit. I had had enough and stomped around him, getting angrier by the second. By the time I was safely out of the car, I'd reached my tipping point. No one deserves to be treated like he'd treated me. "Hey," I said as I turned around to give him a piece of my mind. The trouble was that there was no one in the elevator car.

And now the nurse looked like she could easily continue staring at me for the rest of the night. I wasn't that patient. "Hello...nurse."

"Her name was Velma," Kelly said. "Sarah mentioned it earlier."

"Okay then. So, Velma, how's life?"

"Abbey!" It was Lexi. "You have to be respectful of the dead."

"She's not staring at you like you're dinner. Besides, I'm trying to provoke a reaction." Something I'm generally good at accomplishing.

Lexi grabbed my hand. "Let's do that thing where you bring me into your world. I want to see her."

I had pulled Lexi into my world recently so she was able to see a ghostly clown. I'd tried the same thing with Turner, and he could see the honor guard of clowns down in Iowa. In both cases, I held their hands while I helped them focus. Rather than diminishing it, sharing my ability made it stronger.

I grabbed Lexi's hand and positioned her to face the dead nurse.

"The power of the three," I murmured to no one in particular. My mind, on autopilot, could still connect the dots for me. I grabbed Kelly's hand and gave it a welcoming squeeze.

"Ladies, take a deep breath, close your eyes, and picture an older woman. She's about Kelly's height, has gray hair, and wears glasses with black frames. She's wearing a white nurse's uniform, you know, the kind that has white tights and sensible shoes. She has..." I paused as something had changed. A rivulet of blood now ran down from her hairline.

"There's a little blood on her forehead. Picture Velma as best you can and open your eyes." I drew out the last three words. A sharp intake of breath from Kelly and a squeeze from Lexi's hand told me it worked.

Kelly and Lexi could see the ghost of Velma.

The semi-transparent ghostly figure stared at me, a trickle of blood still running down the nurse's temple.

Suzanna Neri's words came to me. "Close the loop."

I knew what to do. "Grab onto each other's hand. But keep your focus on her."

Kelly and Lexi's fingers fumbled for the other and finally latched on behind the woman. When Kelly and Lexi joined hands, the ghostly woman became significantly more solid within seconds. Her eyes shifted between us. Truth be told, she didn't exactly look comfortable being surrounded by teenage girls. When her eyes returned to me, I spoke.

"Velma, hello. My name is Abbey. Kelly and Lexi are here with us, too." Velma's lips moved, but nothing was being said.

"I'd like you to think back to the carefree days when you worked with Elizabeth regularly. Life was pleasant, and you enjoyed your time here."

The nurse's eyes stopped their darting movement, and she appeared more relaxed. Best of all, the blood was no longer present.

"I need you to help me find something. It would have been here long before you came to work for Elizabeth. It's a box made of wood with gold inlays. I need to find it," I told her. "Do you understand?"

The nurse nodded slightly and opened her mouth. The faintest of creaks was all that came out.

"Pardon me? I couldn't hear you," I told her.

The nurse blinked and nodded. "I'm not used to talking," she replied in the voice of someone who has walked through a desert. It sounded painful to speak, though I knew she was way past the point of feeling anything.

"I'd imagine you don't have many people to chat with."

It was such an odd experience to have a conversation with a ghost. In most cases, I never heard a word from the dead people I encountered. Typically, they were a shy bunch.

"Do you know of the box?"

Velma shook her head. "There's so much here. Maybe if I'd been a housekeeper or a maid, but there are so many rooms I've never even entered. My focus had always been Elizabeth."

Kelly squeezed my hand, trying to get my attention. It was clear she wanted to say something. "Go ahead," I told her.

"Is there anyone else?" she asked tentatively. "Anyone else here that you know of that we could ask?"

The nurse kept her long dead eyes on me as if she hadn't heard Kelly.

But, after a moment's pause, she replied. "There is no one else. Not here, not now."

An idea occurred to me. Certainly a longshot, but worth the try. I pulled out the diary page with the sketch of the spirit box. "This is the box we need to find. Can you go somewhere else, maybe to another time, to ask about it?"

Velma's eyes began to flutter rapidly, and she let out an eerie moan. I sensed the questioning glances from my friends, but this was completely new territory for me. I had no idea what was happening, but I knew I needed to do something.

"Ladies," I began, not quite sure if my next move was an intelligent one. "Focus your thoughts on your hands as we move closer to Velma. We're going to make physical contact with her."

Lexi made a slight noise.

Moving our hands, I reached out for the spirit of the long-dead nurse. My hand began to tingle, while a chill spread across my fingertips when they grazed her ghostly shoulders. I got a palpable feeling that was both disorienting and cold. My peripheral vision became a mass of shifting colors. Our hands rested on Velma's shoulders, and she amazingly felt very solid.

Images, sounds, and smells began to play through my mind. I heard laughter, saw kids running down the halls of the mansion, and saw many girls and a single boy as the memory clips accelerated their pace.

Scenes flew by as I saw the different rooms of the mansion, except now they were full of life as people went about their day. I saw both family members and staff. A garden with a large fountain outside, a game room inside. Horses, stables, dogs running and playing.

As the images raced by, I sensed they were honing in on the boy. Looking to be around my age, I saw him in a bedroom. There was a bed, desk, dresser, and wicker chairs. Stencils of birds in flight lined the top of the walls. Several shotguns leaned in the closet's corner. Dirty fingers prying a loose board. A stash of treasure in a gold and wood box.

We found it.

Having the box's location, we needed to disengage from this blast from the past. But the image cyclone continued to spin as it gathered energy and speed. Everything was a blur, and the sound had become a roar.

Need to disengage.

I feared being consumed by these memories, a lifetime of madness, if I couldn't break free.

Meditation has been an essential part of my life. It brought presence and control to my mind. When you see dead people, a little mind control isn't a bad thing. Just needed to focus...

My mind went back to a family camping trip to the north shore of Lake Superior. We took the ferry from Grand Portage across Lake Superior to the large island of Isle Royale. The hour-and-a-half trip had started nicely with blue skies and calm waters. That was, until a storm blew in. Soon, the lake became choppy, and the boat was thrown around in the heaving waters. It was fun at first, but you can only ride a roller coaster for so long before you start to feel the effects. People were literally turning green and throwing up.

The storm intensified as we made shore, and it took everything we had to grab our gear and make for our campsite. Knowing we had limited daylight, we had no choice but to persevere hiking through the massive storm. Lightning crackled overhead, and the wind dangerously swayed the large evergreens overhead.

Fortunately, as darkness took over, the storm departed. The stars came out as we reached our campsite. After helping set up our tent, I sprawled on the ground, too tired to eat and too wired to sleep. I stared up at the night sky. The shimmering lights of the aurora borealis were breathtaking as they danced across the sky.

I fought to pull my mind away from the cascading scenes of the Glensheen Mansion and instead focus on the memories of the swirling colors of that summer night. My mind filled with the hauntingly beautiful shades of green. My breathing slowed as the aurora borealis pushed everything from my mind, and I pulled away from the ghost of the murdered nurse.

Her eyes stopped fluttering, and she looked back at me with eyes that were very much aware. She uttered a single word. "Robert."

"Thank you," I replied quietly and pulled my fingers from my friends' hands. And she was gone.

"Everyone all right?" I asked as I straightened out my stiff fingers.

"Yeah," Lexi said. "It felt like a roller coaster was running through my head."

"Have to agree with that," Kelly said as she rubbed the back of her neck. "How long were we riding? I feel so wiped out."

Lexi looked at her phone. "No way. We were caught up in there for almost an hour."

Making contact was far more dangerous than I had believed. "It felt like just a few moments passed. Crazy."

"Shhh." Kelly held up a finger.

We listened.

Someone was coming up the stairs—the same stairs we stood next to.

I pointed down the hall, and we raced for the far end. There was an open door, and I headed for that, anxious to get out of the open. Once we were safely inside, I grabbed the door, preventing Kelly from shutting it. We couldn't risk the noise or movement.

We were in a bedroom, but I didn't remember which of the daughter's rooms it was. Not that it mattered because this was where we had to wait. I desperately wanted to know what was happening out in the hallway. I wanted to see who was out there. But we needed to stay put.

Okay, I can do this. I took a deep cleansing breath, willing myself to be calm, relaxed, and in control.

Ugh, I can't take this.

Sometimes, my control is pretty much imaginary.

Venturing a peek, I stuck my head out. There was someone down at the far end of the hall. It was far too dark, and I couldn't tell if the person was big or small, male or female. Living or dead. Spooky girl problems.

Whoever it was, they moved slowly away, running a hand along the wall. The person paused at a bedroom door and stepped inside, now out of sight.

In a flash, I was on my feet, pulling Lexi and Kelly toward the stairwell across the hall. We literally sprinted, and once safely inside, we started up because that's where the spirit box was.

Robert, the name Velma had spoken, was Chester and Clara's son. His bedroom was on the next level. Velma's memories made it clear that the boy ended up with the box.

On the third floor, we moved quickly down the hall. "This is Robert's room," I said. "We need to find his cubby hole. Look for a loose board."

"I don't remember this yellow wallpaper from Velma's memory,"

Kelly said as she moved around the room. "Are you sure it's his room?"

"I bet as Robert grew up and his tastes changed, they redecorated," I said. "His desk is gone, but the fireplace and wicker chairs are still here."

"So indoor wicker chairs must have been in style at some point in history? Who knew?" Lexi said.

I walked over to the window and peeled back a strip of wallpaper, revealing different wallpaper underneath. The familiar-looking birds were there. There was a sense of whimsy to the bird wallpaper that may have been perfect for a boy's room but maybe not for the teenage version of Robert. "This is his room, for sure. Let's find that box."

I ran my fingers along the wall, looking for a loose board. I was on my knees near the window while the other two checked around the room. The problem was that everything felt solidly in place. Then, a break.

"Hang on," Lexi said, standing in the corner next to the bookshelves. "I can feel the board wobble under the wallpaper here. The trouble is, they wallpapered right over it."

"That's no trouble," Kelly said as she flipped open a wicked-looking knife.

"Wait, you just happen to carry around a machete?"

"A girl never knows," Kelly said. "You just never know."

"We have to talk," I said, shaking my head.

Kelly ran the point along the seams of the wallboard. It took her just a moment to pry the board loose. We crowded around the tight space to see what was inside, and we weren't disappointed.

There was a treasure trove of objects in Robert's cubbyhole.

"He's a little hoarder," Lexi exclaimed. "Look at all that stuff."

There was only one thing I wanted. I reached past Kelly, pulling out the gold and wood box. I carried it across the room and reverently placed it on the bed. It was beautiful.

The detail work was amazing. I hadn't noticed it in the sketches, but the gold had patterns etched throughout the strips. Tiny intricate patterns contributed to larger ones, which in turn made up still larger ones. I had never seen anything like it. And then I noticed the wood grain. Rich, swirling strands were interwoven into a hypnotically beautiful mosaic. Looking still closer, it wasn't the wood grain I was admiring. The pattern was produced by countless intricate pieces—probably thousands of intricate pieces—perfectly fitting together like a puzzle. There was no seam, no rough edges, and no sign of even a millimeter of space between the pieces. Astounding craftsmanship.

My friends crowded around me. "Do you feel anything different about the box? It's supposed to attract spiritual energy," Kelly said.

"No, not really. It is attractive, though."

"Attractive," Lexi said. "Nice pun."

"Let's see what's inside," I said, lifting the lid. With a creak of something that hadn't been opened for a century, I opened the lid. Not only did the top lift, but the front part extended out, making the interior part much larger now that the box was open. I couldn't see any sign of how this happened—the wood looked solid. The individual pieces were hinged in some way. Unbelievable. I don't think the space shuttle was as intricate as this centuries-old box appeared to be.

The three of us sat on the bed with the open box between us.

"Wow," Kelly whispered.

"Hey, there's baseball cards," Lexi said as she grabbed a rubber-banded stack. She thumbed through them and said, "They can't be real cards. See this Wagner guy? He apparently played for Pittsburg, but he doesn't look like a baseball player. He looks like a child." She tossed the stack on the bed. "Maybe some kid will want these."

I was barely listening to Lexi's observations as I felt a disturbance.

The spirit box shimmered, and I heard a child's voice off in the distance. The door to Robert's room made a drawn-out creak as we watched the door close on its own. The floorboards creaked as if a weight had been placed on them—a lot of weight—but no one was here with us. A breeze kicked up and swirled my hair around my face.

"Abbey," Lexi said with obvious concern.

The skin on the back of my neck began to crawl. Someone laughed outside our room, but it wasn't a happy sound. It was a villainous, I've-tied-you-to-a train-track-and-here-comes-the-train kind of laugh. I exchanged nervous glances with Kelly.

Something—or someone—was scratching from the inside of the closet door. A very persistent something.

A shadow slid across the wall like someone had walked between the window and the far wall.

"Abbey," Lexi said again, rising panic in her voice.

"Freaks Come Out At Night," I said, quoting the eighties Whodini song.

It was subtle at first, but a luminescence began pouring from the box. As it grew brighter, a greenish tint was cast on everything in the room. Lexi's blonde hair looked like she'd spent way too much time in a chlorinated swimming pool; it had that same greenish tint that pool kids get.

Kelly made a noise that drew my attention away from the box. A gigantic spider crawled up her arm. Kelly usually had a bias for action but looked petrified with fear. In a rare moment of bravery around spiders, I swiped the hairy arachnid off her arm. It scurried across the floor, effortlessly went underneath the closet door, and disappeared out of sight. The persistent scratching abruptly stopped, and we heard something I can only describe as the crunching of bones.

"You have to be kidding me," I said to no one in particular.

"Abbey!"

All subtly was gone from Lexi's voice as she demanded my attention.

"Okay," I told her. "We've got what we need. Let's get out of here before..." I glanced toward the closet door. The thing in the closet scratched with renewed vigor while the greenish light shimmered across the ceiling, and the hallway doorknob moved back and forth.

That would have been bad enough, but add in the sounds of footsteps moving across the wooden floor, the breeze intensifying as it swirled in the bedroom, and the laughter that sounded right on the other side of the door.

Time to close the lid on this box.

But something unseen grabbed my sleeve and pulled my hand back. Frankly, I was not surprised. There was a lot of serious mojo going on around this box. There didn't appear to be much more than a hand and a forearm holding onto me. I struggled with the hand for a moment and then relaxed before darting out with my other hand. I slammed the lid down.

It pays to be smarter than a hand with no brain attached.

The room went silent. Except for the sound of our breathing, nothing moved. We exchanged glances, our relief palpable.

From the closet, the scratching started up again.

We grabbed the box and ran.

9

AT DEATH'S DOOR, I'M GOING TO RING THE DOORBELL AND RUN LIKE HELL

After you die, they throw you a party.

I've been to these parties before. Usually held after the funeral, people gather to share stories and reminisce about the recently departed one. Often held in church basements or someone's home, people come together to share a meal and gain strength from one another. There are tears, laughter, and a lot of hugs. For many, it's the beginning of the road to healing and recovery.

Life had been quiet since escaping with the box in Duluth. No word from Neri, no request for the box to be turned over. For now, it sat on the shelf in my closet, hidden but not forgotten. In the meantime, life had moved on, but unfortunately, so had death.

One of my mom's co-workers at the hospital lost her husband to a car accident. The man had been on a shoulder and was hit by a passing car. He left his shattered bike behind, along with his wife, Sheryl, and eleven-year-old daughter, Jenna.

Tragic.

I went to the after-funeral get-together with my mother, as my father was traveling on assignment. Following introductions, my mom left me to grab a plate while she went to talk with her friends. The food options looked pretty good, and I filled my plate with cold cut sandwiches, some hot dish, fruit, and a delicious-looking dessert bar.

Grabbing a bench seat by a window, I took in my surroundings. The home was older, but that didn't mean it was run down. We were in the Summit Avenue area of Saint Paul, after all. For those unfamiliar with Summit Avenue, it has some of Minnesota's largest, most beautiful, and iconic homes along its manicured streets. From the ginormous mansions located near the Saint Paul Cathedral down to more modest homes on the western side, this was the city's premier avenue. Unlike many homes I've been in, everything looked custom built. Of course, when this home was built, everything was custom. My eyes tracked up the wall to the intricate molding on the ceiling. It was beautiful.

"Lady, are you all right?"

There wasn't a seam in the wood, let alone a nail hole. My grandfather had a woodworking shop in his garage and had taught me a lot about woodworking.

"Maybe she had a stroke or something."

Huh? I glanced away from the ceiling to see a small herd of young girls staring open-mouthed at me. And only then did I realize they were talking about me. A little stunned to be the subject of their fascination, I stared back at them, unsure what to say.

"My dad's a doctor. I can go get him." This suggestion came from the tallest girl in the group. She had long, straight blonde hair. I studied her for a long moment, trying to decide if she was kidding.

"Maybe you better, Avery," a short girl with Latin features said. The ends of her hair were strawberry Kool-Aid colored. As I looked closer, I became convinced that was exactly what she used to color it. Most of the girls had their hair colored the same way. Must be a thing with the tween crowd.

"Okay, watch my plate, Sierra." When Avery stood up, I realized she was being serious.

"Hey, wait," I said, grabbing her sleeve. She stopped and gave me the slow burn look that screamed, "Don't be touching me."

"I think she's coming out of it," Sierra said. "Lady, are you all right?"

I couldn't help but laugh at her earnest expression. "I didn't realize you were talking to me. You kept calling me lady."

Sierra folded her arms across her chest. "Well, my dad said I need to respect my elders."

I reached for my glass of punch. "Wait, how old do you think I am?" I asked her.

The other girls in the group seemed to sense that the situation was beginning to get good and gathered closer.

"I don't know," Sierra said as she studied me. "Maybe 30."

In a perfect world, I wouldn't have taken a drink of my fruit punch when she made her outrageous guess. And I wouldn't have barked out a laugh right then—and for sure, I wouldn't have spit out punch in their direction.

When they get startled, several girls let out a high-pitched squeal that girls of this age do. Clearly, I'd spooked the herd as they all jumped back, afraid for their very lives.

Glancing around the room, I saw all the adults' eyes looking in my direction. The only thing I could do was laugh and give in to it. The girls joined in, and I said, "I'm nowhere near 30. I'm only 14. Not even close to stroke age."

This had the group laughing even harder.

"Oh, Sierra," a girl with dimples said. "She's always getting us in trouble."

Sierra gave a little pout but seemed to enjoy the attention, too. "Whatever," she said with a practiced eye roll.

"You do, though. Remember that time you asked the referee if he swallowed his whistle?"

Sierra made a show of studying her nails.

"We're all on the same team," one of the girls explained. "Soccer," she added.

Now she was speaking my language. "Hey, I play soccer too."

I held out a fist, and she gave it a bump.

"Nice to meet you girls. I'm Abbey." I gave a little wave.

One of the girls said, "I'm Jazzy."

"Cool name."

"Thanks. It's short for Jasmine. We're on Jenna's team."

"She's our goalie," the girl with the dimples said.

I looked around the group. "Where is she? I haven't seen Jenna at all."

The boisterous group quieted. Sierra leaned in and said, "She's over there," nodding towards the edge of the room. Staring straight ahead, Jenna sat in a chair across from a bearded man. He had haunted eyes as he spoke to her.

"She's been like that for a half hour now. Completely ignoring us. Just sitting and staring," Avery said. "Nodding, not saying anything."

"It does look like it's been hard on her," Jazzy said. "I can't imagine losing my father. And if that wasn't bad enough, today is her birthday."

I nodded, not taking my eyes off Jenna. The man sat on the edge of his chair, leaning close to Jenna. It looked like he was trying to soothe her. I studied him for a moment. He had bushy brown hair and one of those genuine smiles that went right to his eyes. His attempts to lighten the mood didn't appear to be cheering up Jenna, though.

"My mom works with her mom. I never met her dad," I said. "Did you guys know him?"

"Her dad was super nice. He'd always be the one to drive Jenna to soccer," Jazzy said.

"He always made us laugh," Sierra added.

"He had a smile that made you feel better about yourself, if you know what I mean," the girl with the dimples said.

"I do. Some people just have a light that burns brilliantly. People are drawn to them," I said as I watched the man animatedly talking to

Jenna. "Say, you wouldn't happen to have a picture of Jenna's dad, would you? You have me curious."

"You must not have gone to the funeral," Jazzy said. "They had a slide show running during the service."

"No, we came straight here," I explained.

Jazzy handed me a folded piece of paper. "There's a picture on the program."

Even though I had begun to suspect it, I was still shocked when I unfolded the program. Smiling, the man in the picture had creases around his eyes, a beard, and bushy brown hair. I lowered the picture and saw the same man sitting across from Jenna.

Jenna's dead father was here.

As odd as it may sound, I don't always recognize ghosts when I first see them. Some ghosts look like everyone else, while others are more transparent, not entirely here in our world. It's the lifelike ones that I can't distinguish from a living, breathing person.

Sierra was looking at me funny again. "Are you okay? You look like you saw a ghost or something."

I shook my head. "It's funny you should say that, though. I need to ask a question that might be a little out there."

The moment when people learn about my unique ability can be bad. Friends I've known and trusted suddenly look at me in fear and want nothing to do with me. It hasn't always been easy being the spooky girl.

One of the good things about maturing is learning to accept the things you cannot change. And you learn that it's okay to be yourself. You're not here to please others or conform to their expectations. Each of us has our gifts and abilities. Some people can play an instrument, while others can sing. Some can write a story that enthralls the world. And some of us see dead people.

I've learned that if you're given a gift, you should use it. Don't worry about what people may think. It took me a long time and some therapy to come to terms with what I could do. I know I'm different.

You may draw well, but I can see the ghost of a girl's dead father. This is who I am and how I roll.

Nodding in Jenna's direction, I asked, "There wouldn't be a man over there talking to Jenna?"

Four heads swiveled in her direction and swiveled right back, confusion coloring their faces. Each of the girls looked as if they wanted to ask something. No one did.

I sighed. "I didn't think so."

Standing up, I handed my plate of mostly uneaten food to Avery. "Hold this for me. I've got some business to attend to."

I didn't wait for a reply but strode across the room and knelt next to Jenna—and her dead father. I gently laid my hand on her knee. She continued to look in her father's direction. "Hi, Jenna," I said softly.

No acknowledgement.

I decided to change tactics and glanced at the funeral program. "Hello...Steven. Nice to see you."

Jenna's father, Steven, looked at me in surprise.

"Yes, I can see you." Looking up into Steven's eyes, I spoke the truth to him. "I'm sorry that your time here on earth ended so abruptly. Life isn't always fair. But you need to let go and let Jenna live her life."

There was a sadness of infinite proportions in his eyes. But there was also something else, some unmet need that held him here. Maybe there was something left to be done, maybe there was a message, or perhaps he simply couldn't let go.

"Let me help you," I said to Steven. "If you have a message for Jenna, I can pass it on."

Steven nodded, tears running down his cheeks.

"I can help, but you need to let Jenna go first," I told him. "Stop talking to her. Let go of the hold you have on her. Can you do that?"

He nodded again.

"Jenna, I'm here to help." I brushed her hair back. "Can you hear me?"

Her eyes fluttered as they lost their withdrawn quality. "Jenna," I said again with determination. "I need you to be here. With me."

Finally responding, Jenna looked in my direction.

"Hi," I said. "Welcome back. I'm Abbey, Katherine's daughter."

Looking like she had just woken up, confusion colored her face. I gave her leg a reassuring squeeze. "This may be difficult to understand, but I can see dead people. Ghosts, spirits, that kind of thing. Are you with me so far?"

Jenna blinked, pausing momentarily, and said, "So, you're like a medium? You hold séances?"

I couldn't help but laugh. "No, I'm real. I don't make up things and tell people what they want to hear. I actually see the spirits of people who've died."

"So, why are you telling me this?" Jenna's forehead wrinkled.

Here we go.

"Jenna, your father is here. He's with us right now."

I waited for her reaction, half expecting her head to whip around as she searched for him. Not Jenna. She knew I was telling the truth. Whether she could see him or not, she looked directly at her father.

"You know he's here, don't you?"

She nodded.

"You can feel his presence, can't you?"

Another nod. Her eyes welled up, tears threatening to break free.

"Your father has been trying to communicate with you. Have you heard what he's been saying to you?" She shook her head.

"That's actually pretty common. It's often difficult to understand what the ghosts are saying. Some people hear indistinct whispering. They'll feel driven to listen because it feels like the whispering is about to come into focus. But it never does."

I took a deep breath. "For some, this is the road to madness. But I'm not going to let that happen to you."

I turned to her father. "Steven, what would you like to say to your daughter?"

His eyes held my gaze. His lip trembled, and his mouth opened slowly. I heard a faint whisper. Not good enough.

Holding up my hand, palm facing Steven, I closed my eyes to help bring him into focus. With one hand on Jenna, I moved my other hand slowly around him as I tried to hone in on his words.

The words began as if it was coming down a long tunnel. And just like that, they became focused and sounded like he was close, whispering just for me.

"I'm so proud of you, Jenna."

"He's so proud of you," I repeat.

"I've watched you grow and mature, becoming more confident as you find your place in the world. I especially like what playing soccer has done for you. It's brought out your competitive nature and, at the same time, showed you the value of being part of a team. I've seen how soccer has made you more resilient. Life will put obstacles in your way, and I know you'll overcome whatever adversity may come your way."

I watched this man speak from his heart. Tears ran down my cheeks, but I had to hold it together for Jenna. Her cheeks were also wet as I conveyed her father's message. This wasn't easy for either of us.

"I bought you a birthday present, but I didn't have the opportunity to give it to you. Since I know how you like to peek, I tucked it in the cabinet directly in front of my car in the garage." The smile that everyone talked about was shining as he spoke.

Addressing her father, I said, "It's time for you to move on. Let your daughter live her life. You will always be a part of her, but it's not good for the dead to interfere with the living. As much as you mean well, you can psychologically damage your daughter with your attempts to communicate with her."

Steven nodded, his smile remaining.

"There's a light, Steven," I told him. "When you look for it, you will find it. This light is bright and welcoming."

Steven nodded again as he looked at his daughter. However, his words weren't so agreeable. "About that. I'm staying right here. This is my home."

Whoa. Big left turn. "Wait, What? You can't possibly stay."

Steven turned and stared at me, his eyes burning with sheer force of will. "There's no one to stop me. Jenna needs me, both my kids need me."

I had entered new territory here. But I refused to be bossed around by a ghost. I folded my arms across my chest and glared at him. I was the picture of defiance.

I was a lioness.

"Here's the thing, Steve. You don't have to enter the light, but you can't stay here. Life is for the living. It's difficult enough for a girl as she hits her teenage years. Trust me, I know what I'm talking about. There's so much going on around you. You're being pulled in so many directions. Friends, family, faith, media, expectations, disappointments, there's so much."

I took a deep breath and held Steven's gaze.

"There's no way all that's happening with her dead father constantly whispering in her ear. She'll be a wreck if you stay." I paused for a moment. "But, if you leave, she'll be a normal, well-adjusted young girl. So, you need to look for that light."

Like a boxer faced with defeat, Steven was on the ropes, his eyes darting back and forth as he looked for a way out.

I was not having it. "Now," I barked.

Something shifted in him as he searched his surroundings, which appeared far beyond this house. As his eyes fixed on a spot, his face relaxed. A smile for the ages lit up his face. His entire face lit up like a late summer's sunset as warm hues danced across his face.

"Mom." Steven's tone was one of unexpected joy. He got to his feet and moved in the direction of his gaze.

"Toby! Come here, boy." He stooped to visit with something I strongly suspected was a dog.

Steven turned to face me. "Thank you. Please tell Jenna goodbye and that I love her desperately."

Warm tears stream down my flushed cheeks. "She knows," I said, looking back at Jenna. "She knows."

When I turned back, Steven had left. But there's a part of him that was still here. I could feel his warm spirit. I knew then that Jenna would always carry a little of her father.

"I'm hungry," Jenna said, looking around.

I held out a hand for her. She took it with a firm grip, and I helped her stand. "Lucky for you, there's an entire buffet right over here. And a soccer team to keep you company."

As she filled her plate, I asked Jenna, "Who is Toby, by the way? Your father mentioned him."

"He was our cocker spaniel. We had to put him down several years ago. My dad adored him."

"It looks like dogs do go to heaven after all." I smiled. "And that's exactly how it should be. Dogs and heaven together."

ᐁᐃ

Afterward, in the car, I had a radio station battle with my mom on our way home. I decided to let her win after she pushed the button for the classical music station. We listened to Mendelssohn for a moment until my mom said, "Wasn't it amazing that they found Jenna's birthday present from her dad? I didn't get the opportunity to check it out. What was it?"

"It was a signed soccer jersey from her idol, Alex Morgan. She plays for the U.S. Women's National Soccer team," I added.

"Very special," Mom said before drifting back into her thoughts.

After a few minutes and several highways, she mentioned, "It makes you wonder how Jenna's friends knew where to look for her present."

My mother, the doubter, holds onto her clinical scientific view of the world. Ghosts and spirits do not fit easily into that world. However, she knows firsthand that I have a connection to the dead.

She may not like it, but she couldn't turn a blind eye when the evidence happened right in front of her. That's not science.

Staring at the road, she said, "Really, it's almost like her father pointed the way."

I shrugged. "It's an amazing world we live in. Anything is possible."

With a knowing smile, Mom echoed my sentiment. "Agreed. Anything is possible."

10

THE NOBLE QUEST

"Unbelievable."

"What?" I asked, seeing my mom check her rearview mirror.

"We're getting pulled over." The exasperation in her voice was evident.

"Technically, you're the one getting pulled over. I'm just an innocent passenger."

"Abbey," she said. Judging by her tone, I was only in the warning stage, so I continued.

"How fast were you going? You do feel the need for speed." I enjoyed teasing my mother, which helped keep her mind off the stress of being an adult. I figured it was my job to lighten the mood whenever I could.

"Abbey," she said again, this time more forcefully. I may have hit a nerve.

My mom's BMW coupe is a thoroughbred among trail-riding ponies. Getting frustrated with the slower-moving cars, she would hit the steering wheel with the palm of her hand, talking to the other drivers, "C'mon, c'mon." And then, when the opening presented itself, she'd rocket into the open space. The engine roaring as she smoothly shifted through the gears. Ahh, the freedom of the open road. At least until the next minivan.

Emergency lights filled the interior of our car with strobing red as my mom moved over to the shoulder. She put the car into neutral and engaged the parking brake. As she put her hands on the top of the steering wheel, she explained, "It calms the officer when they can see both hands."

"Exactly how many times have you been in this situation?" I asked. "Is there something you'd like to share?"

"Abbey," she said with a definite emphasis on each syllable. I knew I was approaching her limit. However, I was saved by the appearance of the highway patrol trooper. A tall man, he had to stoop to look into the car. I wasn't sure about the relationship between law enforcement and mustaches, but almost every cop I've encountered had one. Trooper Dawkins was no exception. In a rare moment of self-control, I chose not to ask him about it.

"Good evening, ma'am. Do you know why I stopped you?"

I'd read that this question was designed to prompt an admission of guilt, but I wisely kept this to myself.

"I must have a taillight out," my well-read mom offered. She clearly knew how the game was played.

"Not that I noticed," the officer said. "But I'll take a look. Actually, I was more concerned about the fire."

"Fire?" Mom asked as she bit the hook.

"Yes, I figured with the speed you were moving, you had to be on the way to a fire," he said, leaning closer. "A big one."

My laugh quickly became a coughing fit when my mom whipped her head around. She fixed me with a look that said, *watch yourself.*

She and I have two completely different senses of humor.

"I'll be okay," I managed to get out.

The trooper cleared his throat. "I'll need your license and proof of insurance. And then you can get to your fire."

I held my tongue as my mom passed over the requested

documents. We sat in silence while the officer returned to his squad car.

After a few moments, there was a tap on her window. The trooper had returned.

"There's a problem with your license," he said when the window was down. "I'm going to need you to step out and come back to my vehicle."

"Should I call Dad?" I asked.

"No," she answered quickly. "It's just a mix-up."

"You're probably right. He doesn't have his handcuffs out," I said, peering out at the officer when my mom opened her door. "No Taser either."

I got the look again, and then she was gone.

It's difficult to say how I felt about seeing my parent being led to a squad car. It was like my foundation had taken a massive tilt, threatening to upheave my world.

A moment later, there was a rap on my side. I jumped, surprised to find another trooper waiting there. Rolling down my window, I glanced at the trooper and was blown away.

"Hello, Abbey," Suzanna Neri said.

"Glitter..." was all my brain could come up with. It made sense to me. You know how once you have something with glitter, no matter where you are or how much time has passed, that glitter keeps turning up? Suzanna Neri had become my glitter.

"We have just a few moments to chat. My partner will delay your mother, giving us time to talk." Dressed in the Minnesota State Patrol's uniform, Neri stood before me. When I last saw her, she was an FBI agent and, before that, an EMT. How...?

She read my hesitation. "I'm not really a state trooper," she said as she polished her badge with a sleeve. "Just go with it, and your mother will be fine."

Yes, I got her implied threat, but I didn't like it. At all. However, she had all the power; I could only nod.

"I have the box. I can give it to you." *And then you go away. For good.*

She gave me a smile that didn't make it to her eyes. The kind of smile a wolverine might make as it sized up its helpless prey. "I figured you'd come up with it. Did you have any trouble? Was there anyone else after the box besides you and your friends?"

I thought of the night at the Glensheen Mansion. How there was someone else moving around in the building. "We weren't the only ones in the mansion that night. Someone else was there, but we stayed out of sight. We weren't discovered, anyway. I thought it may have been a security guard we were evading, but maybe it was your..." I paused, pointing to the scar on her head.

Neri absently touched behind her ear. "Be thankful that you stayed out of sight. There may have been more than one funeral tonight." Her eye twitched slightly, and the corner of her mouth tightened up. Her pseudo-smile clued me in on her attempt to show off her spy skills.

"You're not impressing me," I told her. "It's not difficult to follow someone."

Neri held my gaze for a long moment as she played her intimidation game. She spoke first, which meant I won.

"Hold on to the box for the time being. You can deliver all three at the same time."

"All three?" My stomach started doing the flip-flop thing.

"There are two more boxes you need to find."

"Wait. I need to find them?"

Neri nodded.

Stomach flip-flops plus rising anger were not a winning combination for me. But I had to hold it together—after all, my mother was involved. "And you want me to do your dirty work."

"Don't think of it like that. You're on a noble quest. It's like Harry Potter going after the Horcruxes. Like King Arthur's quest for the holy grail. Think of Indiana Jones' search to find the Lost Ark before the Nazis could use it as a weapon. Even Shrek's quest to rescue the beautiful princess, Fiona."

"Shrek? Are you kidding me?"

"Not at all. But I need to be straight with you. Your quest could be dangerous. The woman who shot me, her name is Olga Vengekov. She's either a current or former Russian intelligence operative—who can tell these days? There's so much chaos over there, and everyone's becoming a contractor because the benefits are better. Anyway, she's also after the spirit boxes. This is not good news. Vengekov is dangerous; she's motivated and has enough resources and connections to find the boxes. But we have something she doesn't. We have Manfred Krug's journal."

"I loved his Shanghai adventures. Manny was amazing."

Neri nodded. "I have to agree. Krug was a remarkable man. His travel journals should give you insight to help you find the remaining boxes," she paused as if studying me. "The journals should also give you fair warning about their capabilities."

"I'll be careful." I nodded, thinking about what may have been in the closet at the Glensheen. "So, why does Vengekov want the spirit boxes? What is her end game?"

"She believes that these artifacts shouldn't be hidden away. She believes that power should be used. The thing with some people is that when they get a taste for power, they will do virtually anything to get more power and to keep it. They won't care how many people get hurt or killed in the process. If you want an example, look at the Russian government."

I nodded. With my dad being a journalist, the New York Times was practically required reading in my house. I was more up-to-date on world events than many politicians.

"Conversely, I believe artifacts like the spirit boxes are too dangerous not to be hidden away. We need to keep these extremely powerful boxes out of Vengekov's hands. We don't want them used for the wrong purpose."

"The wrong purpose?"

Neri shook her head. "Imagine someone bringing these boxes that attract, amplify, and unleash spiritual energy into a public area. Imagine all that energy let loose in Chicago at Soldier Field, the LAX airport, or Times Square. Or even here in Minnesota at the Mall of America."

Pausing for effect, Neri leaned in and rested her arms on my door. Her eyes drilled a hole into me. "That would be a disaster of biblical proportions."

I nodded as a shiver ran up my spine. I know what happened when I raised the lid on the one box for a moment. All three boxes working together for an extended time would not be good.

"I'll think about it, but I'm way behind on my schoolwork." Okay, not really that far behind, but she didn't have to know that.

"Abbey, if it sounds like I'm giving you a choice here, you're dead wrong. You are going to recover the last two spirit boxes. I'm in charge, so consider yourself drafted."

"Everybody Wants to Rule the World," the song by the English pop rock band Tears for Fears, came to mind. I wanted to tell her exactly that but decided a little restraint might play better. So, I settled for "Great."

Neri looked back toward her squad car and gave a nod.

"One last thing," Neri said. "For some reason, the power of the three will only work once with each pair of friends. I'm sorry, but that means no Lexi or Kelly. You'll need to bring someone else along for each box."

"That complicates things." My mind raced, as the circle of friends who knew and trusted my ability was rather small.

Neri passed a small packet through the window. "This is your cover story, should your mother ask why I was visiting with you. You can show your mother this folder and mention we talked about it, but don't let it out of your hands. The details of the last two boxes are tucked inside."

I glanced at the folder and back up at Neri, but she was gone.

The folder read, "Young Law Enforcement: Become a Community Service Trainee."

The door opened, and my mom climbed back in. "No ticket, thankfully. There was a computer glitch with my license, but the trooper got it resolved. We're good to go," she said, throwing the coupe into gear and quickly accelerating away.

What am I being forced into? I didn't like this one bit.

Glancing at the folder in my lap, the statement on the brochure's cover felt decidedly ironic.

"Volunteer today!"

11

THE PARANORMAL DUDES

"I can't believe you've talked me into this. Again." I shook my head.

Lexi lets out a laugh that might be more at home in a cartoon when the villain announces his dastardly plan. "C'mon, it's the perfect idea. We'll be the best ghost hunters there are." She took the ramp onto Highway 36 and merged with the usual horn honking that seemed to follow Lexi's driving wherever we went.

Over the school year, we'd learned that riding with her was a leap of faith. My father would define a leap of faith as believing in or accepting something outside the boundaries of reason. Based on the reactions of the other drivers we encounter, expecting to get to our destination whole and unscathed would seem to fall well beyond the boundaries of reason.

"But why do we want to be ghost hunters in the first place? It's not always as fun as it sounds. Sometimes ghosts are mean." I've met more than my share of those.

Kelly turned around from the passenger seat. "I think it's a brilliant idea. You're the ghost expert. You can totally see them when others can't. And I'm the investigator." Kelly wanted to be a cop like her father. "See? Brilliant."

"Hey, what about me?" Lexi asked.

"You're the comic relief." Kelly patted Lexi's arm, who didn't look like she knew what to think. "People will love you. Heck, people will love us. We'll win the contest for sure."

"Wait, what contest?" I looked at my friends. "This is the first I've heard anything about a contest."

Lexi glanced over to the passenger seat to Kelly.

"Wait, you knew about the contest too?" I asked Lexi.

"Maybe."

"You guys can't hold out on me like this. Spill. I want details." I leaned forward as far as the seatbelt would allow. "The contest," I prompted.

Kelly spoke up. "Have you ever watched that afternoon TV show, *Twin Cities Live?* Sometimes, they send out cameras to a haunted place in the area. I've seen them visit Keys Café and the St. Anthony Main area. But now, their resident ghost hunter has decided to retire, and they've made a contest of finding a replacement. All we need to do is submit a video of us ghost hunting, and they'll choose us."

I was familiar with the local daytime television talk show. Covering a wide range of topics, including lifestyle, entertainment, fashion, and food in the Twin Cities community, it was a fun show to watch. "Us and not anyone else?" I was skeptical. "And you're sure?"

"Yep," Kelly said in her uber-confident way. "With you, we're a lock. With all three, we'll be completely irresistible."

Robert Palmer's classic eighties song, "Simply Irresistible," popped into my head. And when any eighties song shows up in my life soundtrack, I go with it.

"I'm in," I say to the delight of Kelly and Lexi. But there's another advantage to saying yes. It could also remove Neri's threat to expose me since I'll already be known as a ghost hunter. "So where are we going?"

"The Lexington. It's a historic restaurant on Grand and Lexington in Saint Paul. Dates back to the thirties," Kelly said. "Let me read you what the producers sent over. *The Lexington opened in 1935, after the end of prohibition, and was a popular neighborhood bar to gather and socialize. Previously operating as a speakeasy, the expansive wood panels were perfect for hiding a little booze, and one can only imagine the shenanigans going on beyond the hidden staircase behind the coat check.*"

"A hidden staircase? That's so cool," Lexi said. "I wonder where it leads?"

"Most likely, either up or down." I can be funny when I want.

"The show's producer will meet us there to make sure we have all the access we need," Kelly said, totally ignoring my display of humor. "And then we can start exploring."

I have to admit it: I was excited. Outside of our Duluth trip, I haven't had many chances to hang with Kelly and Lexi. And to be exploring an older building with friends and doing what I do best was priceless. And really, what could go wrong?

As it turns out, several things could go wrong.

A bright-eyed younger woman stood inside the Lexington's entrance holding a tablet. Her face lit up when we walked in. "You must be..."

Kelly stepped up. "I'm Kelly. This is Lexi and Abbey," she said, gesturing to us. "We're the Spook Squad."

Wait, what? I glanced at Lexi, who shrugged.

"We needed a team name," Kelly explained. "It was required on the form."

"I'm Tori, a producer from *Twin Cities Live,*" the woman said. "I'm excited to see what you find. We've heard many stories of people experiencing things here. Hopefully, you can document actual ghosts."

Tori looked at her tablet. "We're just waiting for the other team."

I stepped up. This was new information. "There's another team?"

Tori nodded.

"This is news to me," I said. I was looking at Kelly as I said it.

"I didn't know there would be another group here, either," Kelly said.

"It's no big deal," Tori said. "Both teams will be here at the same time, but the Lexington is big enough for everyone. Logistically, it's easier for us to have both groups here. You'll be fine."

Kelly's eyes narrowed. "Who's this other group?"

"They're University of Minnesota students. Physics program."

"What's their name?" Kelly looked perturbed.

Tori looked down at her tablet just as the front door opened. Four boys—who looked like their only hope of kissing a girl was their grandma's cheek—pushed in.

"The Paranormal Dudes have arrived!"

The four boys stood in the classic superhero pose with fists on their hips. They wore matching coveralls with PD written in sharpie marker on the front. Each carried a large black suitcase. Every one of them wore glasses, and I swear, one of them had tape across the bridge.

Kelly rolled her eyes.

Tori smiled and tapped a box on her tablet. "Great, you're both here. We can get started."

She led us into the foyer. "Let me make some introductions. First, I'm Tori Hafner, a producer for *Twin Cities Live*. Our competition is classic boy versus girl. Over here, we have the Paranormal Dudes. They are Ben." A beefy boy with dark brown hair lifted a hand.

"Ernesto." A thin Latin boy nodded.

"Jonas." A redheaded boy with freckles and a toothy smile waved.

"And Kevin." He was the one with tape on his glasses.

"Bring on the ghosts," one of the boys said.

"And then we have the girls, the Spook Squad. They are comprised of Abbey..."

I lifted my hand, not sure I wanted the attention.

"...Kelly..." Arms folded, she nodded confidently.

"...And Lexi." She smiled and reached out to fist bump Jonas, but he let her hang. No one does that to my friend, so I stepped over, glaring at the boy who slighted her. I returned her fist bump.

Tori continued. "Welcome to the historic Lexington, or as it's known to regulars, the Lex. Over the years, we've heard many reports of unexplained things here. Employees hearing voices, getting grabbed by the arm, and things going missing," Tori began. "But that's not all. There's been sightings of figures in vintage clothes, unexplained lights going on and off, or just a creepy feeling that staffers get when they enter the basement."

Beckoning us to follow her, Tori continued. "This is the Williamsburg Room." The room looked like it should be in the Congdon mansion, with its wood-paneled walls, grand piano, and wood-burning fireplace. "This room was a popular spot for hosting wakes during the Lexington's long history. More than 80 years, in fact."

"That's a lot of dead bodies," I said.

"So, here's how this is going to work. Each team will have the run of the place, but I want the teams to stay together. No running around solo. Try to respect the other's space. If someone's already in a room, find a different one. At close to 26,000 square feet, there's plenty of space and plenty of ghosts for all of you."

Tori reached into her bag and pulled out several phones. "These are the latest models of iPhones, with cameras that excel in low light conditions. There's a fully charged one for each team. Use these to document your search and discoveries. By using the same camera, we're leveling the playing field. At the end of the night, I'll take back the phones, and our editors will create essentially a highlight reel of your experiences."

Looking around the room, Tori asked, "Any questions?"

The boy with the taped glasses raised his hand.

"Yes? Ask your question." Tori said.

The boy pointed to Kelly. "Is she single?"

That broke up the room and got his buddies elbowing and chastising him. "Kevin, you're such a dweeb."

"I am, actually. Single."

We all turned in surprise to look at Kelly.

"What? I am."

Tori cleared her throat. "I meant any questions about the paranormal and what you'll be doing?"

"How long do we have to look around?" I asked.

"Good question. After you set up your equipment, I'll start a three-hour timer. When the time is up, you'll pack up, and we can get home for some sleep."

"Where will you be?" This was Lexi who asked.

"I'm going to lock us in, and then I'll be at a table by the front entrance if you need me. I have some work to catch up on. But if I can wrap that up, I might wander around to see how everyone is doing."

She looked around the group. "Sound good?"

Nods all around.

"Okay, this will be your base, so you can unpack your stuff here. Let's get started."

We took off our jackets and set them in a booth. We waited while the Paranormal Dudes boys opened their cases, pulling out various pieces of equipment from the foam lining. One had a silver digital camera, another had a recording device, based on the microphone and headset. The boy with the taped glasses pulled out a small gray device resembling a television remote. The last one had a large video camera.

"Leave the video camera there. I only want you to record on our iPhone." Tori handed Ernesto the phone and handed another to Lexi.

"It's what I use to find orbs," Ernesto said.

"Uh, okay," Tori said, shrugging.

"Where's your gear?" he asked Lexi.

"We don't need no stinkin' gear," she said. "We got her."

Lexi pointed at me. And everyone stared.

I swallowed hard.

Tori cleared her throat. "I'm going to start the time in three, two, one." She pushed a button on her watch. "Go."

We looked at each other, unsure where to go.

"Upstairs." Kelly moved us to the stairway and took a tentative step before stopping. "Abbey, you should lead the way."

She turned to Lexi. "Get this on video. You never know what may happen."

Taking a deep breath, I put a hand on the wood handrail. There was a vibration of energy that reminded me of days long past. Energy that lingered still. Energy that wouldn't let the dead remain entirely dead. At that moment, I knew we would be experiencing paranormal activity.

I kept moving up, the stairs creaking ominously underneath.

At the top of the stairs, red eyes stared down at me.

My first inclination was to turn around and tell Lexi and Kelly that there wasn't anything here. I've spent my life trying to avoid these things. Trying to shield friends and family from their presence. But as I stepped forward, I realized this was right where I should be. With friends who knew all my dirty little secrets and fully embraced my unusual abilities.

I moved up another step, and a second set of glowing red eyes joined the first. There was no actual form that I could make out in the dark. Just the piercing eyes. I had no idea who or what would confront us at the top.

Like moths to the light, a third set of eyes arrived.

Breath. In. Out. Breath. I wanted to calm my mind.

Looking up at the three sets of eyes, they were at differing heights. Perhaps suggesting a family. The feeling I had was not dark. Often, spirits who met a violent end had that darker energy coloring their stay here. They wanted people to know how they died, and that led to traumatic meetings with the humans they encountered. I wasn't getting any of that. There was something there, like curiosity. It felt like they wanted to know about me.

The shortest of the three sets of eyes moved down a step.

"Abbey?" Lexi asked. Her voice cracked as she drew out the syllables of my name. She sounded frightened. She needn't be.

"It's okay, Lexi. These are Caspers. We'll be fine."

"I like friendly ghosts," she said. "They're my favorite."

"Make filming your favorite. You are getting this, aren't you?" Kelly moved next to Lexi.

"Duh, that's why we're here," she said.

While the other two sets hovered on the landing above, the other eyes glided silently down, coming to rest several steps above mine. This put us roughly eye to eye, which meant it was considerably shorter than I was. And I was just five inches over five feet.

This was a child.

I held out my hand, palm up. Two silver coins dropped into my hand.

"Whoa," Kelly said behind me on my right. "Zoom in on this."

Lexi moved closer to my left.

The coins were larger, with Benjamin Franklin in profile. The year 1949 was stamped below his chin. I flipped them over and the liberty bell was on the tails side.

"Thank you," I said. "But you should keep them."

Reaching my hand back out with the coins closed in my fist, I trusted my instincts and opened my hand. The coins dropped. And then vanished.

"Now that's something you don't see every day," Kelly said.

This got us giggling, and when I glanced back up to the landing, all three sets of eyes were gone.

We walked through the upstairs office but found nothing of note. After ten minutes of pointless standing around, we decided to move on and returned to the main floor. Tori had her nose in her laptop and politely waved as we trudged past. The boys from the Paranormal Dudes group were spread out in the bar area.

The bar featured a sweeping wooden bar that curved toward the Williamsburg dining room. Bottles of numerous shapes and sizes lined the wall behind the bar.

Ernesto was taking pictures with the iPhone camera over the long wooden bar. He'd shoot several, flip through the images, and giggle before taking more. This pattern went on for several minutes.

He saw me watching and sauntered over. His smug expression telegraphed his words. "We are SO going to win this competition. I've got so many pictures of orbs. There's so many here."

I glanced around. "Really?"

"Hell, yeah. Those floating balls of paranormal energy are everywhere here. You're going to regret not having the proper equipment along."

"Show me," I said, gesturing to the camera.

"I'll do you one better. I'll take one here," he said, pointing across the room to the leather booths. "Do you see any orbs?"

I didn't even have to look. "Nope. No orbs."

"Watch this," he said and lifted the camera. *Click.* The flash went off. Ernesto turned the camera around and showed the picture. It was a picture of the red leather booths. No orbs in sight.

I shrugged.

"Wait, you have to zoom in." He zoomed the image three or four times and giggled. There was something translucent floating above the table.

Shaking my head, I looked down at my feet. The patterned carpet underneath.

"Do you want to see even more orbs?" I asked.

The other members of both teams had wandered over. Kevin had the iPhone up to record.

"Okay," Ernesto said with a hint of wariness.

"Aim the camera at the same booth. Get ready to take a picture, but wait for my word."

Stepping in front of him, I slid my feet back and forth on the carpet. I moved out of the way. "Now."

Click. And the flash of the digital camera's light.

Everyone crowded around to look at the display. It took only several zooms, but there were now easily a dozen orbs in the picture.

"Ashes to ashes," I began.

"Dust to dust," Kelly finished. "Boys, your orbs are nothing but dust lit up by your camera's flash." She laughed. "Some ghost hunters, you boys are."

The boys exchanged glances and didn't look too happy.

"Orbs," Kelly said, shaking her head.

"Let's find something real. Where to next?" Lexi asked.

"The basement," I said. "There's something there."

"It's always the basement." Lexi didn't look enthused. "Why isn't it ever the sunroom?"

"There's no sunroom, silly. This is a restaurant." I wasn't sure if Kelly was being serious or not.

"I know that," Lexi said. "I was just making a point."

"C'mon, ladies. The basement awaits." I led the way past the boys, who made a point of giving us the stink-eye. Typical boy behavior.

Like all good haunted buildings, the door creaked ominously when I pulled it open. Even better, the stairs groaned as I took a step. The flashlight's beam illuminated the dusty wooden steps as I moved further into the abyss. Catching a glimpse of something moving in the edges of the light, a shiver ran up my spine.

But I couldn't help smiling. I was enjoying this.

"Can you hear that?" Kelly asked, her eyes wide with curiosity and a palpable sense of fear.

We paused halfway down the stairs and listened. There was a conversation happening ahead of us. In the waiting darkness. A man and a woman's voice were talking, but the actual words were indecipherable.

"Interesting."

The voices faded and vanished as we moved down the stairs.

At the bottom of the stairs, we shone our flashlights to survey the room. It was a large space, with several smaller rooms branching off. It looked like a prep kitchen. Metal counters gleamed in the light of our flashlights.

I flipped on the overhead lights.

"Not here," I said and moved through the kitchen, trying to get a sense of the place. Everything said it was well cared for and put in its place. If there were something here, it would be away from the kitchen. I pointed to one of the doors that branched off from the prep area. "Let's explore back here."

The first door was built of sturdy-looking wood with a brass knob. Hand on the knob, I paused. There was a creaking sound behind us that wasn't there before.

"Maybe it's nothing," Lexi said. "These old places..." Her words trailed off.

"I'm definitely hearing something," Kelly said, looking at me. "You're hearing it too, right?"

I nodded, thinking it was ironic that none of us brave ghost hunters had turned around, even though the sound was quite clearly coming from behind us.

"Guys?"

"We should see what's in this room," Kelly said, indicating the door in front of us.

"We do need to be thorough," Lexi added.

The creaking sound continued, but the clink of dishes joined in. Whoever—or whatever—was making the noise wasn't being subtle. Not in the least.

"Guys."

My friends looked at me blankly.

"It won't do us any good to ignore this. We can all hear what's happening behind us. Something is happening."

"But I'm scared." Lexi's wide eyes and trembling lips casted a shadow of vulnerability on her pale, anxious face.

"It's okay. Remember, we're here for moments like this. If we're going to call ourselves the Spook Squad, we damn well better be okay with seeing the occasional spook." I looked at Lexi and then Kelly, holding each of their gazes for a long moment. "Brace yourselves, we're going to turn around. On three."

The current clanking of dishes dwarfed the earlier clinking.

"Two."

It sounded like a dozen people were carelessly tossing dishes onto the counters.

"One."

I took my hand off the knob and turned around.

"What the…?" Kelly said breathlessly.

Lexi moved the iPhone's camera around to capture the scene.

The earlier pristine kitchen had been transformed. Every single cabinet door was wide open. But it wasn't just that, now there were dishes covering every inch of the countertops. Dinner plates here, salad plates there. A blue platter with a porcelain gravy boat resting on top. A stack of soup bowls higher than I could reach if I stood on my tippy toes sat in the middle. Cups of all shapes and sizes were spread around the metal surfaces.

"This was *not* here before," Lexi said.

"I think we have a poltergeist," I said.

"A what?"

"Poltergeist is a German word meaning noisy spirit. They're known for being mischievous. Things go missing. Things show up. They like to mess with us."

"But, what is a German ghost doing here?" Lexi looked perplexed, but I suspected she may be just being silly.

"That's pretty intense." Kelly shook her head.

"Got to agree," I said. "As far as dish stacking spirits go, this is one of the more prolific ones."

"So what do we do?" Lexi asked.

"Nothing. Do you want to put them away?" She shook her head. "I know I don't."

I put my hand back on the doorknob. "Let's keep moving then."

Inside was a large storage area. Dusty furniture sat stacked on one side while boxes lined the far wall. I flipped the light switch, but nothing happened. The only light was from the prep kitchen behind us. Stepping into the room, we spread out and looked around. There was nothing else here. Just boxes, discarded furniture, and dust. Lots of dust.

"Why don't people just throw things away?" Kelly asked. "I mean, look at this place. Doesn't look like anyone has been here for decades, so the stuff down here won't ever be used. Just haul it to the trash."

"So, you want to add to the landfills?" Lexi asked. "That's not going to help anyone. You know as well as anyone, the key is to reuse and recycle."

Kelly looked at our friend like she'd just grown a third eye. "What?"

Kelly had a sparkle in her eye. She relished confrontations.

"Why can't you just haul this to the dump? It's wood and fabric. It'll revert back to nature."

Lexi shook her head. "But why not get it into the hands of someone who could use it? Imagine someone struggling to open a restaurant. They'd be ecstatic to get these tables and chairs."

Kelly didn't look convinced. "Sounds like a lot of trouble."

"But there are organizations that do exactly that. Their mission is to find new homes for things that already exist." Lexi nodded. "And more importantly, we're not using new resources and polluting the planet building new ones when someone uses already made things."

"Since when did you go all soft?"

Lexi stepped forward and looked directly at Kelly. "It's not about being soft. It's about being responsible. You, of all people, should get that concept. You actually enjoy being responsible."

During this exchange, I'd stood there and enjoyed the interchange between my friends. I'd never be bored with Kelly and Lexi in the same room.

Kelly turned to me. "Yes, I'm responsible, but that doesn't mean you don't have to reuse everything." She paused as she pulled a plastic water bottle from her backpack and opened the top to take a drink. "Abbey, help me out here."

I nodded to her water bottle. "You know, Mother Nature sheds a tear every time you open one of those disposable water bottles?"

Kelly shook her head. "That's it. I've gone to hell."

Lexi and I exchanged glances, and we both broke up.

"Let's move on," Kelly said. "This room is a dead end."

I was so (think thumb and forefinger held roughly the size of a miniature marshmallow apart) close to leaving. There didn't seem to be anything worth investigating here until my Spidey sense began tingling. It was a vague but strong sense of something being wrong or dangerous. Holding up a finger, I scanned the room. Nothing had changed, yet everything had changed.

Yeah, I know I can be an enigma.

"Over here," I said, pointing to the two dozen cardboard boxes stacked along the back wall. "Help me move these. There's something about the wall here. I want to see it clearly."

We each grabbed a carton and hefted it over to the adjoining wall. Whatever was in the boxes was heavy. Not vinyl record collection heavy, but certainly heavier than a box of stuffed animals. Not that I ever had stuffed animals other than Reggie, the moose. But I digress.

After several trips with the non-teddy bear cartons, we paused to catch our breath.

"What's up with the wall?" Kelly asked.

"Too early to tell. Let's keep going. We're nearly halfway done."

I grabbed another box and turned to the stack of relocated cartons. Except, there wasn't a stack.

"What the...?" I let the box slide from my fingers to the floor.

All the boxes were stacked back in their original location.

"Maybe I should be recording this." Lexi pulled the phone from her back pocket.

"Maybe you should," I agreed and nodded to Kelly, "Let's get these moved."

We made quick work of the boxes, moving them to the adjacent wall while Lexi filmed the process. When we were done, I pointed to a box. "Sit on this, Lexi, while you record. I don't want them moved again."

Approaching the wall, I studied it. Covered with wood panels, it differed from the concrete blocks that made up the two sides of the room. I put a hand onto the surface. The wood was smooth underneath my palm, yet I felt a tingle.

Working towards the corner, I slid my hand along the way, feeling the bump of each new section. I paused when I felt a breeze on my ankles.

"Here."

Stepping back, I kneeled and searched for the source of the draft. There looked to be a gap where the wall met the floor that wasn't in the other wall sections.

"There's a room behind this wall. I'm sure of it."

Kelly joined me at the wall. "There's a way in if we can find it," she said. "Try pushing on the wall."

Try as we might, the wall wasn't budging.

"Well, damn," Kelly said after a few minutes.

"If there's a room, there's a door. It's here." I put a hand on Kelly's shoulder. "Don't give up."

From behind us, Lexi cleared her throat. "If there's a door, maybe you should try knocking."

Kelly looked at me and rolled her eyes.

"Maybe we should. Why not?" I rapped my knuckles on the wood surface, the sound echoing.

Unexpectedly, the sound of sliding wood and an opening appeared as the middle panel swung silently and slowly inward.

My friends both turned open-mouthed to me.

"Carl Sagan once said that somewhere, something incredible is waiting to be known. I think he was talking about this room."

Lexi slid off her box, the phone held up in front of her as she recorded.

The door continued its silent opening until it thudded softly against the wall. The light from our flashlights shone into the cavernous space behind the wall. It was far larger than the cubbyhole I'd expected.

I stepped inside.

The musty air had to have been trapped in this space for over a decade, if not half a century or more. My skin tingled like a multitude of ants crawling across my bare flesh. Running my hand across my arm brought no ants, though. It was just my senses on overdrive.

I moved further into the room, drawn to the far corner of the space. It was unfazed by my flashlight beam and remained impenetrable to light. The mustiness was joined by another smell, not a bad one, but it wasn't a good smell either. All sound was blanketed, and I swear I heard my pulse race through my body.

Moving closer, a shape awaited just inside the veil of shadow.

"Hello, young lady," a voice that belonged to someone's southern grandma said. "Welcome to my home."

Fighting the urge to say something sarcastic about needing to open a window, I simply nodded.

"Child, you carry the weight of generations." Her tone suggested this was important. But when she didn't elaborate, I spoke.

"The weight? What do you mean?"

"My dear, the weight is the sight. The summoning. The pathway to the dead."

Oh, that weight.

"Yeah. My grandmother had that, too. She could talk to the dead." My grandmother could communicate much like I could. But my mother? Not a chance. She's the show me the scientific proof kind of person. That's why she became a doctor, where everything is studied and proven. She didn't have tolerance for the gray of the spirit world.

The old woman laughed. "We're talking about you, dear. You have the ability. We wouldn't be here in this space if you didn't."

About that. "Why are you in this space? I know why I'm here, but this wouldn't appear to be," I said, looking around, "where I'd want to spend my afterlife. I'd maybe haunt a sidewalk café in Paris or the haunted mansion at Disney, just to be ironic. But why stay cooped up in this dark basement?"

The woman moved to the edge of the shadow, leaving me just on the verge of seeing what she looked like. She stood, unmoving for a moment, then two, and then three. And then she spoke.

"Do you think I wanted to be married off to a pig of a man at 14? Do you think I wanted to endure his blows, his crushing weight, his disgusting breath? Do you think I wanted to move north, to live out my life caring for his six children from his previous wife?" Her voice had gotten louder as she went along. She paused before continuing. "Do you think I wanted to be beaten for the horrible trespass of returning a hello from the man who delivered our feed? Do you think I wanted to be left to die on some dusty basement floor?"

Her dark eyes remained fixed on mine.

She did nothing for a long, awkward moment. Then, the woman stepped out of the shadows. I gasped. The sight of her was enough to make me take a step back. A knot of twisted flesh, her face looked like it had been torn and put back together. Badly.

"Has it occurred to you, dear, that we may not have had a choice in the matter? Any matter, in fact?"

It hadn't.

Before I could even formulate a response or say anything, she was gone. One moment there, the next, gone.

"Abbey? Do you see anything?" Lexi said behind me.

"It looks empty to me," Kelly added.

Turning, I gestured to where the woman had stood. "Did you guys see...? Did you hear...?"

But I could tell from their expressions the woman had come to me alone. How do I even begin to explain the high strangeness of it?

I decided to let it go.

"Let's go back upstairs," I said. "Nothing to see here."

12

MORE THAN A FAT KID
LOVES CAKE

I know life can be unfair.

There will be times when you get slighted or don't get what you've been expecting. It's not your fault—it rarely is. Maybe that's why it feels so unfair. But, that's no reason to treat someone poorly. Nothing gets me angrier than when someone is being a jerk to another human being. When I see it happen, it unleashes the inner Abbey-beast, who becomes the judge, jury, and executioner. I won't rest until the natural balance is restored and the jerk is put back in their place.

Case in point: I was in line at a coffee shop, and the guy in front of me was talking loudly on his phone. Yes, he was one of those. He was so involved in his conversation that when he took a step or two back, he didn't realize I was there. I held up my hand and pushed on his back. "Don't Stand So Close to Me" from The Police, an eighties classic if there ever was one, popped into my head. And then, oddly enough, out my mouth.

"Don't stand so close to me."

I got a grunt in response, but he took a step forward. When he reached the front of the line, he held a finger to the barista when she asked what he'd like. Never mind, another half-dozen people were waiting behind him. After a moment, he said, "Hold on, Bill," He looked over at the waiting barista and said, "I'd like a mocha."

"I'm sorry," she replied, "but it's been an unusually busy morning, and we ran out of mochas." She looked nervous as she said this.

His body tensed as he lowered his precious phone. "You have to be kidding me. I have a mocha every single morning here. How did you even get a job here? Some coffee place this dump is." His voice was getting louder as he went on. "This is total BS. Fine. Just give me a regular coffee." He was still grumbling as he sat down with his drink.

The poor girl's eyes looked watery when it was my turn at the counter. I felt terrible for her while at the same time feeling complete disgust for the jerk. I gave her my best reassuring smile and told her I'd have a latte. When she asked for my name, I knew it was because they would call it out when my drink was ready.

So I told her my name was Mocha.

You should have seen the look on the jerk's face when they called out "Mocha" as I skipped up and grabbed my latte. I glanced at the barista, and her grin made my day.

Several people share this "play nice" sensibility with me. The first is my friend Turner. He has used his delightfully wicked pranks on people who have meanly wronged others. While I may disagree with his tactics, they sure have a perverse fun quality.

The other person is Brian Thompson, my attorney. The only adult willing to help when I was being unfairly treated as a prisoner at summer camp, we became fast friends. It's been too long since we've talked. Life gets hectic in high school — especially when you've been fighting off a horde of clowns.

Having a grownup like Neri not playing nice with me got under my skin and, quite frankly, scared me. But I knew when to ask for help. Ghosts are one thing, government agents are another. So when I needed help, that kind of help, Brian Thompson would always be my best option.

After the phony traffic stop, I couldn't wait to get home and call him. I'd volunteered to take out the trash, and the moment I stepped outside, I made the call.

"This is Brian Thompson. I'm here to help." Answering right away, his words are more than words, they are a lifeline. Palpable relief filled me as he spoke. I've only met a few attorneys, but how many attorneys could you say that about?

"Brian, it's Abbey Hill."

"Abbey, I thought I might be hearing from you."

"Oh, really?" Dropping the garbage bag into the trash can, I paused, hearing a noise behind me.

"Having a very bossy, self-important someone asking about you made me think I'd also be hearing from you. I didn't answer her questions, of course. We do have attorney-client privileges, after all. She got up in my face when I didn't answer. But hey, I'm an attorney. That is an everyday kind of occurrence." Brian paused for a moment. "Does this woman sound like anyone you've met?"

"Yeah, I've met the dragon lady. She's the reason I'm calling. This woman is determined to make my life interesting." One of my trademark understatements.

"How so?"

"She's coercing me into recovering some artifacts brought here from Shanghai." There was the sound again. Closer, now.

"Really? I'm not a big fan of coercion. It raises my attorney hackles."

"I didn't know you had hackles."

"It was a prerequisite for getting into law school. You had to have them. Mine are well-developed after many years of protecting the weak and downtrodden."

"I'm not actually weak, you know." Whatever was out with me in the dark was right around the corner. I grabbed the gardening shovel, feeling better with something in my hand. "And as I think about it, I'm not really that downtrodden."

Brian let out his characteristic belly laugh. "Sorry, just refining my marketing speak. How is this woman coercing you?"

"She's threatened to make my ghostly abilities public if I don't use them to find these Chinese artifacts."

"I see." Brian paused. "Why do you suppose she needs you to get the artifacts?"

"These artifacts were brought to the U.S. around a century ago. Since then, they've been lost, hidden or forgotten. This woman wants to take advantage of my expertise in communicating with people." Hearing it again, I lifted the shovel.

"People?" Brian questioned.

"Sorry. Dead people. Chances are, only dead people would know where these artifacts are hidden away." I stepped closer to the corner, ready to swing the shovel. Ready to protect myself.

A pause. "Ahh, those kind of people." Brian knows of my ability. I had to tell him so he would believe that my knowledge of my kidnapped mom was real. He's a believer now.

"That brings up a question. How would she have learned of your abilities?"

I took another step towards the noise, now just a few feet away. "She said she learned of it after picking up chatter, as she said. Apparently, my friends had discussed the events, and she had figured out there was more to my story."

"Chatter? That sounds like she's with the government. Intelligence, perhaps."

"Government sounds right. She flashed an FBI badge but has also shown up as a paramedic and a state trooper."

Whatever was making the noise was right around the corner.

Brian paused for a long moment. "She could be an intelligence operative—a spy, if you will. They are usually adept at playing roles. It feels like she has significant resources at her disposal."

I nodded into the phone for some reason. "Yeah, she does."

"What else do you know about her?"

"She said her name is Suzanna Neri, and she is a doctor. She also said she had similar abilities as I have, that was until a bullet grazed her skull and took away those abilities. There was a nasty-looking groove behind her ear."

Now was the moment. Shovel ready, I stepped out from the protection of the corner.

A raccoon looked back at me with glowing eyes. It had torn open a trash bag and was feasting. The raccoon hissed at me, clearly not appreciating my intrusion. Stepping back around the corner, I left the raccoon to its dinner.

Brian's hesitation as he processed things was apparent. "I think we should meet up. I can make it to the cities tomorrow." Brian lives in River Falls, Wisconsin, roughly an hour away, depending on traffic and weather. "These artifacts she wants you to retrieve, where is the next one located?"

"It's at the James J. Hill house in Saint Paul. Almost directly across from the Cathedral." I went back inside the house and sat at the kitchen table. The folder from Neri was there under a textbook.

"I've heard of it but have never visited."

"Same." I put Brian on speaker and opened the folder. "I'm reading from the brochure: Rugged stone, massive scale, fine detail, and ingenious mechanical systems recall the powerful presence of James J Hill, builder of the Great Northern Railway." The brochure had pictures that showed an enormous stone building. Why couldn't one of the boxes be nestled in a lovely two-story bungalow?

"I love the sense of history you get from touring these old places. Count me in. I'll help you find the dragon lady's artifact. And possibly a solution to get you out of her clutches."

The first ray of hope hit me like a Saturday morning ray of sunshine. You know the feeling when you wake up without the alarm and realize you don't actually have to get up for school or anything? A great feeling.

"You think there's something you can do?"

I could hear Brian's optimism in his tone. "I know one thing for sure. Having the artifact in your possession puts you in a much stronger place. Negotiation works best when you have something the other wants. She wants the artifacts, and you want your freedom. Maybe we can make that happen."

I couldn't help but let out a squeal of excitement. "Lois Lane may have had her Superman, but you're my hero. Thank you."

"No promises, young lady. But I'll see what I can do."

That was good enough for me.

◊◊

Sitting in the dark of my room as I waited for sleep to take me, I pondered. For Saturday's visit to the James J. Hill house, I needed one more person for the power of the three. The list of potential thirds was short. My parents, Stacia, Carrie, and Turner. I couldn't see bringing my parents along as I removed an artifact from one of Saint Paul's most notable buildings. There would be just too many explanations needed. Stacia and Carrie had been with me at the River Falls camp and saw what I could do. They were both excellent candidates. And then there was Turner. I had shared my first kiss with Turner at camp. But beyond that, he's been with me for several demonstrations of my spooky girl abilities. He was also intelligent, resourceful, and more than a little handsome. Plus, he had a driver's license.

My mind made up, I texted him. After a bit of back and forth, I got to the point and asked him if he'd join Brian and me on Saturday. Without hesitation, Turner said yes. Closing my eyes, feeling the sleep getting close, I pulled up the covers. And smiled.

◊◊

Turner was at my door. Just knowing he was on the other side caused my heart to race. I paused before opening it, deciding it would be best to keep my calm and cool demeanor. A girl shouldn't show too much interest. I pulled open the door and...

Turner stood with his winter coat open, his shirt stretched across his chest. His dark eyes stared into mine, and my calm and cool demeanor went right out the window.

"Turner," I exclaimed and wrapped him up in a hug. While he returned the hug, I took in his scent and luxuriated in his arms. There's a line when a hug becomes awkwardly long, and I knew it was way behind me. I didn't care.

"I missed you too," Turner said.

My words were muffled with my face buried in his shoulder.

"Pardon me?" Turner quizzed. "I didn't catch that." There was a hint of amusement in his voice.

I pulled myself back to the moment and looked up at Turner. My grip on reality was seriously threatened as his gorgeous eyes looked at me. I didn't believe I was capable of speech at that moment. His lips were just inches from mine.

"Oh, hi, Turner," my mom said. "Abbey mentioned you'd be stopping by. How have you been?"

Awkwardly attempting to disengage as Turner answered, I held onto his sleeve. I didn't trust myself to stand on my own just yet. Taking a deep breath, I looked back and forth between Turner and my mom. I had no idea what they were discussing, but found myself nodding along. Briefly, I wondered if I was coming down with some sort of disease. My mind clouded, my heart raced, and I was sweating. Typhoid fever? Possibly malaria?

And what is it with my mom's sense of timing? My lips were still tingling in their near-kiss anticipation. Can lips be disappointed? Is that even a thing?

ᗢ

We rode in Turner's pickup to meet up with Brian Thompson. The truck wasn't new, but there was a comfort to it. The front seat had a bench seat, and the only other seat was a folding jump seat in the back. Shifting smoothly through the gears, Turner glanced over his shoulder as we rocketed down the ramp and merged into the highway traffic. "I like to be at full speed when I merge," he said. "It frustrates me when someone tries to merge when they are going slower than everyone else. It jams everyone up."

"I agree. Some people don't get the merge concept. Those people should have their licenses taken away and be sent back to driving school until they can prove their competence."

"Exactly!" Turner agreed enthusiastically as he slapped the steering wheel with his palm. "Wait," he said and glanced in my direction. "You're teasing me, aren't you?"

"Maybe," I said with a smirk. "Or maybe I really believe anyone driving a little too slow should have their driving privileges revoked. You tell me."

Turner shook his head. "I guess it sounds a little harsh when you put it like that."

"A little?"

"Okay, a lot." Turner grinned. "Listen to you, being the voice of reason."

"It's a role I've become comfortable with." I grinned back at him.

໐໐

We met up with Brian outside the impressive James J. Hill house. With the enormous Cathedral of Saint Paul across the street, it said something when you called the Hill House impressive. Built of stone, with tall peaks over the three-story building, multiple chimneys and a trio of dormers sat over the imposing arched entrance. I counted 50 windows from where I stood.

It was a big house.

Brian waved, and I ran over and hugged him. I was happy to see the man who brought my mom back and forever changed my life for the better.

After we separated and he warmly shook hands with Turner, I made a show of sizing up Brian. "You're looking good," I told him.

"Open casket good, or GQ cover kind of good?" You have to love Brian's sense of humor.

"Somewhere in the middle," I told him. "You look like you've lost weight, too."

Turning sideways, Brian sucked in his stomach. "Getting there. I started running every morning. I hated it at first, but now I just detest it. I consider it a necessary evil on my path to self-actualization. Just trying to be the best me I can."

"So what prompted the lifestyle change?" Turner asked.

"My wife. One morning, she patted my belly and told me there was plenty of me to love. That I didn't need to keep adding more." He laughed.

"That was a diplomatic way of putting it. Got to give her credit for that."

"Yep, she's a good woman. Why she ended up with a blood-sucking attorney, I'll never know." The fact that Brian's eyes got misty as he said this only made me appreciate his warmth and depth more.

I couldn't help but give him another hug. "You are so gosh darn lovable," I told him.

"So, you're saying you love me more than a fat kid loves cake?"

I was laughing so hard that it took a moment to answer. Wiping away my tears of laughter, I told him, "Yep, that pretty much covers it."

"Before we go in, I want you both to hear something," I said, pulling out the well-read pages from my backpack. "These are pages from the travel journal of the man who brought the box from Shanghai to this house."

I pointed to a bench. "Let me tell you a story," I began.

13

SHIP SHAPE

I write this account as the welcome coast of New York is on the horizon. This past week aboard the RMS Aquitania has been an adventure, to say the least. Thanks to the generosity of my benefactors, I've been able to share the luxury with the rest of the first-class passengers. As near as I have been able to make out, there are over 500 of us in first class and a similar number in second class. I've heard tell that there are four times as many in third class. Good lord, they must be packed in below decks!

Our voyage across the Atlantic has taken a week. During this time, I've had the pleasure of meeting some of the world's elite. On our second day out, I shared a table with a New York financier in the first-class dining area. He had spent the summer in England with his wife, Edith, and his two grown daughters, Adeline and Dee Dee.

The first mate had stopped by our table and shared stories of the Cunard superliner. He told us that even though the Aquitania was known as "Ship Beautiful," it also had a reputation as a lucky ship. It was built as Cunard's answer to its Liverpool competitor, White Star Lines RMS Titanic. He bowed his head briefly in remembrance of the tragedy that befell the giant ship on its maiden voyage. Dee Dee had crossed herself.

He said the London press had described the Aquitania as a moving, floating palatial residence of awe-inspiring dimensions topped by four tall scarlet and black stacks. These four funnels gave the impression of great power, especially important for the emigrant trade, which had been so vital.

Indeed, many third-class passengers were embarking on a voyage for a new life in America.

The officer stood proudly—and somewhat pompously—in front of us in his dark uniform with its epaulets and gold buttons as he told us about the ship serving during the Great War. She was a troop transport and a hospital ship. Only in the last several years had she returned to commercial use.

Adeline was particularly taken with the officer. There is power in a man's uniform, I've always believed. Her sister, Dee Dee, had caught my eye, and I was determined to speak with the raven-haired beauty again. Her eyes were dark and magnificent. Her lovely hair was piled high on her head.

As I recall, the first officer, James, told us that London's most famous hotel decorator had designed the first-class dining saloon. It certainly was luxurious—as was much of the ship. Beyond this palatial room, I've seen English gardens, a music hall, and stately rooms decorated in the finest traditions of Paris and London.

My cabin was no exception as it looked like a twin of my Lansdowne House room in London. Several times daily, my cabin is freshened by a trio of the ship's servants. I could get used to traveling like this.

I had managed to pry Dee Dee loose from her family for a stroll on the deck. The evening air was cool as we stepped into the garden lounge, which stretched 150 feet on either side of the public rooms. It was designed to look like an old English garden. The walls resembled stone, and trellises in natural teak were attached to the stone, with ivy making its way upward.

We were chatting about my Asian adventures until a breathless man rushed into the lounge. His wide-eyed look suggested a man on the verge of panic.

"It's out there," he said with hysteria. He was so beside himself that the waiter had no luck calming him down. The man kept glancing toward the door like he expected something monstrous to barge in.

As we were close to the man, I handed him my whiskey. Without so much as a word of thanks, he took the glass and emptied the contents without coming up for air. I held up two fingers and gestured for the waiter to bring over several more.

The man's eyes were locked on the entrance.

"Good lord, man. You look as if you have just seen a ghost."

He whipped his head around and fixed me with a look for the ages.

"Yes!" he exclaimed. "Yes, that's it!"

The waiter returned, and I quickly plucked the whiskies from his tray. I handed one to the panicked man while keeping the other for myself. The man downed this one as quickly as the first one.

"Tell me what you saw," I prompted. The whiskey appeared to help, and with a sideways glance toward the entrance, he told his tale. Many of the other patrons in the lounge moved closer to listen.

The man's voice was low and even, and if it wasn't for the haunted look in his eyes, he could have been discussing the third race at Churchill Downs.

"I had taken dinner in my cabin, and shortly after the steward had dropped off a pitcher of water, I heard a commotion from the adjoining cabin. There were several loud thumps and a shout, followed by a persistent scratching that emanated from the wall. The ferociousness of the scratching made me wonder if a tiger was loose in the next cabin."

Dee Dee looked concerned by the man's account. "Oh, dear. You never can tell what people will have in the 3rd class cabins. Daddy said it's positively a zoo down there."

The man swung around and glared at her, clearly agitated. "Young lady, I am a first-class passenger. I do not stay below deck. In fact, my cabin is just a few yards from the officers' quarters."

A thought crept into my head, and I asked for his cabin number. His reply, C22, made my mouth dry up, and I took another sip of whiskey. My own cabin was C24.

Dee Dee asked him what had happened next.

"There was a haze in my room. A mist seeped in underneath my door. Worried there may be a fire aboard, I threw open the door and stepped out into the corridor. It was so thick, I could not see beyond a few feet."

"Was it smoke?"

The man shook his head. "No, it was cool and had to be fog. And as I tried to wrap my mind around fog being inside the ship, a figure emerged. A man moved towards me. He had a green radiance and was not so much walking as gliding. It was not natural movement. I was transfixed in place as he came into view. Hideously deformed, his face looked like the very skin had been burned off in great patches, leaving gnarled flesh and exposed bone behind." He paused to take another drink before continuing. "It was the most horrible thing I've ever seen, yet I was frozen in place. That was, until he spoke."

There must have been twenty people listening to his story, every one of us wholly riveted.

"Tell me, what did he say?" I questioned as I finished the last of my whiskey, relishing the burning sensation as it went down.

"'The gas,' he had said with a voice like a screeching owl. 'The gas burns.' And he reached for me. I'm not afraid to admit it. That's when I ran. I just couldn't take another second of his voice."

I stood up and announced we needed to go to the first-class cabins.

"No," the man shouted, wrapping his arms around himself as he trembled. It wasn't from the cold, though. The garden lounge was warm.

"We have to know if we're in danger," I explained. "Out here in the ocean, there's no room for error. It would be a devastatingly deadly mistake to allow something like you described loose on the ship. There's no rescue close by."

There was a murmur from the assembled guests as opinions were voiced. Unwilling to wait for a consensus, I said, "Let's move."

Dee Dee, our waiter, and several other men followed me out through the entrance. I noticed the panicked man was not among them. But I knew where to go. After all, his cabin was right next to mine.

I couldn't help but shiver.

I led the way as we raced down the corridor, taking the turns as they came, my dress shoes sliding on the smooth surface. I grabbed Dee Dee's hand, and she ran with me, her heels echoing in the stillness. I wasn't proud of it, but using the situation to get closer to her crossed my mind. She was out of my league, so any advantage I could use felt like the right choice.

It wasn't, as it turned out.

When we rounded the next corner, I knew we were getting close. My cabin was the third one down, but I couldn't see it. The fog was too thick.

"There must be a fire," Dee Dee said behind me.

"It's not a fire, it's too cool. It must be fog. You can feel the dampness in the air."

"But why is it in the ship?" she asked.

"I have an idea," I told her as the fog billowed from the third cabin down the hall. My room. "Maybe there's something I can do, but I need to get to my cabin."

She looked at me with those smoldering eyes of hers. "If you wanted to get me back to your stateroom, you should have just asked," she said.

I turned to her. "Would you have come?"

"Probably not," she said after a moment's hesitation. "But at least things would have been in the open. They're better that way."

"Sometimes," I admitted, "but not all the time. A little mystery can be good, too."

I glanced at the fog and told Dee Dee we'd better get going. Several steps brought us into the mist, and I froze. A pair of eyes glowed at us. Human eyes don't glow like that. Pretty sure I haven't come across anything that has eyes like that.

At the first door, I noticed the voices of the group that came with us had gone silent. Dee Dee's grip felt as if she held on for her life.

Something bumped my foot.

At the second door, the visibility was at arm's length. I reached out in front of me to test my theory, and something brushed across my fingers. I quickly pulled my hand back.

The third door was open, and fog billowed out. The choice to step into the lion's den was made easy as the sound of dozens of birds flapped all around us. I hate birds.

When I stepped into my cabin, the source of the trouble became readily apparent. My trunk was open, and one of the small gold boxes was out. The lid was open.

Clearly, someone had been in my room.

My cabin is not tiny, but it felt like a crowd was jostling me. First one, and then the other shoulder were bumped. As I reached to close the lid on the box, I realized Dee Dee was no longer holding my hand. Turning to see where she was, I became horrified.

In her place was an old woman. I'm not saying that Dee Dee left the room, and a much older woman happened to stop by. No, this was Dee Dee—but it wasn't. This woman wore Dee Dee's clothes. She had her eyes, but the spark was gone. Her pretty face was lined with a half-century of hard living. Her hair had gone gray, and Dee Dee's ready smile became a sneer.

I reached for the box, knowing with complete certainty that I had to close that box.

"Wait." The woman's voice was a loud, screeching sound that echoed unnaturally in the cabin. Her voice was not from this world. "We can be together. Forever."

I couldn't help myself and turned to look at the woman. The look in her eyes convinced me that this was not Dee Dee. And definitely not someone I wanted to be with. Not now and not forever. She grabbed onto my sleeve, pulling me toward her.

I shrugged off my coat, letting the old woman have it. Lunging for the box, I slapped the lid closed.

Time stood still as my cabin returned to its normal state. No fog, no strange noises, and no... I hesitated to turn around and see if the old woman had gone. But I knew I had no choice. With great trepidation, I turned around.

Standing there, still holding my coat, was Dee Dee. The old woman was gone. I looked into her eyes, unsure of things now. Was this the same woman I was so enchanted with? Was I just given a glimpse into the woman she would become?

All I knew was that something had changed, and I was anxious to be free of her.

"Let's get you back to your family," I told her. "They must be getting worried."

"But," she said as she stared at me for a long moment, her eyes going wide and then returning to normal. "I thought we..."

I gestured for Dee Dee to step into the hallway. "We should see if the ship is okay."

We made our way through the corridors, now entirely back to normal. Neither of us spoke as we walked back to the garden lounge. Her family sat at the card game table.

"Would you like to stay and join us?" Dee Dee asked.

I shook my head. "I'm going to turn in."

Dee Dee stood there for a long moment, unsure what to say. I pointed to my coat that was still clutched in her hand. She looked down and appeared to be surprised it was in her hands. Dee Dee held it out, and I was shocked to see the coat sleeve had been sliced into ribbons. If she noticed, Dee Dee hadn't let on.

"Take care," I said, turning away.

"We could've been great together," I heard behind me. Only it wasn't Dee Dee's voice. It was the old woman's voice again.

I ran from the room, anxious to be safely behind the locked door of my cabin. Maybe I'm destined to be unmarried my entire life.

"That's all. That's where the diary ends." I flipped over the page, but the back side was blank.

"That's crazy," Brian said. "That really happened?"

"We may never know for sure. But since it came from the travel journal of Manfred Krug, it must be actual events."

"He is quite the character," Turner said. "I don't care what the commercials say; Manfred *is* the world's most interesting man."

"Can't argue with that," I said, getting to my feet. "Let's go find his box."

14

MEMORIES OF AN OLD MAN

"Welcome, my name is Sophia. You're in the James J. Hill House. He was an important guy. I'll talk more about that as we go along. Thirty-six thousand square feet, nine kids, and lots of servants. It took 300 men three years to build this nice house. Completed in 1891, the family was here until Mrs. Hill's passing. Five years prior, in 1916, Mr. Hill passed away. Despite his business acumen, meticulousness, and detailed record-keeping, he didn't have a will. Five years later, Mrs. Hill passed away. She had a will that wasn't signed. The Hills left behind a seventeen-million-dollar fortune. Six homes across the country and Europe. Massive transportation empire spanning both oceans. Nine kids fighting over it all."

Our tour guide had eaten a sugary cereal for breakfast. She was spewing words like a fire hydrant on a hot July sidewalk.

Sophia tucked a strand of her dark hair behind an ear and moved to a group by the window. "You guys have any other siblings? You know how you fight over dumb things? Can you imagine fighting over $17 million? It got messy. It took over four years to get things sorted out. They decided not to keep the house in the family.

"In 1925, four of the daughters purchased the house from the estate and donated it to the Catholic Church. The Catholic Church had the house for 53 years, from 1925 to 1978. During that time, it was a nun's teacher college, a priest's dormitory, and a school for the deaf. And then church administrative offices.

"The Minnesota Historical Society walked into the house in 1978 after buying it for a whopping $250,000. It was a steal, frankly. And then we spent the next seven years and $3.5 million restoring it, lovingly bringing it back to its original condition. The house is 126 years old, so we ask that you not touch anything or sit on the furniture."

Sophia gestured for the group to move towards the hallway. "Please stay together. The more we stick together, the more you will get to see. It takes a long time to corral people when they wander off."

I leaned close to Turner and whispered, "I suppose she doesn't want us sneaking off to search for missing artifacts."

He shook his head. "No. Probably not."

"Too bad, then. We do what we have to do. Sophia doesn't have a gun-toting government dragon lady threatening her."

As we moved across the hall, Turner noticed it first. "Did you see the motion detectors?"

I shook my head. "That's not the kind of thing I would notice."

"Some burglar you're going to make."

Several replies came to mind, but I let it go. "Why does it matter?"

Turner shook his head. "Because once the building is closed, they arm the security system, activating the motion sensors. Then, when we start searching the place, the alarm will go off, and the cops are called. They show up and arrest us. Not the outcome we were hoping for."

"At least we have a good lawyer," I said, nodding toward Brian. He smiled.

"Fat lot of good that will do us when he's locked up with us." Turner looked frustrated.

"True point," Brian said. "In my humble legal opinion."

Turner continued. "So, we can't search for the box after the building has closed. We're going to have to do it while we're here." He looked at me with those dark eyes of his. "While there are people here."

"That does make our tour a little more interesting," I said.

Our tour guide discussed the pipe organ, which dominated one gallery room wall. Brian listened, asking our guide questions. For her part, Sophia looked more than a little irritated at Brian's persistent questions. However, something about his boyish enthusiasm quickly tore down her wall. He was just so darn likable. Now, instead of short, clipped responses to his questions, she was practically having a conversation with him. I could see why he might be good in a courtroom.

"I think we need a diversion," Turner suggested with a twinkle in his eye.

"I think Brian's a one-person diversion. Look at him," I said. "He raises a question, and she waxes eloquently for several minutes. It's like a late-night talk show."

We watched their interaction for a minute. "I bet she's happy to have someone so interested," Turner said. "Better than another group of bored kids on a field trip."

"You mentioned a diversion," I reminded Turner.

Turner had a half smile and a devious look in his eye. If anyone can create a diversion, it's Turner. We had met at Camp ToughLove, the camp for troubled teens. He was there because of a very elaborate —and hilarious—prank. It turned out he had a history of pranks. I'd hoped he'd learned his lesson and was now using his powers for good. However, the look in his eyes had me worried.

"Promise me no one will get killed."

He held up a hand. "I solemnly swear that no actual people will die as a result."

I narrowed my eyes at him. "No maiming. No flesh wounds. And no lasting psychological scarring."

"Define lasting," Turner said with a grin.

"Anything over two weeks."

He paused, stroking his chin, a thoughtful expression on his face.

"Turner!"

"Okay, nothing longer than two weeks, as long as a strong sedative and professional early intervention therapy is involved." Turner's goofy grin had me.

"Looks like we have an agreement," I said. "What do you need from me?"

"Stall her for a few minutes," he said. "Just have Brian ask our tour guide about ghosts."

"Will do," I agreed.

"And then act surprised when you see it." Turner slid his backpack off his shoulder and disappeared around the corner.

See it? I couldn't wait.

I scribbled a note on my tour receipt and moved next to Brian. He was looking up at the pipe organ when he caught me off guard.

"Is this the largest organ in the Twin Cities?" he asked.

I was the victim of a sudden coughing attack and used the moment to slip the note into Brian's hand.

For his part, Brian kept his cool, turning his back to our guide and putting an arm around me. "Are you okay?" he asked, patting me on the back. He glanced at the note. It read *Ask her about ghosts.*

I flicked my eyes toward our guide, and Brian gave me a wink in return. Game on.

Sophia was gesturing toward the door when Brian held up a finger. "Excuse me, Sophia. One more question. These older homes all have their histories. Joys and sorrows, celebrations and tragedies, births and deaths, and...even murders." Brian paused rather dramatically before continuing. "Let me ask you this: is the James J. Hill house haunted?"

Our guide paused and smiled the smile of someone who's been asked the same question hundreds, if not thousands, of times. "Considering the Catholic Church had the house for 50 years after the Hill family donated it to them, they wouldn't have left any ghosts here. They're used to dealing with that kind of thing." She looked directly at Brian. "So, no ghosts."

She gestured for the group to proceed.

Too soon. I pointed to my wrist, waving a single finger. *I needed one more minute.*

Brian nodded. "Um, Sophia, one more thing. I read up on the house, and several accounts would contradict your well-rehearsed ghost answer. There was even one such account last month."

Sophia paused, looking very much like the deer that our headlights illuminated the other night on the bend of Maple Street.

An older gentleman with a white beard cleared his throat. "I'd like to hear the story."

The group turned away from Sophia and faced Brian, who was very much in his element. I could imagine him addressing a courtroom jury. "There was a wedding held here in September. The bride and her maid of honor were getting ready in one of the bedrooms. The bride, Bella, was enjoying the feeling of her friend stroking her hair. She commented about how relaxing it felt. The trouble was, her friend answered from across the room—and not from behind her. She whipped her head around, but there wasn't anyone there."

"Wow," a college-aged girl whispered.

"That's so cool," the younger girl beside her added. They looked like sisters.

Brian took a step closer to the group. He had their full attention. "There's more from the same wedding, too. The groom and his buddies were all on the back porch smoking stogies. They were doing this sort of cigar toast and blowing smoke into a cloud. The smoke was acting strangely, and everyone watched it intently as it rose in a tight spiral. But then, the smoke stopped its spiral and came down in a plume. Suddenly, a face burst through the smoke cloud and scared the crap out of those boys."

"No way," the younger girl exclaimed.

"Way," Brian said and turned back to Sophia. He paused and waited for her response.

"I may have heard rumors about that," she said. "But, you can't always believe what you hear. I haven't seen anything out of the ordinary. Okay, we better keep moving, or your tour will end before you see everything." She gestured toward the door.

"C'mon, Brian. Don't hold up the tour." I said with a grin.

He shot me a look, and I winked at him.

The guide led us up the stairs to the bedrooms. I spotted Turner at the edge of the group, and he nodded to the first bedroom. Sophia led us to the doorway and talked about the Hill's seven daughters. She gestured for the group to enter, and the sisters went into the room first.

"Oh, my," the older sister exclaimed.

Standing immediately behind the girls, I saw what was going on. Sitting on the bed was a doll with a porcelain head. It looked a little too lifelike, sort of like a mummified baby. A pad of paper sat in its lap with a marker in its hand. "Stay out of the closet" were scribbled on the pad.

We all turned to the closet.

There was a smear of red on the white-painted door. A shock of dark hair stuck out from the closed door. The younger sister let out a shout of fear.

Way to traumatize the kid, Turner.

Something grabbed my hand. I wanted to shout, but it was Turner.

"This is our diversion," he said, handing me the backpack. "Let's get moving."

As everyone pushed into the bedroom to see what was going on, we stepped out. We bounded up the stairs to the third floor, where the three sons had bedrooms. It also housed the schoolroom and servant quarters. I headed for the servant quarters, thinking it would give me more time when the tour resumed.

After several right turns, I came to a bedroom with a rope

stretched across the entrance. It was clear they didn't want anyone entering. I ducked under the rope and moved to the corner to get out of sight. I slid down the wall and sat on the floor while Turner waited outside.

I closed my eyes.

Almost immediately, I opened them as I remembered my emergency preparations. Rummaging through the backpack past the snacks and water bottles, I found my secret weapon. Unwrapping the towel, I pulled out the spirit box and set it on the floor. There was a shimmer of gold that belied the danger contained in the spirit box. I took a deep breath, sighed, and whispered, "Here we go."

I opened the box.

Closing my eyes again, I focused on calming my breathing through meditation. It wouldn't be extreme to say I wouldn't be here if it weren't for meditation. Meditation has become my friend over the years. The quiet grounding kept me in the here and now, remaining calm when confronted with the spirits of dead people. That calm was a gift from God.

A meditation a day keeps the darkness away.

Feeling centered, I opened my eyes. I was alone in the room—for the time being. I held the mental picture of the second box that Manfred Krug gave to his benefactor. There was a detailed illustration of it in his diary pages. Roughly half the size of the larger box in front of me, the gold inlays were much more fluid and elongated than the pattern on this one.

"Where are you?" I said out loud. "Where are you hiding?"

There was a creak by the door, but I didn't turn around.

"I need your help," I said calmly. I hoped someone would come to help.

Then, a shadow slid across the wall. I looked up and saw I wasn't alone anymore. A bald man wearing a long robe joined me. He had a kindly expression; maybe it was his dimpled smile or the twinkle in his eye. If it weren't for the fact that I saw the wall behind him—right through him—I wouldn't have guessed he was a ghost.

"Hello, Father."

He smiled.

"Would you be able to help me?"

This time, he nodded, but still no words.

The floorboard creaked nearby, but I continued holding the father's gaze.

"Abbey?" It was Brian's voice. "Is everything all right?"

"Things are good here, but I could use your help with a little communication problem."

"Sure," Brian said, sounding like he wasn't at all sure.

"C'mon in and have a seat."

"We used to say *pull up some floor*," Brian said as he sat with a groan. "You know you're getting older when you make noises sitting down and getting up."

"I do that, too," Turner said as he sat on my other side.

Grabbing onto their hands, I gave them a squeeze. "Hold each other's hands, too."

I glanced at the father standing over me. "Maybe we should be standing, too."

"Umm, what do you mean, too? Is there someone else here?" Brian looked concerned.

I squeezed his hand. "Yes, we are joined by...Father, I apologize. I don't know your name." Rather than answer, the man in the holy robes simply smiled.

"Oh," was all Brian could say.

We stood in a group surrounding the catholic priest, holding hands.

"Close your eyes," I instructed them.

"You're going to get your mind blown," Turner whispered to Brian.

"Shhh. Your eyes are closed. Your mouth should be closed as well." I said, sounding like a second-grade teacher. "Now, take a moment to focus on your breathing. In... Out... In... Out... Nice and smooth."

The priest looked at me with his kindly eyes.

"Picture in your mind a man. He's probably in his seventies." I got a raised eyebrow from the ghostly father. "Or, he could be in his sixties. Either way, he's wearing a long robe of brownish-gray color. He's wearing wire glasses and is mostly bald. It looks good on him."

The father smiled.

I continued. "Now that I think of it, he looks like Friar Tuck from the Robin Hood cartoons. He has kind eyes."

I waited a long moment to get the image in their minds.

"Keep that picture of a kindly Friar Tuck in your mind and open your eyes."

"Hello," Brian said, a broad smile on his face. Tears ran down Brian's cheeks, but he looked radiant seeing this ghostly man.

"Father," I said. "We're searching for a box. A unique box. It is about six inches long and roughly three inches tall and deep. It's made of wood with gold inlays."

The father held my gaze.

"The box would have been here since the Hill family lived in this house."

Hearing the sound of heavy footsteps in the hall, I pushed the spirit box's lid closed with my toe. We didn't need further ghostly visitors.

"It's like a smaller version of this box," I told him. The father looked as if he was deep in thought. I knew it was time to take the next step.

"We need to make contact," I told Brian and Turner. "We'll need to touch him to harness the power of the three."

I looked up at the priest. "If that's okay with you?"

He nodded.

Bringing up our shared hands, I touched his shoulder. The contact made him more solid like he was more present in our world now.

"Close your eyes and focus on the box," I said, speaking to not only Turner and Brian but also the father.

A memory of the church staff moving into the Hill house flashed into my head—but it wasn't my memory. I can't tell you how strange it is to have someone else's memories in my mind. Actually, I can. It's extremely strange.

The father's memories continued to unfold. I saw other people's reactions to him and could tell he was well liked. I picked up on his name along the way. Father Lavin was clearly a man who lived his faith. He prayed with a multitude of people, as well as praying with other clergy and alone on his knees. His memories gave me a sense of his positivity and his caring.

The memories played out in a rush.

A cardboard box filled with decorations, pictures, knick-knacks, and books was carried to the basement. Piles spread out across the floor as the contents were evaluated and categorized. Many trips up the stairs carrying the cardboard boxes. Boxes being handed to a woman, another to a man in black robes. Still another to a couple dressed in shabby clothes.

Back in the basement, behind a carved picture frame, I see the box. It's the spirit box from Shanghai as a sliver of light glimmers off the gold inlays. Without transition, the box was now on a different shelf, sitting next to other objects. A young girl wearing a uniform is moving along the shelf, picking up each of the objects and examining them. She picks the box off the shelf and sits on the floor with it. The box is open, and a doll sits inside, its legs hanging out.

A man wearing a priest's collar is concerned. His eyes dart to the side as he gets worked up. His hands tremble. A nun cries. Father Lavin looks down at the box on a desk as he crosses himself. The child reaches for the box. The box is put into a leather satchel that looks much like an old doctor's kit. A winter snowstorm, the wind howling, the driven flakes stinging Father Lavin's face as he trudges through the drifted snow. The hulking stone structure of the cathedral in front of him. Treacherous steps on the way to the massive wooden doors. Steps leading down, a musty storage room with wooden shelves. The satchel is tucked onto the top shelf in the corner, cobwebs sticking to the bag as it's pushed back to the wall.

I squeezed the hands in my grasp. We had our answer, but the memories continued. Images, sounds, and sensations kept me rooted in place. I knew I should disengage, but I was too drawn into the moments of Father Lavin's life to stop now. The years raced by and then abruptly slowed as he looked into the concerned faces of those gathered around his bed.

His death bed.

Much like the sky at twilight, the light faded into black. I held my breath, wondering if this was the end. Then, like the dawn of a new day, light flooded into view. No longer confined to his bed, Father Lavin was bounding across a field of daisies. Full of life and energy, his power and grace created a symphony of movement as he jumped and glided through the lush grass and wildflowers, a golden retriever at his side.

The air was fresh and sweet, while the breeze was almost musical, offering a rhythm that encouraged the old man's joyous movement.

A former old man.

I pulled our hands from Father Lavin as we locked eyes.

"Thank you," I told the fading ghost in front of us. I wanted to say to him so much more, ask him so much more, but my words were caught in my emotions.

His lips moved, the words trying to cross the distance between his world and ours. I leaned closer to hear what message he had for us. It was not quite a whisper but a voice from far, far away.

"Love Him in all the people around you." His smile continued until he faded entirely from view. My last sight of him was his twinkling eyes.

I glanced at my dear friends and saw I wasn't the only one crying. My big, strong men.

15

INTO THE DARK

If there's one place in the Twin Cities that makes you feel small, it's the Cathedral. Massive and imposing, the Cathedral is the icon of Saint Paul. The marble, the stained glass, the beautiful alters; the church is like no other I've ever visited. And we were going to steal something from it. Yeah, a proud moment.

None of us spoke during our short walk from the James J. Hill house. When you're given a glimpse of the afterlife, it can have a profound effect. How could it not change something inside you? Talk about your "Total Eclipse of the Heart." Bonnie Tyler's eighties song swam into my mind.

Past the massive door and right inside the entrance, we spotted the stairs. On the lower level, a group gathered around posters of the pictorial history of the Cathedral's construction. I motioned for Turner and Brian to follow as we slipped away from the group. A roped-off area felt like it might lead to the storage area.

You know how you can feel when someone's staring at you? I had that feeling. But casting my gaze on the group, no one looked my way. Brian and Turner stayed to keep watch while I took that moment to duck under the rope. I tried a couple of the doors, but they were locked. Rounding the corner, I found a small stairwell that curved down into the dark. I'd never heard of the Cathedral having a subbasement. But I would find out where it went.

Flipping on my flashlight, I stepped down into the musty stairwell. The cobwebs told me it had been quite some time since anyone had been down there.

But after seeing that the cobwebs kept getting larger and thicker with each step, I started worrying about the size of the spider. The thing had to be ginormous. I grabbed a dusty 2 x 4 and used the board to clear the way. The solid piece of lumber felt good in my hands. You never know if the monster spider might make an appearance. By the time I reached the gravel floor, so many webs were wrapped around the board that it resembled the cotton candy I had at the state fair. Fortunately, there was still no sign of the spider.

Casting the flashlight beam around, all I saw in the murky light was a mass of pipes running overhead and a wall lined with shelves. This had to be the place I saw in Father Lavin's memories. The shelves were full. I wondered if all the other objects were as interesting as the one I was seeking.

I made my way down to the far corner. At the end, the suitcase sat waiting on the top shelf. A little out of my reach, I climbed onto the cobweb-covered shelf. Gross.

And then I saw why.

A giant spider descended in front of me. This thing was huge. Enormous and hairy, it reminded me of my Uncle Ned. I'm kidding, the spider wasn't nearly as hairy as Ned.

It was gross and disgusting. Ghosts are one thing, but spiders are on an entirely different level.

Lunging at the satchel, I wanted to escape this Godzilla-spider as fast as possible. But grabbing it, I lost my balance and fell off the shelves.

I don't know if you've ever had the wind knocked out of you, but it's both painful and terrifying. When you can't get a breath, it feels like you're dying. I was on my back trying to breathe when I heard something.

It was footsteps.

I rolled onto my side, grunting with the effort. Pulling the satchel close, I slipped a hand inside. When my fingers touched the delicate wooden structure, I knew I'd found the second box.

The sound of someone clearing their throat had me moving. On my hands and knees, I looked up. A woman stood looking down at me. Her flashlight shone in my eyes, making it difficult to see anything. However, I did see something clearly enough.

She had a pistol in her hands. This had to be the Russian woman, Olga Vengekov.

She looked familiar. There was something about her angular face that I'd seen before.

"You're late. I was expecting you long before this," I told her. "Did you get lost?"

Put off by my witty banter, I sensed her hesitation. Right then and there, I decided my best strategy would be to keep the woman off balance. Maybe I could wrestle back some advantage. I grabbed my flashlight and stood up.

Holding up the satchel, I challenged her. "These things are difficult to find. It's too bad for you that I found it first."

The woman gestured with the gun. I assumed she wanted me to hand the suitcase over.

I took a step toward her.

The gun gestured down, wanting me to set the bag in front of her. But I didn't like my chances once she had what she wanted.

"I should warn you," I told her. "A battalion of highly trained special forces operatives is waiting outside."

The gun shifted back and forth.

"Would you believe a pair of county sheriff deputies?"

The gun waved back and forth again. She obviously preferred to let the gun do the talking.

"No? How about an angry Chihuahua?" I got nothing from the

gun-toting woman. It occurred to me that I might not be as funny as I thought.

She lowered the flashlight and illuminated a spot on the ground between us.

"Okay..." I moved closer and placed the bag in the indicated spot. Now.

I slapped the flashlight from her hand, and it spun across the floor. Seizing the opportunity, I bolted for the entrance. And then things got worse. She started shooting.

When the shots rang out, they were punctuated by her shouts. It went like this:

Boom. "Da!" Whoa. I really didn't think she would shoot at me.

Boom. "Da!" I don't know much Russian, but I know that Da means Yes.

Boom. "Da!" I swear she was enjoying herself.

Nothing gets a person moving like being shot at. I sprinted for the entrance, wanting to get out before she could pick up her flashlight.

Boom. "Da!" She was giggling now. The horrible woman was enjoying herself as she shot at me.

Boom. "Da!" She shrieked with laughter. I couldn't tell if she was aiming for me or just shooting for the fun of it, but relief flooded me upon reaching the stairs.

The curved stairwell wasn't built for speed, but you find a way when you're sufficiently motivated. I found a way.

I sprinted up the stone steps, and before I knew it, I burst through the door. Turner and Brian stood in front of the posters. They looked surprised to see me running full speed at them.

"We have to get out of here," I shouted. I was sure I looked more than a little spooked as I sprinted with the box tucked under my coat. "Run!"

They didn't hesitate.

16

SO MUCH FOR MY TELEVISION CAREER

"Three, two," the director counted off while gesturing with her hand. Instead of saying one, she simply pointed.

Elizabeth stood center stage, wearing a sleeveless black dress. "Welcome back to *Twin Cities Live*. In this segment, our fearless ghost hunter finalists are here. As you may have heard, Matilda Effervescence, our resident ghost hunter, has retired, and we thought it'd be fun to make a contest to find her replacement. We had four individuals and eight groups enter, and we promptly sent them out to investigate some paranormal hotspots around town."

Speaking of hot spots, it was uncomfortably warm under the bright lights. As I glanced at the live studio audience, I felt a bead of sweat run down my cheek. As subtly as I could, I wiped it away with my sleeve. No one seemed to notice.

What a rollercoaster life had been. Having that crazy Russian woman taking potshots at me and then running for our lives with the second box tucked under an arm felt like so long ago. But it was only a day ago. When Brian, Turner, and I reached our car, Brian got us out of there and onto the freeway as fast as he could. And now here I was, on stage, in front of a live studio audience.

Why settle for normal when I can be me?

Elizabeth continued her introduction. "We provided our contestants a new iPhone to record their ghost-hunting results. Then, our production crew gave each video a professional edit and posted it to our website. Based on your votes, we narrowed down the pool of contestants. Joining us are our two finalists, the Spook Squad," Elizabeth said, gesturing to us. "And the Paranormal Dudes."

At this, they all raised a fist and said, "Dude," in unison. They were wearing their trademark coveralls. Elizabeth laughed.

She turned to us and said, "We have Abbey, Kelly, and Lexi making up the Spook Squad. Thanks for joining us, ladies. We'll begin with you. Here's their video clip from the historic Lexington restaurant."

We turned to the in-studio monitors as our clip began. It opened with a dusk shot of the Lexington's exterior. The next shot was of a darkened staircase. I moved into view as I climbed the stairs. When I hesitated near the top step, Lexi must have moved the camera, and she let out a loud breath as three pairs of glowing eyes came into view. The camera zoomed in on them as the shortest of the three eyes moved down a step.

"Abbey?" Lexi asked. Her voice cracked as she drew out the syllables of my name. She sounded frightened.

"It's okay, Lexi. These are Caspers. We'll be fine."

The audience gasped.

The first eyes glided silently down while the other two sets hovered on the landing above. They paused several steps above me.

The camera zoomed in further as I held out my hand. Two silver coins dropped into my hand.

"Whoa," Kelly said.

Elizabeth gasped.

Lexi moved, and the coins came into focus. The coins were larger, with Benjamin Franklin in profile. Franklin bore a stamp of the year 1949 below his chin. When I flipped them over, the liberty bell showed on the tail side.

"Thank you," I said. My voice sounded like I was talking to a child. "But you should keep them."

My hand reached out with the coins closed in my fist, and as I opened my hand, the coins dropped. And then vanished.

"Now that's something you don't see every day," Kelly said.

The screen went black, and the words "Spook Squad" came up.

The audience cheered.

Elizabeth smiled and turned to our group. "Kelly, what made you want to enter our contest to be our next ghost hunter?"

Kelly, looking surprisingly relaxed, leaned forward and smiled. "Well, Elizabeth. It's simple. We wanted to give back to the community. We understand that not everyone knows how to deal with spirits, let alone communicate with them. If we can help just one person, we've made a difference. What else could anyone ask for, Elizabeth?"

The look on Elizabeth's face suggested she was thinking the same thing I was. Kelly was laying it on thick in a used car salesperson way. But better her talking on camera than me. That was our deal.

"I have to ask," Elizabeth paused as she turned to me. *Uh oh.* Apparently, nobody explained our deal to Elizabeth. "Abbey, how did you know to hold out your hand?"

The lights felt like they just got 20 degrees warmer. And I had to pee.

"Um," I began, ever-so-eloquently.

"Abbey has always—" Lexi said, but Elizabeth held up her hand.

"I want to hear it from her," our host said.

Fine. I'll talk.

"It was a child. And I just knew he had something he was carrying with him, the way kids do."

"You just knew?"

"Yeah. Like when you step outside and know it's going to rain."

Elizabeth shook her head. "Even our staff meteorologist doesn't know for sure if it will rain. Sorry, Ron, but you don't. Yet, Abbey, you simply knew this invisible child had something to give you?"

I shrugged. "My grandmother threw a Halloween party one year. She dressed up as a ghost and asked her guests if they had any messages she could pass on to their dead loved ones. She died in her sleep that very night. Like me, she had a gift for talking to ghosts."

With a smile, Elizabeth nodded. "If you have a gift, you have a gift."

Several in the audience stared at me with their jaws hanging open. You'd think they'd never seen a circus freak before.

"Thank you, girls." She turned away from us. "Next, we have the Paranormal Dudes."

Again, in unison, they raised a fist and said, "Dude."

Laughing, she said, "Please welcome Ben, Jonas, Ernesto, and Kevin." Kevin still had the tape across the bridge of his glasses. He looked nervous, but the other three had the confidence of professional card sharks. "Here's their video."

Again, the video opened with an establishing shot of the Lexington. The camera moved closer and quickly sped up as it zoomed to the door. The next shot opened with Kevin, Ben, and Jonas posing with their gear while wearing sunglasses. Ernesto operating the camera.

"Let's find us some orbs," Jonas said, pointing across Lexington's expansive dining room. The camera swept the room while Jonas continued speaking. "For those not immersed in the paranormal the way we are on a daily basis, let me explain the significance of orbs."

Stepping into the shot, Jonas continued. "Orbs are the souls of the departed. When the soul leaves the body, it forms into a sphere of varying colors. Blue is the most common, while the exceptionally brave tend to have green. Red is associated with evil."

I was pretty sure he was talking about lightsabers, not orbs.

"With even the briefest of glimpses, a trained paranormal investigator can tell you many things about the poor schlep that met their untimely demise. I could tell you if someone was murdered or died of natural causes. I can tell you if they were a good or bad person. I can even tell you if they had a dog or a cat as a pet."

This was categorically right in the center of the false column. None of that was even remotely true. If he'd been hooked up to a lie detector, the technician would be shaking his head as the needle would be buried in the liar section, while the resulting voltage overload would be enough to jumpstart even the deadest heart. Yes, he was lying his ass off on television.

Glancing at Lexi, I shook my head. *These guys.*

The video showed several still pictures of orbs above the red leather booths. These were the shots he'd shown me that night. Of floating balls of paranormal energy, as he'd called them then. Not souls of the departed.

"This is where it gets good," Ernesto narrated the video. "We dug deep and channeled our collective energy to summon more souls."

The still image showed a cloud of orbs, and the crowd gasped. Even Elizabeth looked impressed.

Really? It was the image taken after I slid my feet back and forth on the carpet.

Kate Bush's "Running Up That Hill" floated into my mind. I'd always loved its haunted, atmospheric vibe, but the feeling of running up a hill resonated. I was not going to have much luck convincing people these so-called ghost hunters were actually con artists.

The screen faded to black as their team's name came up, and the audience cheered. Elizabeth turned to the group. "Well, I have to say that was pretty impressive. Ernesto, you mentioned being a trained paranormal investigator. Can you tell us where you trained to get such impressive results?"

If they had any training at all, I would be shocked.

Ernesto paused and stroked his chin. "That's a great question."

He's stalling while he makes something up.

"When we decided there was more to our world than meets the eye, we chose to study under the best. Our pilgrimage brought us to China's Valley of the Peace. There, on top of the mountain at the Jade Palace, we studied under Master Shifu. He was absolutely animated. The experience was as transformational as it was enlightening."

He put his hands together and gave a little bow.

"Wow, just wow," Elizabeth began.

I wasn't sure where things would go, but I had to speak up. I'd hit my limit.

"Excuse me," I said, standing up. I went over and sat on the arm of Ernesto's chair. I wasn't going to be ignored. "I'm calling BS here."

"Umm," Elizabeth said.

"You know that's the plot of Kung Fu Panda, right? And I mean the exact plot. That's where Jack Black's character, Po, studied his kung fu. Under Master Shifu." Elizabeth looked unsure, while Ernesto looked ready to fight. "Look it up," I said to the audience.

"This is our cue to hear from our sponsor, Campanelle Restaurant in Lino Lakes. Local and family-owned."

"And we're clear," the director said.

Producers moved onto the stage and shepherded our groups in different directions.

"Thanks for your time, everyone."

"Wait, that's it?" Kelly asked.

"We're out of time for this segment. We still need to get to our recipe of the week," Elizabeth said.

Staffers pushed out carts while several people wearing aprons stepped into the kitchen set on stage.

"Hold on," Kelly insisted. She looked out into the audience. "Did anyone look up Kung Fu Panda? Was Abbey correct?"

"Yes, she was," someone said.

"That came straight from the movie," another said. "The first one."

"The first movie was the best one," another added.

"I liked the holiday special," still another added.

"People," Elizabeth said. "We need to move on. I'll get with the producers after the show, and we'll decide on how best to move forward. Until then, stay tuned."

We were brought back to the production area to have our microphone packs removed, given a gift bag, and shown the exit. So much for my television career.

Or so I thought.

◑◐

Just after dinner, Kelly called.

"We're still in. They are sending us out one more time to another supposed haunted location. The producers liked what you did on the staircase, but they asked that we glam things up a bit."

Glam? Not liking where this was going.

"They really like the Paranormal Dudes' uniforms. They want us —or you, anyway—to wear something that looks good on television. I have some ideas."

Not liking this. Not one bit.

17

ONE-TRICK PONY

Standing before the historic Mounds Theatre in Saint Paul, I fumed.

"I look ridiculous. It feels like I'm set to get a participation award at the annual Halloween costume contest."

"No way," Kelly, who was wearing the same uniform, said. "We look amazing. And totally badass. Just wait until Lexi gets here. You'll see how much she loves it."

We were at the Mounds Theatre because of *Twin Cities Live.* Another chance to see what we had to offer. Get us on camera, this time with their cameraman. The thought still made my skin crawl.

Lexi arrived, skidding to a stop. Her Ford Escape rocked as she slammed the vehicle into park. She got out singing. "Some people call me a space cowboy. Some call me the gangster of love." She paused and glanced at me. "Something tells me my Halloween costume still needs work."

"That's it." Glaring at Kelly, I started unbuttoning my jacket. "I am so not wearing this. The dorks from the Paranormal Dudes can have the ghost-hunting gig. It's not worth it if we have to dress like circus characters."

Kelly put a hand on my shoulder, concern in her eyes. "I understand why you, of all people, don't like the circus, but this is different. We're not dressing up like a killer clown. But listen, by putting you in the spotlight, it takes the power away from that government woman. She can't hold exposing you over your head."

She held my gaze.

"And that's a good thing, right?"

I nodded. "It is. But."

She shook her head, not willing to relent. Classic Kelly, in other words. "There is no but. Not with this."

"But you know I'm a fly under the radar kind of girl. Things haven't always worked out well when I haven't."

Lexi joined us, no doubt having heard the conversation so far. Kelly nodded to her and continued. "Then things need to change. You need to change. Look at it this way. This is your story, not ours. The hero always changes due to the events she's been thrust into. She adapts, grows, and conquers. Haven't you been paying attention in English Lit?"

"It's my first hour." I shrugged.

"Get some caffeine flowing in your bloodstream, then. Haven't you seen the lines at the Just Java stand?" Kelly asked. "It's the busiest place at school."

"I like their peppermint mocha," Lexi said.

Kelly was not going to be sidetracked. "The point is, you can change. Just because that's how you were before doesn't mean you always have to stay that way. Change, adapt, evolve. Or die."

"That's a little overly dramatic, don't you think?" Lexi asked.

"That's from a quote. Evolve or die." I offered. "But I get it. Embracing change might not be a bad idea."

"It's a good idea," Lexi said.

"Don't undersell it," Kelly said. "It's a brilliant idea."

Holding up my hands, I said, "I give up. I'll wear the costume."

"Uniform," Kelly said with a grin. We headed for the entrance to the theater.

"I'll wear the uniform. But why did you have to make it so…" I hesitated, unsure how to describe what we were wearing. Stepping in front of the glass at the entrance, I studied my reflection. Long sleeve black t-shirt with Spook Squad written in slime green, Lululemon leggings in bright red, and black boots. Top it off with a Secret Service-type earpiece that ran down into my shirt but wasn't actually connected to anything. I looked ridiculous, leaving me at a loss for words.

"We look awesome," Kelly said. "Now, let's get in there and kick some ghostly butt."

Producer Tori was waiting for us inside with her usual tablet in hand. A slightly younger woman with a severe expression stood next to her. She also held a tablet. Tori stepped forward and beamed at us. "Love the outfits. Now you guys totally look the part. The camera is going to love you. Speaking of that, this is our camera guy, Matt."

"Photojournalist, actually. But, nice to meet you, ladies." Matt was a thirty-something guy with dark brown hair and a bushy beard. His ripped skinny jeans and flip-flops said a lot about his relaxed nature. He smiled and lifted the camera. "I want to get a shot of you coming in. Can you step back out and make an entrance?"

We went outside.

"What does he mean when he says make an entrance?" Lexi asked. "Is it different from plain old walking in?"

"Walk This Way," by Aerosmith and Run DMC, popped into my eighties-wired brain, as often happens. "It's all about the attitude," I said. "Just be yourself, but once we walk into the theater, let your inner warrior come out. You are fierce. And the world needs to see it. Can you do that?"

Lexi looked less than sure.

"If it helps, think of the most confident person you know and pretend it's her walking inside. Now, let's do this."

"Sunglasses on," Kelly said.

Sunglasses on, we went in. We didn't hurry, we didn't go slow. We absolutely strutted through the doors.

"Woo, woo!" Tori was ecstatic and clapped gleefully as we made our entrance. Her assistant remained serious.

We paused inside. Flanked by Kelly and Lexi with folded arms, I posed with my fists on my hips. Not sure what else to do, I held still until Matt lowered his camera.

"Perfect," he said.

"I imagined I was you, Kelly," Lexi said. "You're the most confident person I know." Which was funny because I had done the same.

"This is my assistant, Candy, by the way." Tori gestured to the serious woman.

"Candace," she corrected, a little irritation showing.

Tori stepped forward before things got more awkward. "Here's how it's going to work today. You'll have an hour to explore the place while Matt follows you. There may be some moments where he has you wait while he changes angles to give the viewers the best possible view. Don't worry about him, though. He's here to document things, not be part of the story. You can go on stage, check out the basement, or go wherever you want. No part of the building is off limits, so explore to your heart's content. But we have a hard stop at 11. Questions?"

"Will the Paranormal geeks be here too?" Lexi asked.

Tori shook her head. "No, it's just you today. The producers wanted to see how you do on your own."

She shared a glance with Matt.

"I'll give you a moment to strategize, and then we'll get started."

Lexi, Kelly, and I huddled.

"Where to first?" Kelly asked.

The back of my neck itched. But not in the *scratch it, and the itch will go away* kind of itch. Something was up. "Hold on. Something is going on here. Did you see the look they shared when she said we'd be on our own?"

Kelly nodded. Lexi shrugged.

"Well, I saw it. There's something she's not telling us." I ran a hand across the back of my neck. "But whatever it is, we'll just have to roll with it. I can't just go over there and accuse her of hiding something. So, stay on your toes and be ready for darn near anything. We're soccer players and spook hunters. We got this."

Glancing at my friends, the determination in their eyes made my heart melt. I loved these girls.

"We're ready," I called out. "Let the games begin."

One of Tori's eyebrows raised a twitch, but she smiled and offered a thumbs up. Consulting her tablet, Tori said, "Let's begin with you introducing yourselves and explaining why you're here."

Matt stepped forward, his camera raised.

I stepped forward, clearing my throat.

"We're the Spook Squad, your local paranormal investigators. We're here in Saint Paul at the historic Mounds Theatre today because the fine people at *Twin Cities Live* thought it would be a good idea."

Tori waved her arms. I'd seen her looking happier.

"Let's do the intro again. Maybe rather than mention us, say something about the rich paranormal history of the theater. That's why you're here."

I nodded. "Can do." I cleared my throat, and Matt pointed at me. "Hello again. We're the Spook Squad, and we're here at the Mounds Theatre in Saint Paul today. The theater has a rich and spooky history of unexplained events. Many have come here over the years to find answers but left running away in fear. Rumor has it that a local television producer discovered an actual gray hair after a particularly loud bump in the night here."

Tori was waving both hands. Matt lowered the camera.

"What was that about a local television producer? That's not real, is it?"

I shrugged. "I may have elaborated a wee bit. It sounded good, though."

Tori shook her head. "Just stick to the facts for the intro. Try it again."

Matt pointed at me.

"Good evening. We're the Spook Squad, the Twin Cities' leading high school paranormal investigators. We're here at the historic Mounds Theatre in Saint Paul to do what we do best: find the ghosts. With a rich history of unexplained paranormal activity, the theater is the perfect venue for our unique skills."

Tori gave a thumbs up. "Perfect. Now go explore."

Without a clear direction, the stage area felt like the right place to begin. I exchanged glances with my squad and headed toward the stage. One bright light was trained on the stage, the surrounding areas melting into darkness. I felt myself reaching out. It's tough to explain, but it's all senses on high alert when I'm ghosting. It's not just the usual sight, sound, feel, smell and taste. A sixth sense radiates out around me, sensing, exploring, probing. But I wasn't getting anything.

Still, I kept moving, knowing there was a camera trained on me.

Stepping onto the stage, I paused and raised my hand as I turned slowly counterclockwise. Mind you, the raised hand didn't actually do anything. It was for the camera's benefit. Still wasn't feeling anything.

Without warning, the white of the overhead light switched to blood red. Lexi made her startled *ooo* sound, and Kelly crouched as if anticipating some threat coming out of the darkness. Oddly, I felt nothing.

Beyond us, at the edge of the darkness, something caught my eye. A floating head of a man had appeared where there had only been shadow. The old man's face made you think of someone who lived a hard life. His wrinkles were more like deep crevices, and his narrow, dark eyes stared out with suspicion. I stepped toward the man, looking to communicate with him, but with my first step, he winked out of existence. At that, a fierce barking started up in the other direction. Stage right, to be specific.

On the scale of barking dogs, with an attitude-rich chihuahua on one end and a rabid 150-pound junkyard dog on the other, this one was decidedly on the junkyard end. Starting farther, the sound appeared to be leaping closer by the moment. It wasn't like the dog was traveling as much as it was hopping around. There would be a burst of barks, and then the next burst would be closer. Like that.

Hmmm.

Standing my ground felt like the best non-move I could make. Catching the glances of Lexi and Kelly, I shook my head. There wasn't going to be anything coming out of the shadows at us. No vicious drooling rabid fanged Cujo. We were being played, I was sure of it. But we didn't have a choice but to let things play out.

I needed to think this scenario through. If the dog was coming at us, they wanted us to move away from it. A glance toward stage left showed a light that hadn't been there previously. This was clearly our suggested route. I headed that way, and my best friends were with me every step of the way. The light illuminated the top of a staircase leading down into a pitch basement.

Of course. As much as I hated them, dark basements came with the territory.

"Light it up," I said.

When I turned on my flashlight, Lexi and Kelly lit theirs. The light helped for the first few feet but beyond that lay darkness. Carefully placing one foot on the first wooden step, it let out a long creak as I put my weight on it. The next step didn't do me any favors, either. I wouldn't be sneaking up on anyone, but it didn't matter. We were expected.

Reaching the bottom, I paused as the eerie group of figures waiting in the light of our flashlights reminded me of a late-night zombie film. Never a good thing.

Lexi made her *ooo* sound again as my mind tried to make sense of what I was seeing. It suggested I take another step down to get a better look. Of course, there are times when my mind and I don't agree on everything. But I took that step. I had no choice. With me, curiosity wins out every time. The pale figures remained unmoving as our lights slashed across their bodies. There had to be a dozen of them.

"They're mannequins," Lexi exclaimed.

"Spooky," Kelly added as we stepped onto the landing. "Spooky mannequins."

They *were* spooky.

The lighting didn't help any. We've all done it. You're outside at night, gathered around the campfire, maybe sitting in a tent, and you hold your flashlight below your chin, and the light gives such an eerie vibe that the ghost story you're telling can't help but bring shivers to even the most cynical of your friends.

I studied the unmoving mannequins as we moved past, the three of us in a tight group in the crowded space. The featureless faces of each mannequin uniquely creepy in their own special way.

My neck itched. And then began to twitch.

All the mannequins lined up for a fashion show that would never happen. Male face, female face. Eyes without a face. But the one behind them. This one was different. It had the same ultra-pale features, but there was more detail than the others. It had male features. I pointed my light at the odd face to show Lexi and Kelly. And then.

It opened its eyes. And screamed.

That was it. Lexi and Kelly moved back up the stairs. Though "moved" may be downplaying the sheer speed they took each step. I'm pretty confident that if stair dashing were an Olympic event, Kelly and Lexi would be on two of the three podiums for the medal ceremony. My bet would be on gold and silver.

Me? I held my ground and shook my head. "Really? This is not what I signed up for." Halloween haunted houses are lame. And not at all real.

The fake mannequin guy stood there, clearly unsure what to do next. He looked decidedly uncomfortable.

I stared at him, not wanting to validate his life choices.

Mannequin guy fidgeted. "Umm," he said after another awkward pause. "I guess I'll be going then."

"What? So soon?" I said. "Are you done already?"

His heavily pancaked brow furrowed. "That's it, really. I'm a one-trick pony. I stand there, waiting for you to walk up. Then I open my eyes and yell. That's it. There's nothing else for me to do." He hesitated, looking as if he wanted to ask something.

I gestured for him to proceed.

"Well, unless you can think of something else I should try. I mean, I'm new to this. I'm normally a middle manager at a software company. I don't do anything fun or interesting, so on a lark, I answered an ad for an acting gig. Well, and here we are." He shrugged sheepishly.

"And here we are," I echoed.

The middle manager mannequin guy blinked at me. Waiting.

"The opening eyes thing was good. Very effective. You almost had me there. You lost me with the scream."

The middle manager mannequin guy looked hurt. "I thought that was my best part, actually."

Now I felt terrible. "No, I mean, it clearly worked with my two friends. I'm not sure I've ever seen them run so fast. And they're both soccer players. It's just that ghosts are usually the strong, silent type. They're not much for screaming." I hesitated. "And I don't want this to come out the wrong way, but your scream came out a bit on the higher register."

The middle manager mannequin guy looked confused, and I felt the need to elaborate.

"Um, you sounded like...like a..."

Awareness showed in his eyes, quickly followed by doubt and, ultimately, acceptance. "No..."

"Yes, you scream like a girl."

The middle manager mannequin guy's chin dropped to his chest. I hoped he wasn't pouting, but I was pretty sure that was precisely what he was doing. When he stayed like that for an uncomfortably long time, I got concerned. I'm not used to adults acting like children. No one tells you what to do when that happens. I've seen parents at the grocery store offer a lollipop to their moody child, but I hadn't thought ahead enough to bring along bribery candy.

"There, there," I said softly. Brilliant words of wisdom, I know. Shaking my head, I was desperate for a new approach. Then.

"Say, I have an idea. Let's practice your scream for a minute. Then we can go upstairs, and you can try it again. See if you can scare my friends again. Maybe surprise Tori and her assistant."

This worked as he lifted his head, interest playing on his face. Guess I didn't need a lollipop after all. I'll call it a win.

"You'd do that for me? After I scared you so bad?"

His earnestness stopped me from reminding him that I hadn't been scared. In the least. But there was nothing to be gained. "Of course. We're friends now, and that's what friendship is about. We help each other. So, let's hear it again. Give me your best scary ghost scream. Don't hold anything back."

The middle manager mannequin guy closed his eyes and took a deep breath, undoubtedly getting into character.

I waited for it.

He took another breath and held it. Here it comes.

I waited.

Jeez, how long can someone hold their breath? And then.

Eyes popping open, my middle manager mannequin guy's new friend opened his mouth and screamed.

Hmmm.

Did it sound like a cry of terror from the cold, dead soul of a haunted spirit? No, it was more the mortified sound of a 12-year-old who discovered her little brother reading her diary to his obnoxious little buddies.

Over the next minute, I moved him from horrified teen to someone in excruciating pain and finally onto a respectable, if not slightly awkward ghoul. Close enough for horseshoes and hand grenades.

"Follow me up the stairs, and then give it a moment before bursting into the room with your new and improved scream. You'll know when you hear your cue. This will be awesome."

The middle manager mannequin guy nodded. He looked nervous but excited. Kind of like someone who, after singing in their bathroom for years, was ready to step onto the talent show stage.

I turned around and stopped.

In the chaos of the middle manager mannequin guy's appearance, I'd forgotten about Matt, the cameraman. He was still there. The camera raised, and the amber light was on, signaling he was recording. He'd heard everything, including my plan to unleash the amped-up middle manager mannequin guy on Tori and her assistant. I worried about his reaction but relaxed when I saw his grin.

Matt filmed as he moved backward up the stairs. I tried to put a look of determination on my face for the camera but settled for not gloating in anticipation.

At the top of the stairs, I waited for Matt to get into position. I looked back at the middle manager mannequin guy. "Go big. There's no going home," I said and gave him a thumbs up. He returned it.

It was go time.

I burst into the room, waving my arms. Kelly and Lexi stood across from Tori and Candy/Candace. They looked up from their tablets in alarm.

"They're here," I said. "And they're mad as hell. Run!"

No one looked like they had an idea what to do next. Hopefully, my middle manager mannequin friend might offer some inspiration. At that moment, he crashed the door open and lurched into the room with arms outstretched, letting loose a terrifying scream that any horror movie director worth their salt would applaud.

Pandemonium broke loose. No one could handle it.

Tori and Candy/Candace dropped their precious tablets and sprinted for the door. It was an all-out heat that would have left

Usain Bolt in a distant third place. They fought for position at the door to see who could squeeze out first. Tori won after a well-placed elbow knocked her assistant into the doorframe. This didn't deter her as Candy/Candace was rapidly out the door and out of sight right on Tori's heels.

A moment later, there was a roar of an engine and squealing tires. Wow, that worked better than I'd hoped.

My friends didn't do much better. With wild eyes, they turned away from each other and then, in a moment of cartoon-inspired lunacy, turned back and ran into each other. My middle manager mannequin friend took the opportunity to lurch in their direction, hands out like he was going to drag them back to his grave.

"Hell, no," Kelly said. She grabbed Lexi's hand and pulled her toward the door. Lexi, for her part, was more than willing to get the heck out of dodge.

I sighed and turned to Matt's camera.

"That was my friends, the fearless ghost hunters of the Spook Squad. Of course, the television producers didn't exactly come out looking any too brave here either. Especially considering that this entire visit to the supposedly haunted Mounds Theatre was a setup. Yes, they rigged the place with haunted house effects to scare us. Even had someone hiding in a basement mannequin posse to jump out and frighten us."

Moving closer to the camera, I paused and smiled. "The funny thing is, I used their own scare tactic against them. I got him hyped up and unleashed him on the producers." I gestured for my middle manager mannequin friend to join me. "Say hi to the audience."

Clearing his throat, he said, "Hello, I'm Murray. I'm a manager with a software company." He looked at me. "Can I give a shout-out to my people at work?" His eagerness was infectious, and I couldn't say no.

"Of course." It's not like it was my television show.

Murray lifted his hand and made the thumb and pinky gesture. "Shout out to the peeps at Liberty Software."

Reaching out a hand, I said, "You did great today. You nailed your part."

Eyes looking a tad misty, Murray smiled. "Not bad for a one-trick pony."

"Not bad at all." I squeezed his hand. "Stay golden, ponyboy."

And I was out to look for my "fearless" friends.

18

MANNY'S ONE-TRACK MIND

I t was time.

No use in putting it off. With one last box to locate and recover, I could finally get out from under the Neri woman's oppressive government thumb. I understood the *why* of using me to retrieve the spirit box, but the how irked me. With her threats and being offered no choice, it was a dangerous game she played. There's a saying about cornered animals.

Neri's threats to expose me were meant to scare me. But I am not afraid. Let me explain why. My friend from camp, Renata, said they talk about fear differently in Spanish. In Spanish, they don't say we *are* afraid. Instead, they say we have fear (tengo miedo) or we are *with* fear (estoy con miedo). The beauty of this is that fear doesn't become you; it's something you can let go of. It was such an encouraging way to look at things, and it gave me a new perspective. Considering what we went through there, I was happy she taught me that.

With my television career going down in flames in such a spectacular fashion, I had the time to focus on finishing this quest. But would I miss being in front of the camera with cheering crowds celebrating my gift?

As if.

That's not who I am. Never was, never will be. I'm just a girl. But not just a girl, either.

One with confidence.

One with strength.

One with the resiliency to overcome whatever challenges or obstacles were placed in front of me.

My father once told me I could go from princess to warrior faster than anyone he'd ever seen. I'm assuming he meant it as a compliment.

Anywho.

Pulling the last pages of Manny's diary out from their hiding place, I laid them on the table in front of me. I've grown to have mad respect for this man who lived and died a century ago. What he went through and accomplished back in the days before phones and computers was incredible. I wish I could've met him.

My friends in this final chapter of my search were important ones from last summer: Stacia and Carrie.

I'd met Stacia and Carrie last summer at Camp ToughLove, the summer home for wayward teens. We'd been trapped in a burning dormitory together and survived by leaning on each other. Harrowing experiences like that create a bond that can overcome time, distance, and different high schools.

Though they were the same age, the two girls couldn't have been more different. Stacia was as thin as a candy cane and just as sweet. With a flair for the dramatic, she had tried to fool us into believing she had a twin sister with nothing but a blue cardigan and an outrageous French accent. It had worked for a while, too.

On the other hand, Carrie could be summed up in three words. Driven, competitive, popular. Carrie played volleyball at her school and was as fit as any Olympic athlete. With her glasses and no-nonsense hairstyle, you might miss the fierceness hiding just below her surface. But it was most certainly there.

With as crazy and harrowing as it was at the cathedral, I would make sure my friends were kept safe and out of harm's way on this quest.

This quest.

Maybe not King Arthur's quest for the holy grail, but it had been surprisingly epic. Tom Petty had a hit in the eighties, "Runnin' Down a Dream." Talk about totally fitting. I found myself singing it as I leaned over the pages of Manny's diary. As I read through the earlier sections of the Manny pages, I found myself connecting with him. I guess good writing can do that to a person. But, even more, something about the man and his outlook captivated me. Even though the events took place a century ago, I felt his spirit as I read his words.

I'm writing this a changed man aboard the Chicago Limited. I boarded this passenger train in New York City yesterday, and from what I understand, we're not far from Chicago. From there, I will switch trains and head northwest to Saint Paul.

Due to my benefactor's generosity, I am again riding in the first-class section. Luxury is everywhere as we make our way across the country. The finest wood and brass fixtures adorn every surface. Sitting in the plush dining car last evening, I particularly enjoyed the luxury sitting across from me. She was beautiful.

Her dark auburn hair cascaded around her bewitching hazel eyes. She looked back at me appraisingly over the top of her wine glass. Desiree was her name. We'd met as we boarded at Grand Central Station. When I first saw her magnificent...hair in front of me, I maneuvered to get closer. We started talking, and I was instantly taken with her husky laugh. I invited her to join me for dinner and was pleased when she accepted.

The dining car was a crowded affair. Tables for four sat on one side, while tables for two were across the aisle. White-coated waiters kept the food and drink flowing. To sit in a luxurious traveling restaurant while watching the countryside roll on by was an excellent way to pass the time.

Especially in the company of a beautiful woman. There was a twinkle in her eye that I liked. It spoke of promise.

A promise that wasn't meant to be.

It turned out she wasn't as open to my suggestion for dessert as I had hoped. After nursing my black eye, I'd turned in for the evening, resigned to a quiet night. Surprisingly, this is when my night turned interesting.

I don't remember the exact moment I became awake, but it was a moment I won't forget any time soon—no matter how much I'd like to.

As my eyes fluttered open, I found a strange paralysis had taken over my body. Try as I might, I couldn't move a single finger. Only my eyes would move. Nothing I could do made a lick of difference. As you read this, you may be wondering why it was so important that I move. I guess I need to tell you about the other part. The terrifying part.

Leaning over me was the old woman from the RMS Aquitania. Her tangled white hair dangled into my face as she studied me. Her cataract-filled eyes walked up and down my rigid body. The lines on her face were as deep as caverns. When she smiled, her thin lips pulled back to reveal numerous missing teeth. But when she cackled... I'm not saying her breath was horrible, but it could knock a buzzard off a shit wagon.

I struggled to turn away to no avail.

When the old hag straightened up, I saw she wasn't the only one in the room. A freakishly tall man appeared to be gliding around the small space. His hat bumped the ceiling as he floated from here to there. When I saw his face, it looked pale and sunken, as if life had left it decades past. One time, when he came particularly close, I noticed that his fingers were impossibly long.

My eyes were drawn to the third person in the room. This man faced the corner and looked as frozen in place as any cigar store Indian I've seen. What he was doing in the corner was anyone's guess. He simply stood there.

The entire time I took in the freak show, I felt my chest heaving quickly from the effort of trying to move. It was my growing panic that kept me fighting the paralysis of my own body. I had to get up and get far away from these strange beings.

The old woman spoke for the first time as she placed a gnarled hand on my chest.

"Your heart pounds for me. There has been many a man whose heart raced for me."

She paused and then frowned.

"You don't believe me?"

I couldn't possibly convey a positive or negative, so I wasn't confirming anything for her. But I wouldn't say I liked where she was headed.

"Let me show you." As she leaned over, her hair once again obscured my vision. I felt something in my chest, a sensation of pressure and pulling, but there was no pain.

When the hag straightened up with a triumphant smile, she cradled something in her hands. Her cackle was both grating and horrific as she placed something on my chest. I glanced down and saw a wet mass about the size of a fist that clenched and unclenched rapidly. With dawning horror, I realized what I was looking at.

It was my heart.

Contracting.

Uncontracting.

The speedy pace of my beating heart could be understood, given how terrified I was.

The tall man floated over to the side of my bed. Dressed in a black suit, tie, and bowler hat, he was well-dressed for the occasion. He reached toward my heart, his fingers fluttering as he went to grab hold of it.

The hag slapped his hand away.

The man in the corner stood there, unmoving.

I found it impossible to look away from my heart. Although it was beating, the pace had slowed considerably.

I'm dying, I realized. My heart slowed, and soon, it would stop altogether.

The hag leaned in further, mesmerized.

The tall man's fingers clenched and unclenched with the rhythm of my heart.

The man in the corner stood there, deathly still.

I will admit here, in writing, that I have never been a man of God. I don't go to church or read the bible. However, even I know there is more to our world than we can comprehend. Someone has to be responsible for all this—and I was going to talk to him.

I glanced around.

The hag's tongue darted around behind her missing teeth as she watched me die.

The floating man bobbed side to side.

The man in the corner stood there, unwaveringly still.

I closed my eyes.

I've never prayed before, but I've heard that you're simply talking to God inside your head.

"God, this is me, Manfred Krug. I need your help right now. In the name of everything holy, please make this freak show disappear. I don't want to die here in Ohio. Please, anywhere else."

I kept my eyes closed while I continued.

"I know I haven't been a faithful servant, but that can change. I know I could make a difference if I lived. Please save me, Lord. We could make a great team. Think about it, but I'm afraid this is a limited-time offer."

I didn't know what else to say, so I lay there with my eyes closed. Since I was new to the praying thing, I wasn't sure how I would receive God's response. Would he tap me on the shoulder and say, rise, faithful servant? Would I feel the spirit wash over me? Would I smell a burning bush? I didn't know, so I kept my eyes tightly shut.

However, after several long minutes, I heard something.

I strained my ears, wanting to understand what I heard.

It was...snoring.

Someone was snoring not too far from my deathbed.

This was most certainly an unusual development. At least, it might explain what the man in the corner had been doing.

I cracked open one eyelid, not wanting to see too much. But I didn't see anyone.

I opened my eye all the way. Still, nothing to see, so I opened my other eye.

Amazingly, there wasn't anyone standing over me. No hag with bad teeth and worse breath. No floating man doing his impression of a bobber. And the man in the corner was still there—no, not really. He had finally moved and was also gone.

I sat right up and threw a hand to my breast. I could feel my heart hammering in my chest. I was relieved to find it back where it belonged.

The snoring continued. My gaze landed on the man in the opposite berth. I'd forgotten I shared a sleeping berth with the investment banker, Reginald Scripner. Old Reggie was sawing more logs than all the lumber mills back in Minnesota.

I sat up. I'd had enough sleep for one evening. Best to get away from those cursed spirit boxes. There was little doubt they were the cause of my problems. Maybe the dining car would be a better—and safer—place to be. One thing was for sure: it would be quiet at this hour.

Which was good. After tonight, I had a lot of thinking to do.

19

ON THE OTHER SIDE OF FEAR

The final and smallest spirit box had been given to another of Manny's benefactors. Dr. Dutcher lived in an upscale neighborhood several miles from Pine Ridge High School. The majestic old-money homes were clustered around the shores of White Bear Lake. According to the notes from Special Agent Neri, the house had remained in the Dutcher family after his death. It had recently been passed on to his granddaughter and her family.

And here we were, ringing their doorbell.

The English cottage-style house was a two-story—quite possibly the most enormous two-story I had ever seen. I counted 28 windows across the front as I staked out the place. To put it in perspective, my house has just six windows across the front. The Dutcher house was cream with green trim and didn't look particularly foreboding.

Looks can be deceiving.

The girl who opened the door was several years younger than me. Her brown hair was pulled back into a ponytail, and she wore athletic clothes. But it was her eyes that stood out. The mixture of relief and excitement in them had me wondering if showing up unannounced was a good idea.

"Mom, they're here," she called as she stepped aside. The house was beautiful, with polished wooden floors, stunning woodwork, and works of art adorning the walls. A grand staircase led to the second floor. A glance across the corner showed a hallway with a kitchen at the far end.

The girl who let us in clearly thought we were someone else. I held my tongue as I turned to Stacia and Carrie. Both nodded, understanding the need not to say anything. When life gives you an opening, you need to embrace it.

Stacia, Carrie, and I waited for the girl's mother to join us.

A breathless woman came down the kitchen hall toward us. She was of the age that my mother and all my friends' mothers appear to be. Her dark hair was pulled back, and she wrapped her sweater tighter as she approached us. She looked like she hadn't slept in days. Except for the dark bags under her eyes, she was beautiful.

"You got here early, thank you." Her eyes didn't seem to focus as she gazed past the three of us. "Come in, please."

She swept down the hall and led us to a sitting room off the kitchen. Her daughter trailed us.

"Ella, why don't you keep them company while I bring us some tea? You can fill them in on our recent events."

Her words hung in the air as Ella gestured for us to sit. Stacia and Carrie took the small couch across from the crackling fire. I sat on a blue wingback chair with a flower pattern from a bygone era. Ella sat in a matching chair with a small table and lamp between us.

I studied Ella. Her delicate features reminded me of her mother, and I was confident she would be equally beautiful one day. As Ella wrung her hands, I caught sight of her fingernails, which were chewed to the nubs. She looked to be lost in thought. There was tension in this house.

"Ella, your mom mentioned recent events," I said after a moment. My voice startled her back to the present.

She hesitated before speaking. "Yes, those." Her eyes stared into the fire, and she began to tell her story.

"We've been in this house for nearly three years, and plenty of odd things have happened. I'm sure you've seen that before in your investigations."

I glanced at my friends. *Investigations? Who did she think we were?*

I cleared my throat. "Trust me, we've seen it all."

"People can do strange things," Carrie added.

Ella's face clouded. "It's not people I'm worried about. At least, I don't think so."

"Why don't you tell us what happened?" It's been my experience that it's better to rip the band-aid off.

Ella shivered and nodded. "Honestly, I've never believed in that stuff, but living here has changed my view of ghosts and the paranormal. It brought us all from skeptics to believers. But, you're the paranormal investigators. You must see strange things all the time."

Paranormal investigators? Did she see us on TV?

The irony of the moment was not lost on any of us. Not only did I deal with the paranormal all the time, but I was using the paranormal to track powerful ancient artifacts—artifacts with the power to gather and amplify spiritual energy. I don't need to investigate anything to discover if the paranormal is real. I know it is.

But maybe she saw us on the television program, auditioning for the *Twin Cities Live* contest.

"We've seen it all," Stacia said. "Stuff that would scare most rational people to death." That might be a bit over the top.

I put a hand over Ella's as her mom came in with a serving tray. "My apologies," her mother interrupted, handing us a cup of tea. "I'm Isabel, by the way, and this is my youngest daughter, Ella. My other daughter, Lily, is away at college." We introduced ourselves and waited while Ella took a sip of tea.

"Go ahead," I said, encouraging her to continue.

"At first, it was doors slamming, keyboards typing, and chairs sliding. Even the occasional glimpse of a shadowy figure. We'd seen these ghostly figures multiple times, but for some reason, we were never bothered by them. They were friendly ghosts—until recently," she added.

"It was maybe two months after we moved here from Connecticut, and I was coming down the stairs when I saw a face through the railing. It was a demented-looking old lady, and she nearly scared the piss right out of me. I flew down the stairs, but she was gone when I got to the main floor." She shook her head with the memory.

Ella continued, setting down her tea. "We had accepted that we weren't alone in the house. It was just something we got used to." She folded her arms across her chest, still staring at the dancing flames.

"But everything changed last month. Mom, Lily, and I had just gotten home from the grocery store and had set the bags on the kitchen counter when we heard the distinct voice of a man. When the man yelled, 'Norah,' we all froze, groceries in hand, and looked at each other."

The flames danced in Ella's eyes as she continued. "The man yelled again, 'Norah. Where are you goin', Norah?' He was upstairs, and it was terrifying."

Isabel's hand trembled as she took a sip of tea.

"That's when we grabbed knives, and I whispered to Mom to call the police. Lily and I tried to carry on a conversation so the man wouldn't hear her on the phone. We feared he'd get mad and come down and hurt us."

I glanced at Stacia and Carrie. They were both wide-eyed as they listened to Ella's story.

"It was only six minutes before the sheriff arrived, but it felt like forever. With guns drawn, the two burly deputies stood at the bottom of the stairs and called up, 'Ramsey County Sheriff. Is anyone up there?'"

Ella shivered. "A man's voice announced, 'Yeah, I'm here.' The reply sounded like it came from the first bedroom at the top of the stairs—my bedroom." Ella wrapped her arms around herself and shivered again.

"That confirmed that someone was indeed in our house. The sheriff's deputies commanded the man to show himself. But instead of showing himself, the voice called out, 'I'm right here.' But no one was visible."

The bulb in the lamp next to me crackled and flickered.

"Don't worry about that, it happens to all the lights here." Isabel Dutcher said. "It must be the wiring here."

Or it's the ghosts.

Ella shrugged and continued. "I could see how tense the law officers were as they whispered between themselves. We were led out to the porch as other police cars arrived. Soon, at least six squads were parked in front of our house. Every officer had a weapon drawn as they surrounded our house. The deputy told us they would send the K-9 unit upstairs as they worried the intruder may be armed.

"It was a large German shepherd, and he strained at his leash to get inside. When his handler let him loose, he raced through the open door.

"We were relieved when the dog began barking, thinking the man had been cornered. But the handler told us the dog had been trained to bark first. He said it was a psychological tactic to scare perpetrators into showing themselves. People are afraid they're going to get bit or mauled."

"It would scare me," Stacia whispered. "Big dogs scare me."

"Since the man didn't react, the handler signaled the dog to go upstairs. It bounded up, taking three steps at a time. But the dog didn't find anyone up there. By this time, the county SWAT team arrived and stormed through every room in the house. They didn't find anyone, either. The windows were all shut and couldn't be latched from the outside. And with so many officers surrounding our house, there wasn't any way for someone to escape."

Ella paused to sip her tea, her eyes never leaving the fire. She reminded me of a blind person in how she talked without making eye contact as she told her story.

"So, next, the police used thermal cameras, thinking the intruder must be hiding in the walls. They were incredibly thorough, going through all the bedrooms, closets, and storage rooms. But they didn't find anyone."

Isabel spoke up. "I knew something was wrong when the police came out of the house and were visibly shaken. The head sheriff pulled us aside and said nothing like this had ever happened in his 35 years of law enforcement. I could see the fear in his eyes.

"He advised us to leave and waited while we packed some clothes. When we left, there wasn't a single squad car remaining other than the sheriff's car. And as soon as we were safely in our car, he rocketed off, too."

I shook my head, thinking how horrible it would be to be chased from your own house. "But you came back," I said. "What changed?"

Isabel answered as she set down her cup of tea. Her hand trembled, and some of the tea sloshed over the side. She didn't appear to notice. "We went to one of the hotels on the interstate. We were all scared and so relieved to be away from the house. But, after a couple of days, we needed clean clothes. And we were sick of being stuck in a hotel room. So we stopped at the house, thinking we would grab a change of clothes. But it was Ella that changed our minds."

She smiled at her daughter. "Tell them."

Ella smiled shyly. "When we walked in, with all of us on edge, I called out, 'Norah, we're home.' Everyone burst out laughing, and the spell was broken. No way we were going back to the hotel."

"Did you ever hear from the man again?"

The Dutcher women shook their heads, but I picked up on a wariness that contradicted their denials. If I had to guess, both had encountered the man again but didn't want to scare the other.

Isabel spoke first. "But we wanted paranormal investigators like yourselves to check out the house. We know we're not alone here, but we need to know if we're safe."

Paranormal investigators. The thing was, I had never talked to this woman before. After watching the house on and off for a week, I decided to try the direct approach with Stacia and Carrie. After sitting in the car for an hour as we watched the house, we simply went to their door and rang the bell. Sometimes, coincidences can work to your advantage.

"We decided that we couldn't continue living the way we have, and when I saw a Facebook post about your services, I had to call. I was sure St. Croix Paranormal Investigations could give us answers."

"Answers are good," I offered. At least we knew who was supposed to be here.

"How do you like to work?" Isabel asked. "Do you want Ella and me to leave so you can do your thing?"

I shook my head. "Spirits tend to attach themselves to people or places, though an object can also be responsible for hauntings. To be safe, I'd like you to stay down here while we go up." I nodded toward the stairs. "It feels like the energy is upstairs, so that's where we'll begin."

Isabel looked comfortable with my answer. We got up and moved toward the door.

"Wait," Ella said. "I watch those ghost hunter shows. Don't you need lots of equipment?"

I started to answer, but Carrie held up a hand. "I got this."

She gestured in my direction and said, "You don't need all those gadgets when you have the original spooky girl. Abbey sees more ghosts than cops see donuts. She's the real deal."

Isabel smiled wearily. "Well, we're glad you're here. It's exhausting living in fear."

"It's time to conquer those fears, then," I said, trying to sound braver than I felt. I hoped my goosebumps wouldn't give me away.

20

WE DON'T EVEN HAVE A
BLINKING LIGHT THINGY

"Honestly, we're as sketchy as a waffle house at 2 a.m.," Stacia said. "Do you think she believed us?"

We stood at the base of the magnificent staircase that opened to the second level. Waiting at the top of the carpeted stairs were arched stained glass windows. They were stunningly beautiful.

"It doesn't matter. I know I can help this family more than some amateur ghost hunter. Anyone can claim they're a paranormal investigator. There's no licensing involved. All you need is to carry around some device with blinking lights, and suddenly, you're authorized to walk around someone's house." *The Paranormal Dudes, for instance.*

"But we don't even have a blinking light thingy," Stacia said.

"You've missed the point completely. I don't need a blinking light to see a ghost. But, if it makes you feel better, I can turn my flashlight on and off pretty darn quickly."

Stacia smiled and let it go.

"I'm more concerned about the other paranormal investigators," Carrie said. "The Dutchers were expecting them to show up. Won't there be awkward questions if they show up while we're here?"

"Then we'd better hurry up," I said. Though it would be funny if the Paranormal Dudes showed up.

Running my fingers along the cherry wood banister, an energy grew with every step. Looking back, Stacia was rooted to the spot. I waved for her to catch up with Carrie and me.

She shook her head. "You two can joke all you want, but I'm scared. What if that man doesn't want us here?"

I retreated down the steps and took Stacia's hand. I brushed back her hair. "Everything you want is on the other side of fear. We'll push past it together."

◅◅

Fear had to be the theme of the day. Earlier, as we had sat in Carrie's car watching the Dutcher house, we discussed our fears. The discussion had begun with Stacia's question.

"Don't these ghosts ever scare you?"

I laughed, which is all you can do sometimes. "Of course, they scare me. Not all of them. Some are actually funny or sweet. Others are confused spirits needing my help. But there are mean ones and others that weren't ever human. Those scare me."

"It doesn't stop you, though."

I thought about it for a moment. "Fear doesn't have to stop you. Fear is more about making sure you take something seriously. My dad would say courage isn't the absence of fear but the triumph over it. My take on it is that it's okay to be scared. Just don't let fear stop you from living."

Stacia nodded and turned to Carrie. "I don't think you ever get scared. You are so...invincible. You're popular, driven, and never settle for second best. You are an alpha."

Carrie nodded, her short brown hair bouncing with the motion. She pushed up her glasses but didn't say anything.

But Stacia wasn't going to let it alone. "Aren't you scared of things like the rest of us?"

Carrie's face was unreadable as she looked at the Dutcher house. After a few long moments, she spoke quietly. "When I was seven, my dad left. No words, no note, no explanation. He had packed up his suits, golf clubs, and life, leaving ours behind. Long after the pain became numbness, my mom lost her job, and then we lost our house. We were homeless."

"Carrie..."

"For the most part, we spent nights in shelters, but the days...we were on the streets. And we became invisible. Hundreds, if not thousands of people, passed us every day, but no one seemed to see us. No one looked us in the eye, and no one would acknowledge us. We were truly invisible.

"Eventually, my mom found a new job and met someone. My new father is a successful businessman, and he loves us. But...I still lay awake at night thinking of those days on the streets, and when I finally fall asleep, I often have nightmares of fading from sight and becoming invisible.

"Maybe that's why I am the way I am. If I'm relentless in everything, I can't be ignored. People have to see me. I'm not offering them a choice."

I laughed. "Trust me, no one is going to ignore you. That would be like ignoring a 7.0 magnitude earthquake while your house is coming down around you. Not going to happen."

Carrie turned to Stacia. "What about you? What are you afraid of?"

With a theatrical flip of her hair, Stacia said, "Darling, when you look like I do, you have nothing to fear."

"You can never be too rich or too thin," I said.

"Exactly, darling," she said with a bat of her eyes.

"You might be too thin if I'm being honest," Carrie squad after a moment.

"Like a candy cane," I added.

"You're saying I'm sweet and twisted?" Stacia asked with a grin.

"Your words, not mine, but I'm not disagreeing." I paused. "Let me go out on a limb here with a question. Do you have an eating disorder?"

Stacia looked like she had a quick reply, but I held up a finger. "After all we've been through, you can be honest. This is a judgment-free zone."

Stacia held my gaze for the longest time and didn't say anything. It was the hardest thing not to prompt her. My father interviewed people all the time in his job as a writer. He said you have to give them the space to breathe. That way, the answers will come from the heart rather than the head.

Eventually, Stacia began speaking. Quietly. "I was always a city girl. We lived in Saint Paul, where you knew everyone on your block. You lived around them, played with them, and went to school with them. Same for most of the people in the surrounding blocks. We grew up together, playing jump rope, tag, four square, sardines, ghost in the graveyard," she said, giving me a sideways glance before continuing. "We understood each other.

"That all changed when we moved to the suburbs. He was always worried about crime, but the suburbs were worse than crime. My father thought we'd be happier living away from the city. He was wrong. Everything was different at my new school. Which meant I was different. I didn't fit in—not anymore."

Stacia took a breath and continued. "I didn't have friends, and people were mean to me. The teachers were frustrated because I wouldn't know things that the other kids did. I tried to explain that we hadn't even learned those things yet at my previous school. That just made it worse. I had no hope and no control over my life. But, I found if I controlled my weight, I was in control of something."

"But, were you healthy?"

Smiling wryly, Stacia said, "That wasn't important to me. Being in control was. It still is."

"So, your biggest fear is being different and not being in control? That's why you're doing what you're doing?"

It was a long moment before Stacia answered. Her voice cracked with emotion. "I'm afraid of where I would be without my...disorder. What would I do without running miles each and every day? Where would I be without the number on the scale giving me my worth?"

She was crying now.

"What would people think of me if I wasn't striving to be perfect?"

"Stacia, we're your friends and not looking for perfection. We're certainly not perfect ourselves." I reached for her hand and held it while Stacia composed herself. After an awkward group hug in the front seat of Carrie's car, we turned back to the Dutcher house.

"C'mon," I said, opening the door. "We're going to ring the doorbell and see what happens. Life is too short and precious to wait. Let's do this."

"This is Abbey, in full-on-beast mode," Carrie announced. "Watch out."

Stacia laughed. "Nothing scares this girl."

I couldn't help but think how wrong she was. I was scared. My mother completely vanished on a mission trip to Venezuela a few years ago. Almost a year later, she had been miraculously found and returned to us. But during that year, she was gone...

It had been devastating to lose someone I loved. I was sure it didn't help that I had lost many childhood friends when they discovered how different I was. They were afraid of me. Suddenly, they didn't want anything to do with me.

As we approached the door of the Dutcher house, I turned to my friends. They gave a nod that signaled they were with me, no matter what.

The thing is, I have fear. I fear losing those closest to me. And I was going to make damn sure that didn't happen again.

◑◐

Together, the three of us climbed the grand staircase while the Dutcher family anxiously waited. We joined hands briefly when we reached the second-floor landing. Gazing into Stacia's and Carrie's eyes, I nodded. They both nodded in return. Let's do this.

The walls were adorned with beautiful paintings, landscapes of long-gone days surrounded by gold leaf frames. Hallways went off in either direction. Something struck me as odd—the hallways looked to run on forever. The house was big from the outside but not this big.

After peeking into a few of the rooms, I turned us around. "Let's go to Ella's room. It feels like the answer may be there."

As we passed the staircase to our left, I stopped.

"This is a two-story house, isn't it?"

Both girls nodded. But to our right, another staircase rose into darkness. Stacia and Carrie's jaws quite literally dropped. "Wait. Where do those go?" Stacia asked.

"Looks like they go up." I led them to the base of the stairs. "How often do stairs just magically appear? We have to check it out," I said and clicked on the flashlight. It didn't do much. The darkness swallowed the light before it could find anything to illuminate. Tendrils of fog snaked down the steps from the inky blackness above.

I took another step and felt the energy in the air.

The next step let out a groan of protest, but I kept us moving up. Slow, but steady. A glance behind showed that my friends were right with me. True friends.

Something moved in the shadows ahead, but I couldn't get a sense of what it was. But when we arrived at the landing, nothing waited for us. Cool, foggy mist obscured our feet. Unlike the second-floor landing with beautiful stained-glass windows, we faced a rough-hewn stone wall.

"Strange decorating choice," Stacia said as she ran her fingers over the stone.

The stairs continued up to the right, and a faint glow emanated from the top, shimmering like desert heat. Ironically enough, I couldn't help but shiver.

The soft glow illuminated well enough that I didn't need my flashlight. I clicked it off but held onto it. It felt reassuring in my hand. We walked down the hallway on rough planks. The carpet from the second floor was gone. Narrow and long, the hallway stretched on. In the distance, an amber light beckoned us.

We went.

I heard the whispers first. Indistinct words that floated like bubbles around us. Then came the touches. Little flutters of sensation as if a flock of butterflies were bumping into me. It brought a smile to my face.

But then everything changed.

A strong wind kicked up—odd, considering we were inside a house. The floor was wet and made squishy sounds as we continued. A musty smell invaded my nose and quickly became disgusting. It was at this point that I decided I really would rather be back on the second floor.

I clutched Stacia's and Carrie's hands as the assault on our senses continued. I squeezed my eyes shut and kept putting one foot in front of the other.

Then, I felt different.

I know different can mean a lot of things to a lot of people, but the feeling I had was absolutely palpable. I was cold but also tingling. It left me in an altered state, far from normal. Normal had left the building and was happy with its life choices.

Judging by the intense hand squeezes from my friends, I knew they were experiencing the same thing. At the height of it, I wondered how much more we could endure. And then, much as it began, it ended with a quick fade.

I opened my eyes. The hallway was now deathly still.

"What was that?" Stacia asked, her voice trembling.

"That was the ghostly equivalent of a locomotive running through us."

"See? I knew your one-track mind would get us into trouble," Stacia said as she elbowed me. As tense as the moment was, her comment broke us into laughter.

Then, a light grew in brilliance from a room down to our right.

"That's our sign."

Carrie, who was closest, said, "I got this." She determinedly headed for the room while Stacia and I followed.

The light began pulsing from the room's interior. Silhouetted by the light, Carrie stepped inside and paused. Something shifted in her body language when she crossed the threshold. Her confidence was gone, and she looked timid as she stepped forward, frequently glancing about.

"Is everything all right?" I asked, but knowing things were not all right with her.

Showing no sign that she had heard me, Carrie didn't respond. I exchanged glances with Stacia. Something was wrong here. We watched as Carrie circled the room and turned back towards the doorway where we waited. Her expression straddled the line between confusion and distress.

"Are you okay?" Stacia asked.

Carrie trembled as she looked at us. "Don't you see me?" she asked, her voice cracked with emotion. "I'm right here."

"She can't hear us."

I knew Carrie needed us, but when I stepped forward, something stopped me. Confused, I tried to reach my friend, but I was in a giant bubble. A solid bubble. The transparent membrane gave a little but wouldn't let me enter the room.

"Carrie! I'm right here. I can't get in."

I was frustrated and angry at my inability to reach my hurting friend. She stood just feet away, but it might as well have been miles.

Tears ran down Carrie's cheeks. "Why won't you say anything?" she cried out. "You have to see me."

We pushed against the barrier, but it kept us back. I took a few steps back and launched myself at the membrane. It held with just the slightest of ripples at the point of impact.

"Carrie, we're here," Stacia yelled.

Inside the room, Carrie stared at us with a look of despair. Her lips trembled as tears ran down her face. Her eyes had a haunted look that tore into my heart. I needed to help my friend.

Carrie held up a hand, and her despair melted into horror as she stared at her raised hand. We could see right through it. Carrie was fading away right before our eyes.

"No, no, this can't be happening," she wailed. "Not again." She said with resignation and slumped down to her knees. "No one will ever see me again."

There was no way I was giving up on my friend. In my life, the few friends I'd made were precious beyond belief. "C'mon, we have to get to her," I said. Time after time, we both threw ourselves at the barrier, but it held. Stacia dropped to her knees, exhausted.

I looked at my sad friend, so close but still a world away.

The light in the room appeared to be dimming. I couldn't make out the details of the far side anymore. The light was fading. Fading on my friend.

Carrie's head was down, staring at her clasped hands.

At that moment, I knew what was happening. Carrie's nightmare of a childhood, the childhood that defined her, was becoming her reality in that room.

I refused to give up, not on my friend, not on anything.

"Hold my hand," I directed Stacia as I got down on my knees next to her. Wiping away her tears, she grabbed my hand. The tears on her hand felt like they created a stronger bond as we squeezed each other's hands.

Lord, give me strength.

And then, amazingly enough, there it was. *Hope.*

A childhood prayer resurfaced in my mind. *Light shines in the darkness, and the darkness has not overcome it.*

Getting to my feet, I pulled out my flashlight and aimed it at Carrie's hands. When she stiffened, I knew she had seen the light.

"Carrie, we're here. Be strong, girl. Push past the fear, push past the pain, past the doubts. Fear is a liar, a deceiver. It keeps you from achieving the things you were made to accomplish."

"Yes," Stacia agreed quietly.

"You are strong. Fear is a barrier between you and where you need to go. You can push past this."

"Yes, you can," Stacia said a little louder this time.

"You've got this. You are the strongest of us. Where many shrink back, you are bold. You are powerful."

Carrie's hands separated and then became fists.

"Yes," I screamed.

Carrie got to her feet; resolve on her face. She took a step toward the doorway.

"C'mon, girl. You are a badass."

Carrie stepped up to the barrier, her eyes narrowed with fierce determination that I'd seen before. We'd competed against each other at camp, and when Carrie was in her warrior mode, there was no stopping her.

With a single step, Carrie crossed through the barrier.

"Nothing to see in there," she said casually.

I threw my arms around her and gave her the biggest hug of my life.

"I knew you could do it," I said.

"Once a fighter, always a fighter," Carrie said. She glanced around. "Hey, where's Stacia?"

Wait, what? Stacia was just here.

21

MEAN GHOSTS SUCK

here had Stacia gone?

"She was just here. Right next to me." *Why would she leave?*

I spun toward the hallway. She had to have stepped out of the room. "Stacia," I called out in the empty hallway, holding Carrie's gaze. She looked as worried as I felt.

A sudden shriek chilled me to the bone. It came from the darkness further down the hallway. Without hesitation, we sprinted toward the sound.

I know it didn't make sense, but the faster we ran and the further we went, the farther away we were. I put a hand out to stop Carrie, and we both came to an abrupt stop.

"We need to be smart about this." No monster house was going to outfox this girl. I held out an arm for Carrie. "Let's take a stroll, shall we?" Carrie latched on.

Unfortunately, our levity didn't last. A pain ripped into my arm, and I yanked it away from the wall.

"What the..." Blood soaked into my shredded sleeve. Jagged pieces of glass protruded from the wall.

Carrie pointed at the floor. Spikes jutted up at odd angles. They weren't there moments ago. Something wanted to keep us from Stacia.

Tough. We were going.

Stepping over a spike, I moved around another on the left. A razor-sharp blade stuck out from the wall to my right. *Careful.* Touching that could have sliced my arm right off.

It was step after agonizing step down the long hallway of horrors.

As we made our way, Stacia's voice became clearer. She sounded fragile and psychologically wounded.

"I am not," she said.

Who was she talking to?

"Why would you say that? That's mean."

We found Stacia on the floor, her legs tucked underneath. She looked tiny. I couldn't see anyone there, but she was talking to someone.

We weren't alone. There were others here.

Closing my eyes, I took in a long, slow breath. Then, I took another deep breath and opened my eyes. A shock like an electric current ran down my spine.

There wasn't *a* ghost berating Stacia, no, there were *four* of them. One was an old woman who was more shadow than substance. There were two girls, one dressed in a country-style blue and white peasant blouse, the other was decked out for a night of clubbing. The fourth woman was in her early forties. Hair pinned up, wearing a sweater, pants, and an I-just-sucked-on-a-lemon face. She was the one speaking.

"What a disappointment you are. Have some respect for yourself. Don't you care what your family thinks?" The woman didn't wait for an answer as she leaned close to my friend. "It's no wonder your family despises you. Look at what you've become."

Anyone who knows me knows I won't tolerate bullying. Picking on someone, demeaning them, and tearing down someone's self-worth is the lowest of the low. These people are whale shit. Pond scum. I absolutely won't stand for this demoralizing abuse. Stepping forward, I addressed the woman.

"Hey." She looked up, surprise coloring her face. "Yeah, you."

She opened her mouth to reply, but I held a finger to her lips to silence her.

"Stop. Whatever idiotic thing you were going to say can wait. You're going to listen to me." I stepped even closer.

"What you're doing is wrong. It's hateful and has no place here—or anywhere else, for that matter. Leave my friend alone. She is a beautiful person. She has a heart like no other and doesn't deserve your repulsive words."

I locked eyes with this woman—the ghost of cruel relatives everywhere.

"I need you to listen carefully," I continued. "You are going to leave this place. You're not to bother anyone living ever again. Do you understand me?"

The woman stared back at me. I was so in the moment that I could reach out and poke her.

"Answer me."

Wide-eyed, she nodded. I glanced at Stacia, and the woman was gone when I looked back.

Carrie gave me a thumbs-up. But then things got worse.

The two girls were now in Stacia's face.

"Hey, tubby, where are you going in your plus-size clothes? Going to clean out the barn?"

The other girl in the designer clothes spoke up.

"Shopping the clearance racks at Goodwill again? Nice."

Stacia had tears welling in her eyes. "I'm not..."

"Hey, lard butt," the country girl angrily interrupted. "No one wants to hear you."

"But..."

"Please." This time, it was the designer girl that cut her off. "If we wanted to talk to a thrift store hussy, we'd go talk to your mom. But I'm sure she's busy entertaining the local migrant workers."

The exchange literally had taken a moment, but it was already way too long. If anyone could put mean girls in their place, it was Carrie. Reaching back, I grabbed onto her hand.

"Close your eyes," I told her. "Picture a Wizard of Oz Dorothy clone and a Mean Girls casting reject. And once you have that image fixed in your mind, open your eyes."

Her eyes fluttered open after a moment, and she squeezed my hand.

"Hello, girls," she said coolly. I imagined this was like a shark meeting lunch.

Both turned to see where the new voice came from. And since it came from my small but mighty friend, Carrie, they had better watch out. Carrie was more than capable of kicking their tails back to whatever rock they crawled out from. Stepping closer, she dragged me along for the ride.

"I know you think you're better than everyone else, but you'd be wrong."

"Dead wrong," I chimed in.

"Your meanness is a symptom of your insecurity. You tear down others to build yourself because you don't believe in yourself. Climbing up on the bodies of your victims is not how you get ahead. It's simply not right."

"It's dead wrong."

Carrie shot me a look and continued. "I need you to leave."

The girl in the designer clothes shot Carrie a defiant look. "I don't think you could make us."

"Well then," Carrie said as her eyes twinkled, "you'd be wrong."

"Dead wrong," I said, holding up my pointer finger. The ghostly girl followed it with her eyes as I reached out and touched her forehead. Her eyes widened.

She became a believer at that moment, and both girls winked out of existence.

"We need to get Stacia out of here," I said. She didn't look good.

But the voice of ten thousand cigarettes spoke from the corner.

With a rough and deep voice, she had an accent that reminded me of the gypsy women in old horror movies. "Not so fast."

She stepped from the shadows. The old woman's long gray hair hung in her face, with just her hooknose protruding. But it was her wings and claws where her hands should have been that shocked me into silence. Her wings unfolded, and Carrie gasped behind me.

"She's an angel," Carrie said with awe, clearly misunderstanding the wings.

The old woman cackled, a sound that ranked pretty high on my sounds-I-hate-more-than-the-dentist-drill list. Her wings twitched as she stood over our friend. "Whatever you think, dear." There was no warmth in her voice.

When Carrie started moving toward the woman, I held her back. "Don't let her wings fool you. She's no angel."

With a snarl that would make a honey badger proud, the woman swung a clawed hand at us. I pulled back, saving us from being sliced open.

"Definitely no angel. She's a harpy." I had read of the harpy monster from Greek mythology. They were described as having a human woman's head and body and a bird's wings and claws. But who knew they were real?

I shouldn't be surprised by anything that crawled, slithered, or otherwise appeared around me. Being a spook magnet brought out the freak show.

The harpy held a claw at Stacia's throat and waved the other like a knife. "This one belongs to me."

According to Greek lore, harpies were often agents of punishment, abducting people and torturing them on their way to Hades' domain. I couldn't let that happen.

The problem was, I wasn't sure how to stop her. If I focused enough to enable contact with her, she could also touch me. I knew I didn't want to face the business end of her claws.

When you can't win by physical force, you need to use your

brain. A favorite quote of mine was, *The supreme art of war is to subdue the enemy without fighting.*

This gave me an idea, and I held up my hands. "I'm not going to fight you over this. You are far too powerful."

The harpy looked at me warily but didn't say anything.

"But, are you smarter than me?"

The harpy made a sound that resembled scoffing. She clearly believed she had me in the brains department as well.

I took a step toward her.

"I admit that you've been around a lot longer than I have and most likely have learned a few tricks along the way. But I'm pretty clever. Maybe even more clever than you, old woman." I needed her to take the bait.

She stared at me for a long moment and then burst into a cackle of laughter. "Do you dare to challenge me? Me, who has been around for thousands of years. Me, who has bested the mightiest and the brightest? You wish to battle me, armed only with your wits?"

I nodded meekly.

She roared with laughter. "This is too good. When I best you and your naïve little mind, I'm coming back for your friend there," she said as she looked Carrie up and down.

"And if I win..."

"Yes?" the harpy asked.

"You leave and go away empty-handed."

The old woman's eyes narrowed. "I wasn't born yesterday."

"Clearly," Carrie said quietly.

"If you try to trick me, you will pay. All of you."

I held up my palms. "There's no trick. I'm simply going to ask you a series of riddles. To show you how easy they are, here's the first one. See if you can figure out the answer."

Her eyes were locked on mine like a bird of prey sizing up dinner. I had her full attention and took another step toward her. Time to set the hook.

"There's an airplane, a large cargo plane that's traveling across the face of the planet. It's carrying a load of bricks. There's 500 bricks on the plane when one falls out."

I paused. "How many bricks are left on the plane?"

I stared at her while waiting for her answer. Her forehead tightened, and I imagined she was asking herself if the answer could be this obvious. Finally, she answered. "499 bricks."

"Is that your final answer?" I asked.

"499," she said again.

"You are...correct," I told her. "You got the first one right. I'm surprised. Most people don't. I may have underestimated you."

The harpy looked like it was trying to smile. It didn't work.

"There are five more riddles in the series. To win, all you need to do is get one more correct. Just one more out of five."

The harpy looked confident as she lowered the claw from Stacia's throat. "Ask me your riddles then," she croaked. "And the girls are mine."

"Or...you go away if I win. Agreed?"

"Oh, yes, I agree," she cackled. "This is going to be most satisfying. Begin."

The hook set, I recited the next riddle in the series.

"What are the three steps to putting an elephant in the refrigerator?"

The harpy paused, stroking her chin with a claw. It creeped me out. After a long moment, she spoke. "I don't believe an elephant could fit, so I don't know this answer."

She waved a claw for me to continue.

"There are three steps to putting an elephant in the refrigerator. First, open the door. Second, put the elephant inside. Third, close the door." I tried not to smile.

"I see," she said. "I was overthinking your simplistic riddle. Next one."

Stacia stared at me, but I avoided her gaze. I needed my focus.

"What are the four steps to putting a giraffe in the refrigerator?"

"I have this," the harpy cackled. "You, child, are no match for me.

The four steps are open the door; slice off the animal's neck and put it inside. And then close the door."

The harpy's confidence diminished quickly as I answered. "Wrong. And I must say your answer was more than a little disturbing. The correct answer is to open the door. Take out the elephant. Push the giraffe inside. Close the door. No slicing involved."

"You have your way, and I have mine."

Ignoring her retort, I continued. "Next one. The Lion King is having a birthday party, and he invites every animal in the world to attend. Every animal makes it to the party except one. Which animal didn't make it and why?"

I watched her face as she mulled over the question. Her strategy was evident as she started to name animals and watched me intently for a sign that she was correct. "Hmmm, it could be the donkey because they are slow and meandering. Or, it could be the tree frog because it never leaves the forest. Or, perhaps it's the hyena because it stops to fill its belly." She stared at me, trying to read my expression. I gave her nothing.

"I was testing you," she said triumphantly. "Clearly, it was the female lion because she doesn't bow down to anyone."

"You are wrong. Again. It was the giraffe. He was stuck in the refrigerator."

The harpy didn't say anything. She just slowly wagged her claw at me as if scolding me. "I have two more chances. More than enough for me. Next riddle."

"Okay then. Emily wanted to cross an alligator-infested river. Unfortunately, the only way to get across was to swim. So, that's what she does, yet she makes it safely across. Why?"

"Hmmm," the harpy said as she absently scratched her chin with a claw. "I know what I would do if I were the alligator. I'd wait for her to get across, and just when the girl thought she was safely across, I would pounce. That's my answer. They were waiting for her."

I shook my head.

The harpy was furious. "What? Why not?"

"The alligators were all at the birthday party. Remember?"

The old woman's mouth opened, and it looked like she had a "duh" moment.

I continued right away with the final riddle of the series. "But Emily died anyway. Why?"

Over the next half minute, the harpy began to say something and then stopped. This happened at least a dozen times. Finally, she gestured with a claw for me to answer.

"Emily was hit on the head by a falling brick."

I was trying not to smile, but the corners of my mouth were not fully cooperating. "The Genius of Love" by the Tom Tom Club, a band that could only have surfaced in the eighties, danced through my ecstatic mind.

The harpy looked down at Stacia as she ran a claw along her cheek. "It would have been amazing," she said. "The pain would have been so exquisite for us both."

Not today. Not ever.

"You are most clever," she said to me. "But remember, clever won't always save you."

And with that, she faded from view.

"Clever has worked so far," I said as we helped our friend to her feet and hugged her tightly. The harpy's last two words stuck with me as I held my friends.

"So far..."

2 2

IT IS WELL

The smell was decidedly worse in the hallway. Not quite breathe through your mouth worse, but headed in that direction. It was the musty smell of death and decay.

Light flared at the end of the hallway, silhouetting two figures. As I studied them, they grew in size. It hit me then that they were only getting larger because they were getting closer. They were coming toward me.

"Do you guys see that?" I asked. "There are two of them. Now what?"

When I didn't get a reply, I turned around. Stacia and Carrie were gone.

What the...?

"Guys," I said, stepping back into the room. Only it was empty. My friends were gone.

But there was something on the floor. It was Stacia's scarf. As I picked it up, I heard a crunch underfoot. It was Carrie's glasses.

There was no way she would leave them behind. My heart sank with the realization that the harpy had broken her word and returned. Damn. If you can't trust a harpy, who can you trust?

A howling wind blew my hair back when I stepped back into the hallway. Berlin's eighties classic, "Take My Breath Away," came into my head as I fought to take a breath as the gale grew in intensity. The two figures, one considerably taller than the other, hadn't gotten any closer while I was in the room. That could only mean one thing: they were meant for me.

Still silhouetted, the space behind the pair appeared to melt away as they passed. It was as if reality itself didn't matter after they passed. That was the moment a feeling of dawning horror washed over me. These two couldn't be...

"Mom? Dad?"

It was my parents. They were dressed as I saw them at breakfast this morning. My mom was in her favorite cream sweater and jeans, and my father wore a work shirt and chinos.

It was only when my mom got closer that I realized I could see right through her. Shifting my gaze to my father, the curls of peeling wallpaper were visible behind him.

But how?

There was only one reason. These were the ghosts of my parents.

Tears flowed, and sobs overcame me. First, I lost my two friends to that harpy bitch, and now...

My parents. I fell to my knees. In one fell swoop, everything was gone. Four people I loved and counted on were taken from me. I felt hollow, like everything that made me who I was had been gutted. How could I possibly continue? How could I go on with life, let alone have the strength to escape from this house of horrors?

My parents stood over me. Others joined them, but I didn't have the strength to look up. I knew who they were. The thought of looking at the ghosts of the people who loved me filled me with terror. I was going to be alone.

Dear God, how can I continue?

And then, something changed.

It is well.

I had grown up waiting for the fear to go away before I took any chances. I lived my life playing the "if, when/then" game. It was always *when I was no longer afraid, then I could*. But it never worked. I was always scared. Finally, I realized the fear of any situation faded when I confronted it.

It is well with my soul.

As I told Stacia earlier, everything I wanted was on the other side of fear, and I had to confront these ghosts if I wanted my fear to go away.

It wasn't easy, but I got to my feet, my legs wobbly. My parents looked at me while Carrie and Stacia stood alongside Brian and Turner.

For in death as in life, thou shalt whisper peace to my soul.

As I stood before the people I love, I knew something. They weren't real. This wasn't them. It was this damn house.

I closed my eyes, willing myself to slow my racing heart and ragged breathing. Blessed assurance that this was not my reality. This was a construct of the house. Fake news.

When, in my heart of hearts, I knew this to be true, I opened my eyes.

I was alone in the hallway.

"Abbey," Stacia called out. "Where did you go?"

"I think she's out here," Carrie replied as they stepped into the hall.

I grabbed onto my dear friends and didn't let go until well into the awkward stage.

But I didn't mind. At all.

23

ON A MISSION

"We have to get off this floor. It's literally the Monday of this house."

I gestured to my friends, who looked confused by my clever wordplay, and we quickly made our way down to the second floor. It was a relief to be away from the little floor of horrors.

Ella's door opened with a horror movie creak as we stepped inside. The only light was a small desk lamp. There was another creak, this time from her slowly opening the closet door. Stacia and Carrie stood at my side as the door swung open.

"Hungry Like the Wolf" from Duran Duran played in my brain's jukebox as a man stepped into view. The first thing I noticed was his size. Looking immense enough to play tackle for the Vikings, the top of his head nearly touched the doorframe. Big and broad, he had to weigh over 300 pounds. Sunken eyes, a beard that would best be trimmed with hedge clippers, and a nose broken more times than a purity vow, he looked like he would be at home in a traveling carnival working as the bear wrestler.

Moving lightly—which, considering he was a ghost after all, shouldn't come as a huge surprise—he crossed the front of Ella's bed and came toward us. He never looked at our eyes, and I guessed it was because no one had looked at his for a hundred years. His beefy hunk of a hand reached for Stacia's arm.

"Uh uh," I warned.

He paused before pulling his hand back. I waited as he waited, and then he reached for her again.

"Don't," I said.

This time, he jerked his hand back and stared at me. His eyes were wide with surprise.

"Norah," he bellowed. "You do what I tell you to do."

For the third time, he reached for Stacia. For the third time, I defied him.

"Leave her alone."

We made eye contact then. He didn't look happy as his eyes twitched and his fists clenched and unclenched. But he left Stacia alone. I held Stacia's and Carrie's hands, squeezing them as I instructed them to close their eyes. I wanted them to see the man.

"Picture a bearded giant of a man dressed in a red flannel shirt. He could have been a lumberjack or a bear wrestler in his previous life." I paused and told them to go ahead and open their eyes.

By the sharp intake of breath on either side of me, I knew they saw the ghost of Grizzly Adams—or at least his doppelgänger.

"We're here for an important reason," I told the man.

"We're on a mission from God," Stacia added, quoting from her favorite movie.

"We're looking for a small box built of wood and gold," I told the man. "I suspect you can feel its power in this house, and I'm confident you can lead us to it."

I needed him to voluntarily lead us to the box, as I didn't want to make contact with him. The traumatic adventure upstairs had taken a lot out of me, and I couldn't be sure I would be strong enough to disengage once his floodgates of memories opened up.

"Please. Won't you take us there?"

His face softened, and he nodded. He gestured for us to go back out into the hall. When we turned, he was already waiting for us, and we made our way down to the first floor.

He turned right at the base of the stairs and strode down the hall. Ella stuck her head out of the kitchen, looking as if she was going to ask a question.

"Hang on," I told her, "we're on the trail of something."

"Yeah, apparently, we're on a mission from God," Carrie added.

We followed the giant down the carpeted hallway to the living room. A large red brick fireplace dominated the far side of the room. Carved banister posts framed the structure and were attached to a wooden mantle. Above that, a large mirror spanned the width of the brick.

When the giant man stopped in front of the fireplace, he turned toward us and nodded. His reflection wasn't in the mirror.

If the box was here, it wasn't out in the open. Stacia and Carrie both had the same look of confusion I felt.

"Wait, where is the box?" I asked.

Once again, the man nodded toward the fireplace.

I slid my fingers along the fireplace, looking for a loose brick. Stacia studied the structure, while Carrie tried to see if any of the wood parts moved. If the box was there, it was well hidden.

"Wait," I called to the man, who had started to walk away. "You have to show us where the box is."

The ghostly giant hesitated, a look of annoyance on his face. Carrie crooked a finger at him.

"Come show us where it is."

"Pretty please," Stacia added. "It's not like you have much else to do."

With an air of exasperation, he strode quickly toward us. Before we could move out of his way, he walked right through us.

"Whoa," I said as the atmosphere became thick and charged. Every hair on my body stood on end. The ghost raised a giant fist, and with the swing of a professional fighter, his knuckles connected with the mirror.

The sound of the shattered mirror was loud, and glass pieces flew everywhere. He reached a large paw of a hand into the open space behind the mirror. When he turned around, a small box was in his hand. He handed it to me.

The third box.

The detail was astounding. Thin strips of wood joined with gold inlays to form a seamless box. There was a tiny clasp on the front but no sign of hinges on the back. Tiny delicate feet were in the corners on the underside.

Excited, I glanced at my friends. But, instead of admiring the box, they were looking toward the hall. Then I saw why.

Ella and Isabel joined us, accompanied by another woman. Her long gray hair was pulled back, showing her angular face. It was a face I'd seen before.

The tension was incredible as they stared at the broken mirror. Ella spoke first.

"Umm, this woman says she's the paranormal investigator. So, who are you then?"

24

NOT AS GLAMOROUS AS IT SOUNDS

"Well, this is awkward."

I glanced around, surveying the broken mirror, the shattered glass across the floor, and the box in my hands. The only explanation I could give was the truth. I walked over to the three women.

"I've been living with ghosts for as long as I can remember. And if you ask my parents, even before that. You could say I'm a spook magnet, as ghosts are attracted to me for some reason. They come to me to share a story or to ask for help."

I shook my head. "It's not as glamorous as it sounds. You try having a horde of ghost clowns come after you. That'll change your mind about it being glamorous in a hurry."

I tucked a stray strand of hair behind an ear. "As I've gotten older, I've realized I could help people with my abilities. So, now I use them to interact with dead people to resolve the situation and effect positive change."

Isabel pointed to the woman. "But, she offered to help us. She said she could cleanse our home of everything bad."

"I'm sure she did," I said, keeping my gaze on the woman. She stared right back at me. I recognized her from the Glensheen Mansion. It was Cruella de Vil, otherwise known as Olga Vengekov, the Russian intelligence woman. I was also pretty sure we had crossed paths—and bullets—at the Cathedral.

The situation had just gone from awkward to dangerous. This woman liked to shoot people.

"It doesn't matter." I held up the box. "This is the cause of your ghostly problems. This little box has unusual properties that gather and amplify spiritual energy. Having it hidden away in your home effectively turned it into spook central."

I glanced at the broken mirror. "Sorry about that. Sometimes ghosts can lose all sense of subtlety."

"I think you'll find most if not all, spirits will leave when I take the box away. Life can return to normal, and you can feel comfortable here again."

"Not so fast," Vengekov said. Her Russian accent was very distinct. She stepped around Ella and her mother, a vicious-looking pistol in her hand.

"Janie's Got a Gun," I said, Aerosmith's eighties song shooting into my head.

"I came for that box," the woman said with more than a hint of menace. "You see, I have been tracking you for quite some time. I knew if I waited, you would do my work for me."

"So, you admit you're lazy. Talk about a lack of work ethic. What is the younger generation coming to?"

Vengekov looked at me like she smelled something offensive.

"I was right behind you at the Glensheen Mansion when you found the first prizrak box." She paused. "That's Russian for ghost box. And I should have had the second one at the Cathedral, save for your cleverness. Your cleverness may get you into trouble someday."

"Been working for me so far," I said quietly.

"And now, I'll have the most powerful one of them all," she said, eyeing the box in my hands. "Its powers are incalculable. Especially in the right hands."

"And yours are the right hands?" I shook my head. "I don't think so."

The angular-faced woman smiled and lifted her pistol.

"There's an old saying in Russia. Might makes right. And since I hold the pistol, I am right."

"That's where you're wrong." It was Carrie. "Every totalitarian thinks just because they are heavily armed, that they are right. In an enlightened civilization, the reverse is true. We don't turn over the keys to the city to a bully. And we're not going to roll over for you."

Carrie folded her arms, the picture of defiance.

"What do you mean?" the Russian asked in her heavily accented voice.

"She means you're not getting the damn box." I can be as defiant as anyone.

"Really." The woman glanced around at the five of us, sizing up her odds. She waved the pistol around. "I have six rounds in this magazine and another in the chamber. Even if I was to miss—and I never do—I'm going to kill half of you easily. Is the box worth that cost?"

The Russian made a good point, but there was no way I would tell her that. I wasn't giving it up without a fight. My father said warriors are not the ones who always win but are the ones willing to fight. I am a warrior.

With an idea, I needed Vengekov's focus elsewhere while my fingers searched for the small latch on the box.

"We don't like bullies much, do we, Stacia?"

She gave me the *why are you throwing me under the bus* look. I mouthed the word stall, and she appeared to catch on.

"I was bullied once," she said, stepping in front of me. "And I hated it. You know how mean kids can be in middle school. Heather was the meanest of the mean—even by middle school standards. She'd make fun of the way you looked, the way you talked, the clothes you wore, even the way she imagined you smelled. But that wasn't the end of her tactics. She lived to inflict physical pain on her victims. It might be a pinch to the back of your arm, a rabbit punch to your back, a poke to the chest, or a heavy boot to your toes. She knew her craft."

Oddly enough, Stacia had the Russian's complete attention. It allowed me to rotate the box in my hands as I felt along the seams. I kept sliding my fingers until...yes, I had it.

"One time, I was in line for something or another. We were always in line for something at school, and as Heather passed, she caught my thigh with the tip of her pencil. She claimed it was an accident, but if you saw how she had chiseled her pencil to a point, you'd know she'd planned it."

"I have done this myself," Vengekov said with a look of fond remembrance. "It was a slow-acting poison delivered with a pen on a crowded subway platform."

My fingers slid over the top of the latch but didn't gain purchase. It wasn't until the fourth attempt that I felt the latch slide free. I opened the box and waited.

"The thing is, karma can be a real bitch." Stacia had everybody captivated. "Every bully is going to end up eating it someday. Every bully eventually wakes up and discovers they are no longer on top of the food chain. There's someone bigger, stronger, meaner that comes along. But even more rewarding than that is when the victim decides enough is enough. They reach the point when something ignites inside. That's exactly what happened to me one day. I was walking home from school when Heather rode by and slapped the back of my head."

Stacia reached back and redid her ponytail. "She had hit me like that dozens of times, but that day was different. I frickin' lost it. I ran after her and knocked her off her bike. It didn't stop there, as the fire had been smoldering inside me for a long time. I pounced on top of her and pummeled her until a grown-up ran over and pulled me off her. Not once after that did Heather ever look me in the eye. Not once."

"She must have been Soviet," Vengekov said. "The vanquished in my country never make eye contact. They are never the same again."

At this moment, Vengekov noticed the box I had set down in front of her with the lid raised. The opening faced her, and a light glowed from the box's interior.

I grabbed Stacia and Carrie's hands, and they joined with Ella and Isabel. The five of us faced the spirit box. The Russian stood in front of the box, mesmerized. Her pistol slowly lowered to her side.

That was when I closed my eyes.

It had become easy to slip into my meditative state. First, my breathing slowed, while my heart slowed to the ultra-slow resting heart rate of an Olympic athlete. I willed my facial muscles to relax, followed by my neck and shoulders. I was in my zone.

It's difficult to explain what I reached out *with*, but I felt for a presence when I did. I searched, felt, and welcomed the presence of the dead.

And there were plenty here.

I opened my eyes to find the Russian staring into the box as light beams cascaded from its interior onto the walls, ceiling, and her face. A mist swirled around her feet.

"Close your eyes," I said evenly as I gave a squeeze to each of my friends. "Close your eyes and try to relax. Picture us five girls as we hold on to each other, as our energy flows from one to another. Picture that energy as a warm light, growing and nurturing us. Picture that light as it envelops and protects each of us."

While I was talking, shadows grew from the edges of the room. Shapes danced in my peripheral vision. The wooden floor creaked with the arrival of a horde of spirits. I had never seen anything like it.

There were ghosts of every shape and size. Old men and older women, younger teens, and mere children. Tall, short, thin, fat. Some looked pristine—almost alive—while others were mostly decomposed as if they had crawled out of the ground after decades of being buried. Some walked, some glided, while others shuffled, swayed, or stumbled.

But it wasn't just the ghosts of people. There were animals, too. Dogs followed alongside people, and cats wove in and out between legs. The sound of great leathery wings beat the air as something dark darted above the large room. More and more spirits poured into the room.

It was like Noah's ark on acid.

The light from the spirit box intensified as beams of green and amber light shot out. It felt like I was watching a laser light show at a rock concert.

Vengekov stared into the box, a crooked smile on her face. She didn't notice the ghostly horde surrounding her. That was until a hand reached out and tugged on her long gray hair. She was fast and graceful as she spun around with a pistol in a two-handed shooting stance.

Eyes wide, she pivoted while searching for a target. She didn't appear to find one.

Another hand grabbed her sleeve. She spun in that direction. An old woman leaned in and whispered in Vengekov's ear. She spun again. An oily, wet tentacle wrapped itself around her leg. She tried to pull free from its grasp but couldn't dislodge its hold. A broad man with a beard bumped into her, while another ghost leaned into her face just to breathe on her.

Vengekov lost it. With a snarl of rage, she opened fire. Spraying bullets all around the room, she kept pulling the trigger until the gun was empty. None of the bullets had touched us.

Her eyes landed on me. "You. You did this."

I nodded.

"I'm going to kill you for this," Vengekov said. She winced and glanced down at her ensnarled leg. The tentacle had moved up her leg and was now wrapped above her knee. For the first time, I saw a crack in her confidence as a flicker of fear crossed her face.

"That might be hard to do without any bullets." I'd become familiar with pistols recently through Kelly's policeman father.

"Oh, I have more bullets," she said, reaching for her side pocket. Her hand emerged with a new magazine.

The large man behind her reached over her and knocked the magazine out of her hand.

Undaunted, Vengekov reached into her other pocket and pulled out another magazine. With a smooth motion, she ejected the old magazine from her pistol and replaced it with the new one. Her smile returned.

"You are dead." She leveled the pistol's barrel directly at me. Man, I hate guns.

I tensed, waiting for the bullet. The movies always made it look like it hurt a lot.

"There's already too many dead people in here," Suzanna Neri said as she appeared out of nowhere and deftly plucked the pistol from Vengekov's hand. "No more."

She leveled Vengekov's own pistol at her.

"Can't say it's a pleasure to see you again," Neri said to Vengekov.

"It's the same for me," the Russian replied. "I would have killed your protégé had you not shown up."

"This I knew. You've never valued human life." Neri looked at me and said, "Abbey, the box."

I let go of my friends and poked the lid closed with my toe. Immediately, the room's ghostly occupants began to fade away. The large man and a young girl remained as the rest departed to wherever the departed go.

I was relieved to see them drift away.

The tentacle still hung onto Vengekov but faded slowly as I watched.

Neri looked at Vengekov and shook her head. "I was always the better chess player. You're thinking one or two moves ahead, while my game kept me five moves in front of you. That's why I set things up the way I did. I knew I could get the boxes and draw you in."

I froze. *Wait, I was the bait?*

Neri appeared to realize that she had said too much. "Abbey, the situation was always controlled."

It didn't feel like it.

"Pull out the other two boxes," Neri directed me.

"Wait, you brought the other two boxes here?" Vengekov shook her head. "You do like to live dangerously."

Slipping the backpack from my shoulder, I pulled out the other two boxes, each a little larger than the other. Setting them next to the small one, together they were an exquisitely matched set of beauty and peril.

"Like I said, it's all controlled." Neri knelt, the butt of Vengekov's pistol sticking from her waistband. Moving quickly, Neri opened the medium-sized box and placed the smallest one inside. From there, she closed the top and placed the medium box inside its largest counterpart.

Next, she pulled out a pair of zip ties and used one to secure the large box. "We can't have this opening again. It's simply too dangerous."

She handed the other zip tie to me. "That's to bind our friend Olga."

When I turned to Olga Vengekov, my blood froze. Not only had the tentacle vanished, but Vengekov now held a wicked-looking knife. The knife was poised to stab Neri in the back.

I had to act.

Not thinking, only reacting, I pulled the pistol from Neri's waistband. My finger found the trigger as Vengekov was in mid-swing, the blade arcing toward Neri's unprotected back.

I pulled the trigger.

The explosion was deafening as the gun fired.

Vengekov dropped the knife and held both hands to her belly as she went down. She landed on her back, her eyes locked on mine.

My ears rang as I stood with the pistol held limply in my hand. Neri took the gun. If she was surprised by the turn of events, she didn't show it.

"Take your friends and the Dutchers. Go wait in the kitchen." She wiped the pistol with her shirt.

I was too stunned to say anything, so I simply gestured toward the kitchen. The four women headed down the hall, but I couldn't bring myself to leave.

I stared at Olga Vengekov as she clutched her stomach.

"Go. I have this." I watched as Neri gripped the pistol tightly in her hand before setting it on the table.

I went.

25

KISSING MY COMFORT ZONE GOODBYE

For those of you keeping score at home, that makes two people who've been shot in front of me. First, it was Bri shooting the psycho killer clown, and now it was me pulling the trigger. I know you're supposed to feel remorse after this kind of thing, but I didn't. Both had killed before, and both were going to kill again. Both deserved what they got. As Stacia said, karma can be a real bitch.

Three people—two men and a woman—entered the house without ringing the bell. "Which way?" they asked. We pointed in the direction of the shooting.

Several minutes later, they carried out the Russian. I couldn't tell if Olga Vengekov was alive...or not alive. Either way, I didn't want to see her again.

Neri and the woman joined us in the kitchen. Everyone looked a little numb as we sat there. No one had said a word since we had left the scene of the shooting.

Sitting across from us, Neri studied each of us. I put a hand on top of Stacia's and Ella's, who sat on either side of me. *It's going to be okay.*

"What happened here tonight was a matter of national security,"

Neri said. "Having a rogue Russian agent running around in America's heartland is not the most ideal of circumstances. It's not behavior we'd care to encourage, so your discretion is required."

She took a moment to make eye contact with each of us.

"It was courageous of you all to hold her off until I could get here. Your country thanks you. It was unfortunate that she got the drop on me, but fortunately, I was able to use Olga Vengekov's own pistol to stop her."

My eyes went wide at her words.

Looking directly at me, Neri held up a finger before I could say anything.

"That *is* what happened. My official report will say exactly that." She turned to the Dutcher family, took a deep breath, and continued.

"I need to apologize to you both. I'm sorry that you got caught up in this. Uncle Sam will take care of the damage to your mirror and walls. And to your rug." I winced and dropped my eyes down.

"But on the bright side, you now have a third level to your home," Stacia blurted, as she often did when she wanted to lighten the mood. I've always liked that about her.

"What?" Ella asked in wonder. "A third level?"

"There's just the two." Isabel's confusion was adorable.

"Care to explain?" Neri asked.

"I got this," I said. "When we went to the top floor, we surprisingly discovered another staircase. This one brought us up to another level."

"Really?" Ella's eyes were wide.

"Really. But it wasn't up to the high standards of the rest of the house. Okay, it was a dump."

I shook my head. "And the people weren't especially nice."

"People?"

"Well, former people, anyway. But I'm sure they're gone now. It was a harrowing experience up there, facing our fears."

"It's not all bad to face your fears," Neri said. "You grow when you get away from your comfort zone."

"My comfort zone was so far away that I couldn't possibly see it," I said. "It was more like 'The Danger Zone.' But I've learned over the years that bravery isn't the absence of fear. It's finding a way through it."

"Way to go." Neri looked proud of me. Actually proud. Go figure.

"And I've conquered my fear of ghosts," Stacia said.

"That's the spirit!"

"Wait, where?" Stacia looked around frantically before cracking up. It was our running joke since camp. It never failed to satisfy.

Ella spoke up. "Are all the dead people gone now?" Her eyes looked moist.

"Mostly, but that reminds me of something I still need to take care of. Talk amongst yourselves," I said and headed for the stairs.

Behind me, Stacia said, "So, how about a snack?" The laughter from the kitchen warmed me.

Running my finger along the smooth banister, I wondered how many people had taken these stairs over the last hundred years. Pushing open the door to Ella's room, I stepped inside. I ignored the light switch and waited. They knew I was there.

One moment, I was alone. The next, I had company. The large man stood by the window while the girl sat on the bed. Her blonde hair was in pigtails, and she had a playful look on her face. As if to accentuate this, she stuck out her tongue at me and giggled.

I smiled at her and turned to the large man.

"I'm okay with you being here, but you absolutely can't be scaring the family living here."

"It's my house," he said gruffly. He had the look of someone used to getting their way.

I shook my head. "It's their house, too. It's been in their family forever. The Dutcher family built the place. They are Dutchers."

The man's face softened. "I'm a Dutcher, too."

I nodded with relief. "Then we don't have a problem. You're all family."

Pausing at the door, I stuck my tongue out at the girl. I couldn't help but play along with her.

"All taken care of," I said when I returned to the kitchen. I grabbed a chocolate chip cookie from the tray and sat. "I came to an understanding with your ghosts. As it turned out, the man who scared you is also a Dutcher. Once I explained that you were Dutchers, too, he relaxed. After all, family is family. You won't have any more trouble—not with him, anyway."

Everybody stared at me.

"What do you mean, not with him, anyway?"

I couldn't help but grin. "He's not the only ghost in your house. There's a precocious young girl here, too. But nothing you can't handle."

I pointed at the tray of cookies. "See what I mean?"

Instead of being spread out like they had been, the cookies were now stacked on the tray. I held my breath, waiting for their reaction.

Ella laughed, breaking the tension. "This is so cool. It'll be like having an invisible little sister."

Her mom hugged Ella, and I knew life at the Dutcher house would be okay from now on.

"A word, Abbey." Isabel's expression was unreadable, but there was something unusual there. She gestured for me to follow her into the hallway. When we'd gotten out of earshot of the others, she turned to me. "I got a phone call. From St. Croix Paranormal Investigations, saying they couldn't make it today as one of the two lead investigators had come down with something."

"It is the cold and flu season," I said. "You shouldn't hold it against them."

"But that's not the issue." Isabel studied me, her face a palette of curiosity and wonder. "I know that Russian woman wasn't who she claimed to be, but who *are* you? You arrived when we needed help, and even more importantly, you solved our problem. You have..." she paused as if searching for the correct word. "You have most unusual abilities. I've seen the Ghost Hunter shows. It's usually a bunch of weekend warriors with questionable technology. But you're different."

"Calling me different may be like calling the Grand Canyon sizable."

Isabel laughed as she touched my arm. "But it's not just what you can do. You see things differently."

"Well, I've been around ghosts all my life. I've been scratched, and I've been burned. I've witnessed people levitating and seen people thrown around. I've seen people's eyes change from normal to completely black," I said. "That kinda shit transforms how you look at things."

"But," Isabel prompted.

I knew she was looking for an answer, and I hadn't yet given her one. "Me? I'm just a spooky girl who thinks it's important to do the right thing. If I can make a difference with these crazy abilities of mine, then that's the right thing to do. And that's what brought me here tonight."

"I may never know the full extent of what happened here tonight, but I'm thankful for your help." With misty eyes, Isabel hugged me. "Thank you."

◡◡

"What's going to happen to the spirit boxes?" Carrie asked after we left the house. A sliver of moon peeked out from behind the clouds. Neri was carrying the zip-tied boxes as we walked to our cars.

"I had planned on tucking them away someplace," Neri said. "As you can imagine, the government has thousands of warehouses spread around the country. Put the box in a plain cardboard carton, stick it on a shelf with the wrong inventory label, and it may never get touched again."

She pulled her hair back. I could see the groove of the bullet that served as a reminder of how unpredictable life could be. "But I've reconsidered. The second box had been doing just fine in the

Cathedral basement. There was no bleeding of spiritual energy causing ghostly problems there. Maybe the church has the spiritual thing under control."

"Abbey, what do you think?" Neri asked.

I was surprised she wanted my opinion. So much of our relationship had been her ordering me around and threatening me. This was a step in the right direction.

"Our guide at the James J. Hill house said the Catholic Church knew how to deal with ghosts. And if you saw the cobwebs—and the size of the spiders—you'd know that no one ever visits the Cathedral basement."

Suzanna Neri smiled and handed me the spirit boxes. "Then I think you should put them back in the Cathedral basement. And I'll sleep better knowing our world is a little safer."

I took the boxes.

Neri opened her car door, the moon reflecting on the sleek black roof.

"Ladies, thank you for your service."

She slipped inside and shut the door, her engine roaring to life. As she backed up, she paused and lowered her window. "Thank you, Abbey. Until the next time..."

Neri accelerated away, kicking up gravel.

Wait, what?

The next time?

26
LOOSE ENDS

There's nothing like descending into a dark basement to get me reflecting on the life choices that brought me to this point. I may see dead people, clowns, and harpies, but I love my life.

Take, for instance, the seeming disaster that was my television career. I never wanted to be on television as a ghost hunter. After all, it went entirely against my low-profile, don't-get-noticed, keep-my-head-down-at-all-costs life goal. But as Kelly pointed out, we need to adapt to our changing circumstances. And the Neri woman had presented unique and dangerous circumstances.

Nearly deadly circumstances, as it happened.

So, I adapted and went with the Spook Squad ghost hunter thing to replace the retiring paranormal investigator who did regular features on *Twin Cities Live*. Happy to be teamed up with Kelly and Lexi. Anytime I'm with them, it's an adventure, but throw in some ghosts and look out. Spooky fun at its best.

But when the show's producers set up a fake haunted house at the Mounds Theater, I was angry, frustrated, and done. After sending Murray to scare the producer and her assistant, my television career was over. Or so I thought.

Kelly got a surprise call, though.

We were invited to join the studio audience for the taping of the next *Twin Cities Live*. Our consolation prize for getting booted from the contest for making a mockery of their haunted house twist, I assumed. So, we'd be in the audience as those frauds, the Paranormal Dudes, were announced as the contest winners. No, thank you. But Kelly said the producers insisted we come, not just because it was in our contract, as they pointed out, but because they had gifts for us.

Okay, then. I was running low on lavender hand soap, anyway.

We were escorted to seats in the front row but on the side. Still, not horrible. How often do you get to sit in the front for anything?

The show opened with the usual fanfare, and Elizabeth greeted the audience with a big smile and mock surprise at the audience's enthusiasm. After talking about the discovery of rare and surprisingly valuable baseball cards at a certain mansion in Duluth, she teased out the show's program, which included winter getaways, the latest trends in office attire, and how to prepare your toddler for Halloween. After that, she paused. "And finally, we have some resolution in our surprisingly popular search for our next ghost hunter. You're not going to want to miss this. We have some video that might scare you. But first, a word from my favorite Woodbury restaurant, Angelina's Kitchen."

The director announced we were clear, and the production staff hurried to move things around for the next segment.

"Do you think she's going to mention us?" Lexi asked. "I mean, we didn't exactly look great on camera, did we? But it doesn't matter. I'm excited to see the winter getaways. I so need a vacation."

We both turned to stare at Lexi, who sat in between us.

"What?" she asked. "Life's been stressful. I need a spa getaway. This girl needs a little pampering."

"It doesn't sound so bad," I offered.

"You two," Kelly said as she shook her head in mock disapproval. "We need to keep focused on our new business."

"Wait a minute. You think we should keep the Spook Squad

going even after we got bounced out of the competition?" I hadn't considered the possibility.

After all, I'd only agreed to the contest to make my friends happy. The idea that we could market our services to people suffering from ghosts and paranormal activity never entered my mind. It was intriguing. But only if I didn't have to wear the uniform ever again.

"Technically, we didn't get bounced. It's more like we took ourselves out of contention when we went after the show's producers."

"They started it." I shook my head, getting angry at the thought. "If they hadn't tried to set us up to be scared, then I wouldn't have sent Murray after them."

"Ahh, Murray," Lexi said. "The most terrifying middle manager I've ever met."

"Have you met a lot of middle managers?" Kelly asked. She looked genuinely curious.

"Well, no. But that's not the point." Lexi leaned back, stretching her long legs. "I've never had a manager yell at me. Except that one McDonald's manager."

Kelly laughed. "You deserved that. Trying to pass that phony two-dollar bill. He even called mall security on you."

I was confused. "Wait, what?"

But before either could answer, the show's director counted Elizabeth back in. "Three. Two." And then he held up a finger for one and pointed to our host.

"Welcome back. Our in-studio audience is buzzing with excitement about the winter getaways. I know it's only November, but winter is nearly here. By February, nearly everyone in Minnesota will be ready to find a cozy cabin with a fireplace, a luxurious spa, or a tropical beach to recharge and rejuvenate. This is how you survive and thrive in our Minnesota winter. Here's our roaming lifestyle correspondent, Cassidy Clements, with a look at the hottest winter getaways."

It was easy to tune out the words as I watched the gorgeous

scenery play on the studio monitors. Autumn in Minnesota can be stunningly beautiful with its vivid color-changing trees, mild weather, and complete lack of bloodsucking mosquitos. In a couple of months, I'd sing a different tune when the arctic weather blew in, but until then, I was happy.

But still, there was something to be said for palm tree-lined white sandy beaches on the shimmering aqua and turquoise ocean.

The next segment on office fashion came and went. Since I don't work in an office, there was little to hold my attention. Contrary to how I look pretty much every day, I do give a surprising amount of thought to what I wear. Finding the ideal t-shirt to fit my mood and ensemble is an art. However, my parents may have differing opinions of my choices. Just last week, my father studied me as I walked out of my room and shared a glance with my mother. She lowered the medical journal she'd been studying and asked, "Do you prefer 'fashion victim' or 'ensemble-challenged?'"

As if.

During the commercial break, I leaned over. "Tell me about the two-dollar-bill incident. You said they were phony. I'm confused, why would anyone make a phony two-dollar bill?"

"Exactly. That was my point," Lexi exclaimed.

"You're such a drama llama, Lex." Kelly shook her with an exasperated look.

"I am not."

"Tell me the story," I hissed.

Lexi smiled. "I went to the McDonald's at the mall and ordered a two-cheeseburger meal. All I had in my billfold were my two-dollar bills from my grandmother. When I handed it to the cashier, he looked at it funny. He held the bills for a moment like he was unsure what to do with them. So, he called over the manager, whose nameplate said Duane. Duane and the cashier whispered back and forth for a moment. Then Duane asked if I had another bill. When I asked him why, he said we don't take this kind of money here."

"Wait, what?"

"I know. It gets better, too. I told him it's considered legal tender in the United States, and he had to take it. He didn't like that at all. He tells me that if I insist on passing funny money, he'll call mall security."

"Ooo, mall security," I said.

"Exactly," Lexi said. "I told him to go ahead. He got angry and loudly said I should be ashamed of myself. I told him I'm a proud, confident woman, and he should call all the local authorities he wants."

"Way to go."

"And then he stormed off to make his call. After a few moments of waiting and enduring his hostile glares, a mall cop walks in and joins us." Lexi paused as the lights flashed, signaling we were about to go live again. "I'll finish the story after," she said.

Next was a chat with a child psychologist who was there to talk about how to prepare toddlers for Halloween. The psychologist, Dr. Carolina Maranon, had gorgeous long dark hair and was elegantly dressed in a skirt and heels. Her high heels had red bottoms that were unusually cool. All the while, a slideshow of adorable kids in Halloween costumes played in the background on the monitors. Even though I prefer to see kids dressed as ghosts instead of real ghosts, I'm not convinced anyone wearing a sheet is a good look these days.

Then, finally, the interview was finished.

"Next up, we have an exciting conclusion to our surprisingly popular search for our next ghost hunter. You're not going to want to miss this. And a warning to our young or sensitive viewers, the video might be scary. Right after this break."

The director waved that the cameras were off. The crew went to work and moved the set around. The crew placed four chairs opposite Elizabeth's.

"So, anyway," Lexi continued. "The mall cop asks, 'What do we have, Duane?' He looks like someone hoping for something interesting but isn't getting his hopes up. 'Someone's trying to pass phony money,' Duane tells him. 'Her,' he said, thrusting an accusing finger at me. The mall cop looked more interested and asked to see the bills. Duane hands them over. The mall cop holds them up to the light and squints for a moment before turning them over. He rubs them between his thumb and index finger. When he turns back to Duane, he looks perplexed, saying he doesn't see anything wrong with the money."

I saw where the story was going.

"'But there's no such thing as a two-dollar bill,' Duane insists. The look on the mall cop's face is priceless. He asks Duane for my meal and hands over my two-cheeseburger meal along with my two-dollar bills. 'Here,' he says. 'Don't sue us.' And then he turns to a shocked Duane, telling him they need to talk."

"That's phenomenal," I said. "He really didn't know that they were a thing?"

"Nope," Lexi said and sat back with a smile. "And I got a free lunch out of it, too."

The director counted in the show, and Elizabeth moved to the front of the audience.

"When our resident ghost hunter, the fabulous Matilda Effervescence, announced her retirement, we decided to make a contest to find her replacement. What took us by surprise was your response. It was massive, on a scale we never could have predicted. There's something about ghosts that's universal. We're all interested and want to know why these spirits are here. But then throw in two of the most interesting contestants you could find, and the entire thing went nuclear. We got tons of voicemails, emails, and even snail mail. And the votes. Oh, my."

Elizabeth moved to her chair and sat, picking up her mug. After a sip, she continued. "It was obvious that two contestants—both groups, instead of individuals—caught your attention. We narrowed the field to just those two groups. The Paranormal Dudes and the Spook Squad."

Group pictures went up on the studio monitors to thunderous applause.

"Here's where things got interesting," Elizabeth said with a smile that Mona Lisa might recognize from one of her selfies. Leaning forward, eyes blazing, Elizabeth continued. "We sent the teams to the epically haunted Mounds Theatre in Saint Paul. A word of warning to our sensitive viewers. There may be moments in the following video that might startle or cause distress. Buckle up."

A spooky narrator spoke as the screen showed the Mounds Theatre from a distance. "Saint Paul's Mounds Theatre has always had a haunted history, but since it's a theater, we decided to take a few liberties. We wanted to enhance our investigators' experience and see if they could tell the difference between real ghosts and our ghosts."

The camera zoomed in at a dizzying rate as the theater's door flew open.

"After all, anyone can claim they see something. But how will they react when something scary jumps out at them?"

The camera moved into the building, where the Paranormal Dudes unpacked their equipment.

"Submitted for your approval, a group of young paranormal investigators, The Paranormal Dudes. Seemingly fearless as they face death head-on, they have armed themselves with the latest technology to resolve the age-old question of what happens after we die."

The camera appeared to be positioned backstage as the boys made their way to the stage. When the light illuminating the stage switched to red, the boys froze. That is, except for Kevin, who went into some martial arts routine.

"Be ready for anything. This feels like Cleveland in '75," he said.

The audience cheered. *But really, 1975? Like he was there.*

The same floating head we saw appeared, and all four boys took multiple steps backward. But, the camera zoomed in to show the head was a video projected onto a piece of glass angled at 45 degrees.

"However, not all is as it seems. The ghost is really our show's executive producer, albeit heavily made up."

A montage of the producer before, during, and after the make-up was shown.

"For the next part, our special effects wizards wired speakers to simulate the approach of a barking dog. But not just any dog, we wanted a scary one. Its job was to shepherd the boys to the basement."

It clearly worked as they looked panicked, any thoughts of using their state-of-the-art technology forgotten. The shot changed as the Paranormal Dudes slunk down the stairs.

"Dude, I don't want to go down here."

"Neither do I, but I don't want to meet that dog even more."

"I know. It sounded huge."

"Like a rabid Clifford."

"Exactly."

The lights played on the mannequins' feet and quickly moved up.

"Holy crap!"

"Let's get out of here."

"Wait, they're just department store mannequins."

"I just wet myself."

"Kevin!"

"Look at these mannequins. They'd be scary if—"

That's when Murray, the middle manager, did his thing. And the results were fabulous. The Paranormal Dudes ABSOLUTELY lost their shit. Ernesto, Ben, Jonas, and Kevin dropped their gear and ran for the stairs. Once they got done fighting each other to get out the door first, they were gone.

The camera rapidly ascended the stairs and swept past the startled producers, moving out to the parking lot. A van screeched out of the lot.

The only sound as the screen faded to black was the laughter of the cameraman.

The producer counted us to a commercial break.

Lexi, Kelly, and I exchanged glances. "Not what I was expecting," Lexi said.

"They did not handle that well." Kelly shook her head.

"It's a good thing none of us ran away like that," I said.

Neither of my friends said anything.

Sitting back, I folded my arms and smiled, eager to see the following video. Maybe this was going to go better than I'd thought.

After the break, Elizabeth was back. "Well, that's not what I was expecting from our intrepid ghost hunters. We put our second group to the same test. Let's see if they fared any better."

The shot opened with us walking into the theater. Fortunately, they showed the clip when we strutted in wearing our sunglasses.

"Again, for your approval, we present the Spook Squad."

The audience cheered as the camera zoomed in on me.

"Good evening. We're the Spook Squad, the Twin Cities' leading high school paranormal investigators. We're here at the historic Mounds Theatre in St. Paul to do what we do best: find the ghosts. With a rich history of unexplained paranormal activity, the theater is the perfect venue for our unique skills."

The scene switched to us approaching the stage, focusing on me with my hand in the air. When the light changed, and the floating head appeared, Elizabeth spoke. "Notice that, unlike their male counterparts, the Spook Squad moves forward to investigate the head."

After the head blinked out of existence and the vicious dog barking started, the camera pulled back as if expecting us to move away. We didn't. Then the light went on by the basement stairwell, and we went that way. "Light it up," I said, turning on our flashlights.

It looked badass, and the crowd loved it.

The video followed us down into the basement as we discovered the mannequins. The camera pulled back as Murray did his yelling thing and followed Kelly and Lexi as they sprinted up the stairs. The camera turned back as I said, "Really? This is not what I signed up for."

The camera caught the awkward moments as Murray and I sized each other up. The audience laughed as I worked with Murray to perfect his scream as it transformed from an aghast teenage girl to a respectable spook. The scene transitioned as the camera moved up the steps, filming backward as I took each step with a look of fierce determination.

When I burst into the room waving my arms and yelling, the audience gasped as the chaos of the producers and my friends' panicked exit played out. The camera tried to follow it, but the rapid direction changes added to the pandemonium. After their hasty exit, the camera zoomed on me.

"That was my friends, the fearless ghost hunters of the Spook Squad. Of course, the television producers didn't exactly come out looking any too brave here either. Especially considering that this entire visit to the supposedly haunted Mounds Theatre was a setup. Yes, they rigged the place with haunted house effects to scare us. Even had someone hiding in a basement mannequin posse to jump out and frighten us."

I stepped to the camera and smiled. "The funny thing is, I used their own scare tactic against them. I got him hyped up and unleashed him on the producers." I gestured to my middle manager mannequin friend and asked him to say hello.

Murray lifted his hand and said hi to his work peeps.

Grabbing his hand, I said, "You did great today. You nailed your part."

Murray smiled. "Not bad for a one-trick pony."

"Not bad at all." The camera zoomed in as I squeezed his hand. "Stay golden, ponyboy."

The screen faded to black, and the audience erupted with cheers. All around me, people were on their feet. "Please welcome the winners of our ghost hunter contest, Abbey, Kelly, and Lexi: the Spook Squad."

No way. We looked at each other, our mouths hanging open.

The theme from Ghostbusters played as a producer gestured for us to move onto the stage as the cheers and applause grew. Apparently, despite my efforts to the contrary, my television career was just beginning.

Life was full of unexpected twists and turns. I couldn't stop smiling.

27

A WATERSHED MOMENT

Back to the basement. Descending into the gloom, I ducked to avoid a low-hanging cobweb. Man, I hated spiders.

Even though the quest for the spirit boxes was forced on me, I completed it on my terms. I was able to bring my friends along to help. Having Kelly and Lexi come to Duluth and explore the Glensheen Mansion together was perfect. I especially loved how excited Lexi was listening to Manfred Krug's story. She told me on the drive home that she wouldn't settle for anything less in a boyfriend than someone as interesting as Manny.

Only one boy had caught my attention, and having Turner along to search for the second box was great. Turner and Brian Thompson, my attorney, made the tour of the James J. Hill house that much more memorable.

After getting the second box from the Cathedral, reuniting with Stacia and Carrie was ideal. They were riveted by Manny's crazy story on his train trip. Together, we had pushed through our fears. We emerged on the other side stronger and ready for anything that life—or death—could throw at us. We were warriors.

The forced quest turned out to be a good thing. Having a spirit box, let alone three, fall into Olga Vengekov's wicked hands would not be good for anyone.

As they say, it would be a disaster of biblical proportions. The dead rising from the grave. Human sacrifice, dogs and cats living together. Mass hysteria.

Stepping onto the stone floor of the Cathedral's sub-basement, the nested boxes were tucked under my arm. It was deathly quiet, and only the cool, damp air on my cheeks reminded me I was alive.

Brian had wanted me to use the boxes for leverage, saying that it would give us negotiating power with Neri and force her to leave me alone. But here's the thing: I was glad to help. And in some strange way, I was looking forward to using my odd abilities to help others again. Television was one thing, but I wanted to make a difference. If I could help save people from larger threats, then all the better. I was no longer afraid to let my light shine.

There was a quote that spoke to me when I first read it: *Your work is to discover who you are, and then with all your heart, give your light to the world.*

When I lifted the flashlight, shadows sprang up. I scanned the room, hoping nothing would be moving. From what I could see, I was alone.

Except for several dozen ginormous spiders, which made me shiver.

Moving carefully past boxes, decorations, dusty chairs, and retired pews, I went to the far corner where Father Lavin had shown where the spirit box was hidden. One unexpected thing about tapping into a spirit's memories like Turner, Brian, and I had done is they stay with you. It was like Father Lavin's memories were mine now. Getting those glimpses into his well-lived life left quite an impression. I wished I'd had the chance to meet him.

I flashed the light around the floor, knowing it should still be there. There wasn't any reason for her to have taken it with her. Another step, and there it was. The satchel.

It had been quite a ride, but it was time to put away these boxes.

Opening the satchel, I carefully placed the nested boxes inside. Winding through the decades of discarded clutter, I saw that the empty spot remained on the top shelf. Using my best two-handed granny basketball shooting technique, I tossed the bag.

The satchel rotated once before hitting the stone wall and bouncing onto the shelf. The momentum carried it forward as it threatened to fall back down.

Time froze while I watched it teeter. But, it fell back, perfectly in place on the shelf.

Yes! Abbey sinks the three-point shot!

It's good to celebrate the wins in life, and I did my fist pump dance. But when I turned, I stopped dancing.

I was no longer alone.

A figure of a man stood nearby. With an almost luminous glow surrounding him, I knew right away I was looking at a dead man. My flashlight made it more difficult to make out his features—as the light beam penetrated him rather than illuminate him. I clicked it off.

The rest of the basement disappeared with that click, and the only thing that remained was the glowing man. He had a kind face and not much hair left. His bald head was offset by his bushy eyebrows. This was a face I had seen earlier, and once I saw his priest's collar, I knew who it was.

Father Lavin.

His eyes twinkled as he smiled, and I couldn't help but return his smile. Over the years, I'd had ghosts try to scare, choke, shove, or slice me rather than talk to me. Communication was often more of a blunt instrument than a nuanced dialogue of ideas. I didn't know if we'd be able to have a conversation or not.

Almost like wiring a series of batteries, Neri's power of the three had helped strengthen the communication. But I was alone now. I had to do this by myself.

"Hello, Father. Nice to see you again."

He nodded at me. But gave me nothing else.

After several more attempts to talk to him, and him only smiling,

I grew frustrated. I got more communication from my dog—especially if a dog biscuit was involved. I was half-tempted to check my pockets for a treat. There was something about the randomness of the thought that cracked me up.

I couldn't help but giggle.

Father Lavin's puzzled expression made it even funnier, and I couldn't hold it in. One thing you may not know about me is that I'm a snorter. Some may giggle, while others chuckle. Me, I snort laugh. It can be embarrassing, but I was usually too caught up in the moment to care.

This was one of those moments.

Doubled over, I reflexively reached out to steady myself. I made contact—actual physical contact—with the earthly spirit of Father Lavin. I was touching a ghost.

Surprisingly, Father Lavin was laughing as well. It wasn't the reserved chuckle of a member of the clergy, as I would have expected. No, it was the belly laugh of a man who loved life and lived it to the fullest. I instantly gained a new respect for the man.

As I wiped away the tears of laughter, I carefully maintained our physical connection.

"Sorry, Father. When something strikes me as funny, I can't help it."

"No need to apologize for being yourself, child. We are meant for joy and laughter."

He spoke to me. This was good.

"I brought back the spirit box, Father. Plus two more. They are safer here than anywhere else I can think of."

"They are powerful things. The spirit boxes can alter lives, both for the good and for the bad. It's better that they are here. Thank you for bringing them safely home."

I nodded, thinking about Father Lavin's memories again.

"Father, may I ask you something?"

His eyes twinkled again. "You already have, but ask away. I have some free time."

I couldn't help but smile. A ghost with a sense of humor can't be a bad thing.

"Father, when we met at the James J. Hill House, I saw glimpses of your memories while experiencing parts of your life. What made you decide to become a priest? It feels like you were born for this. Did you always know?"

Father Lavin gave me a shake of his head, saying, "No, I had been going down a completely different path. Then, I had a watershed moment."

"A watershed moment?"

As he spoke, I got a sense of his fondness for teaching. "A watershed moment is a turning point. A moment in time when the direction of your life changes forever. It's a moment from which things will never be the same."

Thinking back to my time at the ToughLove summer camp, I knew exactly the kind of experience he meant. "I've had a moment or so like that in my life. You see everything differently after that."

He laughed. "Exactly. My moment happened on a train. I'd woken up to a supernatural experience that terrified me to my very soul. It was at that moment I prayed for the very first time. After God answered my desperate pleas for help, I found that I viewed things differently. I saw my life in a whole new light."

His eyes sparkled. "From that moment on, I made a conscious choice to be a light for God."

It was as if his words were the key, moving the tumblers of my mind into place. But before I could say anything, he continued.

"I came back to Saint Paul with my mind made up. And in the tradition of the apostles, I changed my name. From that moment on, I was a new person." His eyes danced as he remembered his turning point.

"You were no longer Manfred Krug."

He had a look of astonishment on his face.

"How did you...?"

I smiled, thinking of the quest I'd been on. "Manny, you have no idea what a long, strange journey I've been on."

He accepted my words with a nod. "There was a quote that hung for years on my office wall. *Purpose is the reason you journey. Passion is the fire that lights your way. There is great meaning in life for those willing to journey.* I sincerely hope you enjoy the ride, young lady."

With a tender smile, he moved his arm, breaking our connection.

His chuckle lingered as he faded away, leaving me alone in the dark. But I didn't care.

I frickin' love the ride.

"Sweet Dreams (Are Made of This)" by the Eurythmics played in my eighties soundtrack-filled head as I headed back up the stairs. As ever, I couldn't help but sing along.

ACKNOWLEDGMENTS

When characters write themselves, it certainly makes a writer's life easier. To flip that on its head, I'm letting my Abbey character write these acknowledgments for me.

Hello, people of the real world! I'm Abbey and it's nice to meet you here.

First, congratulations on finishing this book. Now, go post a review. Allan swears it's not an ego thing, but it's important in getting this book noticed and finding a wider audience. I'll wait here until you're back.

[*Checking watch...*]

Thank you for leaving an honest review. It's much appreciated.

Onward. My author (handler, puppet master, creative genius, etc.) has shared how much help and inspiration goes into the writing of a novel. Clearly, your help was needed, and Allan is eternally thankful.

Allan's family is important to him, and he wants you to know that having a family of loved ones behind him is the secret to his success. Thank you, Jen, as well as Abbey (hey, same name, a coincidence, I think not), Andrew, Ben, Cade, Dan, and Suzanna, for supporting, caring, and listening to his near-endless plot ideas. Also, thanks to his mother, Eleanor, who is a rockstar proofreader, and brother, Mark; in-laws Russ and Jerrie; and brother-in-law, Bill. And Tucker, his Cavalier King Charles spaniel. A magnificent beast if there ever was one.

Allan really wants to thank everyone at Immortal Works Press.

This boutique (small) publisher puts out some amazing literary works. And this book. Specifically, Allan mentions his editor, John M. Olsen, for sticking with him for four books now. Staci Olsen for taking a chance on Allan in the first place, as well as her legendary layout skills. Creative Manager, Ashley Literski for her beautiful cover design. Chief Editor Holli Anderson for being a great chief. And Publisher Jason King for sending over that multi-million-dollar contract in the first place. Allan's happy to travel and research the world on your dime.

Other people he'd like to thank (honestly, this guy won't stop talking) include the coaching family and players of the St. Croix Soccer Club. Local bookstores near him, such as Valley Booksellers in Stillwater, Lake Country Booksellers in White Bear Lake, and Magers & Quinn Booksellers in Minneapolis for your support. Author John Sandford and his Prey series for motivating Allan to write in the first place. His fellow Immortal Works authors. Ian Punnett (who we lost in 2023), the fine people at 3rd Act in Woodbury for hosting some fabulous author events. And anyone that has made his usual peppermint mocha at any of the coffee shops he frequents.

Thank you to the real-life Kelly, Lexi, and Stacia who inspired my best friends. Manfred Krug was named after a real chef with the same name. Allan took his cooking class and was inspired by the man's charm and character. Brian Thompson is based on someone who had an impact on Allan's life. You are missed.

Thanks to all the friends who inspired many of this book's characters. To paraphrase a common legal disclaimer, any resemblance to actual persons, living or dead, is meant to be a compliment. Love to you all.

The Twin Cities Live show in the book is based on the real KSTP-TV program. It offers a delightful mix of entertainment, lifestyle features, and local news, capturing the essence of what makes the Twin Cities so unique and exciting. (I so should be in marketing when I grow up.)

Okay, he's done. Finally.

I have just one important thank you of my own: thanks to all you producers who are thinking about this story's potential for a film or series. I think Sydney Sweeney or Jenna Ortega would make a fabulous Abbey. Give it some thought, maybe sleep on it.

All the best, Abbey Hill (for Allan).

ABOUT THE AUTHOR

Author Allan Evans has been busy. His debut novel, *Abnormally Abbey*, was published in 2020, followed by the highly anticipated *Class Clown* in 2022. His first two installments in a thrilling serial killer series, *Killer Blonde* and *Killer Smile*, were published in 2021 and 2023, respectively.

Son of famed Twin Cities jazz musician Doc Evans, Allan has written advertising and marketing for nearly two decades. A soccer coach, he can often be found on the field teaching kids about soccer and life. Allan lives in the Twin Cities.

Visit evanswriter.com to learn more. All of his social accounts are under evanswriter.

This has been an
Immortal Production

www.ingramcontent.com/pod-product-compliance
Lightning Source LLC
Chambersburg PA
CBHW061800190726
48289CB00007B/2013